Diana sipped her tea delicately before answering. 'Surely the reason for my being here is obvious, my lord?'

'Perhaps to make enquiries about your two sisters?'

'That was my first concern, yes.'

'And your second?' That nerve was once again pulsing in Gabriel's jaw, and if he was not mistaken he was developing a twitch in his left eyelid too!

Diana sat forward to carefully place her empty teacup down upon the silver tray, that slight adjustment in her pose revealing more of the deep swell of her creamy breasts. Full and plump breasts, Gabriel noted admiringly, and slightly at odds with the slenderness of the rest of her, revealed by the cut of her gown. Born and raised in the country or not, Diana Copeland was every inch a lady, he noted as his gaze trailed down her graceful slim arms and her elegant hands in their white lace gloves. A self-confident and outspoken young lady who—

'My second reason for awaiting your arrival here is, of course, that I have decided to accept your offer of marriage.'

AUTHOR NOTE

I've always delighted in reading stories of love and adventure set in the Regency period, and it really is a dream come true for me to now be able to write these stories myself. To be able to indulge that love to the full, to live in that period for months at a time, if only in my imagination. In fact, it's sometimes been a shock to come back to the reality of modern times and realise that, yes, I do have washing to put on, food shopping to do, and dinner to cook for my husband and all those sons!

I really hope that you enjoy reading Diana's story, and about the unlikely Earl who falls in love with her, as much as I have enjoyed being a part of their lives.

Look for

The Lady Confesses
Coming soon in
The Copeland Sisters

THE LADY FORFEITS

Carole Mortimer

First published in Great Britain 2011
by Mills & Boon, an imprint of Harlequin (UK) Limited.
Harlequin (UK) Limited, Eton House, 18-24 Paradise Road,
Richmond, Surrey TW9 1SR

© Carole Mortimer 2011

ISBN: 978 0 263 88816 4

Harlequin (UK) policy is to use papers that are natural, renewable and recyclable products and made from wood grown in sustainable forests. The logging and manufacturing process conform to the legal environmental regulations of the country of origin.

Printed and bound in Spain
by Blackprint CPI, Barcelona

Carole Mortimer was born in England, the youngest of three children. She began writing in 1978, and has now written over one hundred and fifty books for Harlequin Mills & Boon®. Carole has six sons: Matthew, Joshua, Timothy, Michael, David and Peter. She says, 'I'm happily married to Peter senior; we're best friends as well as lovers, which is probably the best recipe for a successful relationship. We live in a lovely part of England.'

Previous novels by the same author:

In Mills & Boon® Historical Romance:

THE DUKE'S CINDERELLA BRIDE*
THE RAKE'S INDECENT PROPOSAL*
THE ROGUE'S DISGRACED LADY*
LADY ARABELLA'S SCANDALOUS MARRIAGE*
THE LADY GAMBLES**

*The Notorious St Claires
**The Copeland Sisters

You've read about *The Notorious St Claires* in Regency times. Now you can read about the new generation in Mills & Boon® Modern™ Romance:

The Scandalous St Claires
Three arrogant aristocrats—ready to be tamed!
JORDAN ST CLAIRE: DARK AND DANGEROUS
THE RELUCTANT DUKE
TAMING THE LAST ST CLAIRE

Carole Mortimer has written a further 150 novels for Modern™ Romance.

And in Mills & Boon® Historical *Undone!* eBooks:

AT THE DUKE'S SERVICE
CONVENIENT WIFE, PLEASURED LADY

With thanks to all at HMB
for helping to make my dream a reality.

Chapter One

'Good God, Nathaniel, what have you done to yourself?' Lord Gabriel Faulkner, Earl of Westbourne, exclaimed with less than his usual haughty aplomb.

Gabriel had come to an abrupt halt in the doorway of the bedchamber on first sighting his friend as he lay prostrate upon the bed. Lord Nathaniel Thorne's, Earl of Osbourne's, face was an array of cuts and rainbow-coloured bruises; a wide bandage about the bareness of his muscled chest attested to the possibility of several ribs also being broken.

'Begging your pardon, ma'am.' Gabriel recovered himself enough to turn and give an apologetic bow to the lady standing in the hallway beside him.

'Not at all, my lord,' Mrs Gertrude Wilson, Osbourne's aunt, dismissed briskly. 'I suffered the same feelings of shock upon first seeing the extent of my nephew's injuries four days ago.'

'Would the two of you stop discussing me as if I were not here?' The patient was obviously less than pleased with this development.

'The physician said you are to rest, Nathaniel,' his aunt instructed sternly before turning that same steely-eyed attention on Gabriel. 'I will leave the two of you to talk now, my lord. But for no longer than ten minutes,' she warned. 'As you see, Nathaniel is more in need of peace and quiet than conversation.' She turned back into the hallway. 'Come along, Betsy,' she added. 'It is time for Hector's walk.'

Gabriel was rendered completely mystified by this last comment until another figure stepped out from the shadows of the hallway: a young, slender girl, with ebony curls surrounding the pale oval of a face made beautiful by huge blue eyes, clutching a small white dog in her arms.

'If I have to suffer much more of this mollycoddling I will very likely resort to wringing someone's neck,' Nathaniel grumbled as soon as his aunt and her companion had departed and the two gentlemen were at last left alone in the bedchamber. 'It is so good to see you, Gabe,' he added more warmly as he struggled to sit up, the grimace on his face evidence, despite his denials, that it was a painful business.

'Stay where you are, man.' Gabriel crossed to his friend's bedside, the usual look of determination now back upon a haughtily handsome face dominated by shrewd midnight-blue eyes. Tall and dark, and dressed in a perfectly tailored black superfine, silver waistcoat and grey pantaloons above black Hessians, the Earl of Westbourne gave every appearance of being the fashionable English gentleman, despite having spent the last eight years roaming the Continent.

Osbourne relaxed back against the many pillows behind him. 'I had thought it was your intention to go straight to Shoreley Park when you arrived from Venice, rather than come up to London, Gabe? Which begs the question—?'

'I believe your aunt has advised that you rest, Nate,' Gabriel murmured, arching one arrogant brow.

Osbourne scowled. 'Having summarily removed me from my own home and into her own cloying care, I believe if my Aunt Gertrude were to have her way she would now have me tied to the bed and all visitors refused entry.'

Despite his friend's grumbling, Gabriel realised Nate's aunt had done the correct thing as Nate so obviously found any movement extremely painful and couldn't fend for himself. 'What happened to you, Nate?' he asked as he folded his elegant length on to the chair placed beside the bed.

The other man grimaced. 'Well, despite what you said when you first saw me, I certainly did not do this to myself.'

But having served with Osbourne in the King's army for five years, Gabriel knew better than most how proficient Osbourne was with both sword and pistol. 'So how did it happen then?'

'A little…disagreement outside Dominic's new club,

with four pairs of fists and the same amount of hob-nailed boots.'

'Ah.' Gabriel nodded. 'And would these four sets of fists and hobnailed boots have any connection to the gossip now circulating about town concerning the sudden demise of a certain Mr Nicholas Brown?'

The other man gave him an appreciative grin. 'You have seen Dominic, then?' He referred to their mutual friend, Dominic Vaughn, Earl of Blackstone, who had won a gambling club called Nick's off a rogue named Nicholas Brown, who had then tried to sabotage and threaten Dominic any way he could until Dominic had had to deal with him in no uncertain terms.

'Unfortunately not. I called at Blackstone House on my arrival in town earlier this morning and was informed that Dominic was not at home. That he has, in fact, gone into the country for several days.' Gabriel looked thoughtful.

The three men had been friends since their school-days together, that friendship continuing despite Gabriel's sudden banishment to the Continent eight years ago. He dearly hoped that Dominic's sudden departure from town did not mean his friend was about to face the same fate after being forced to shoot dead that scoundrel Nicholas Brown…

'It is not at all what you think, Gabe.' Nathaniel's grin had widened as he reached for the letter on the bedside table and handed it to the other man. 'The authorities have accepted Dominic's account of what took place between himself and Brown; it would appear that Dominic is even now travelling into Hampshire with the intention of visiting the family of the woman he has every intention of making his wife. Look, see what he wrote to me before he left.'

Gabriel quickly scanned the contents of the missive from their friend. A brief, unhelpful letter, obviously written in a hurry, with little real information—apart from the news that Dominic had indeed gone into Hampshire with the intention of asking permission from this woman's guardian for the two of them to marry. 'And who, pray, is Miss Morton?' He placed Dominic's letter lightly back on the bedside table.

'An absolute beauty.' Osbourne's eyes lit up appreciatively. 'Not that it was apparent immediately, of course, because of the jewelled mask and ebony wig she wore when I first saw her. But once they had been removed—'

'She was wearing a *mask* and *wig*?' Gabriel repeated in astonishment.

Osbourne looked less sure of himself in the face of that Gabriel's utter incredulity. 'She was singing at Nick's the evening the fight broke out, and so Dom and I had no choice but to step in and—' He broke off as Gabriel raised a silencing hand.

'Let me see if I have understood you correctly,' Gabriel said grimly. 'Are you really telling me that Blackstone is about to ask for the hand in marriage of a woman who, until a short time ago, sang in a gentlemen's gambling club disguised in a jewelled mask and ebony wig?' His tone had gone positively icy with disapproval.

'I—well—yes, I suppose I am…' Osbourne confirmed uneasily.

'Has Dominic completely taken leave of his senses? Or perhaps he also received a blow to the head from one of those fists or hobnailed boots?' Gabriel exploded. He could envisage no other explanation for his incredibly eligible friend even contemplating proposing marriage to a singer in a gambling club—no matter how beautiful she was!

Nathaniel gave a shrug. 'His letter says he will explain all upon his return to town.'

'By which time it will no doubt be too late to save him from this reckless venture; no guardian of such a woman would even consider turning down an offer of marriage from an earl. In fact, I would not be at all surprised if Dominic does not return to town already married to the chit.' Gabriel scowled his displeasure at the thought of his friend's obvious entrapment by this "absolute beauty".

'I had not thought of it in quite that way.' Nathaniel frowned his own concern. 'She seemed very much the lady of quality when I spoke with her.'

'My dear Nate, I may have been absent from London society for some years,' Gabriel drawled drily, 'but I do not believe it has changed so much that ladies of quality now seek employment in gentlemen's gambling clubs.'

'Hmm.' Nathaniel considered the matter further.

'Perhaps, as you are travelling into Hampshire yourself, you might seek Dominic out and—'

'My original plan to go to Shoreley Park no longer stands.' Gabriel's mouth tightened at the thought of the conversation that had taken place earlier that morning in the offices of his lawyer, that had succeeded in altering all his plans. 'I arrived back in England only hours ago, to find an envoy from my lawyer awaiting me upon the quayside in possession of a letter requesting that I come to town immediately and meet with him. It would appear that the three Lady Copelands—having, as you are well aware, all decided to refuse my offer of marriage—have now chosen to absent themselves from Shoreley Park completely. No doubt in anticipation of my arrival there.'

It was an occurrence that did not please Gabriel in the slightest. Insult enough that his offer of marriage to one of his wards had been refused, sight unseen, without his now being put to the trouble of having to seek out all three of the rebellious chits!

The previous two Westbourne heirs having died at Waterloo, Gabriel had surprisingly come into the title of the Earl of Westbourne six months ago, along with guardianship of the previous earl's three unmarried daughters. In the circumstances, and as he had a complete lack of interest in taking any other woman as his wife, Gabriel had deemed it appropriate to offer marriage to one of those daughters. Not only had they all refused him, but, to add insult to injury, they had now

all taken it into their heads to defy even his guardianship. A defiance Gabriel had no intention of tolerating!

'I called upon Dominic earlier with the intention
of taking him up on his offer that I stay at Blackstone
House with him when I returned to town.' Gabriel
shrugged. 'It appears, in light of his disappearance into
the country, that I shall have to make Westbourne House
my home, after all.'

'It's been closed up these past ten years,' Nathaniel
grimaced. 'It's nothing but a mausoleum and it's probably full of mice and other rodents, too.'

Gabriel was well aware of the dereliction of Westbourne House. It was the very reason he had been putting off his arrival there all morning. Once he had
finished talking to his lawyer he had first called upon
Dominic at Blackstone House, only to learn of the other
man's disappearance into the country. A similar visit
to Nathaniel's residence had garnered the information
that he was currently residing at the home of his aunt,
Mrs Gertrude Wilson, meaning he couldn't stay with
him either.

'There's absolutely no reason why you cannot stay
at Osbourne House in my absence,' the earl assured
him, as if suddenly aware of his thoughts. 'We could
have both moved back there if my aunt had not taken
it into her head to remove me to the country later this
afternoon.' He looked less than happy with the arrangements. 'Take my advice, Gabe—never let a woman get
the upper hand; she's apt to take advantage while a
man's down.'

Gabriel had no intention of allowing a woman, any woman, to take advantage of him ever again, having learnt that hard lesson only too well eight years ago...

'Oh, I say!' Osbourne instantly looked contrite. 'I did not mean to imply—'

'No implication taken, Nate, I assure you. And kind as your offer is, I fear, as I must take up residence at Westbourne House at some time, it may as well be now.' Gabriel rose languidly to his feet. 'I will see if I can find someone suitable to go into Hampshire and locate Dominic, and hopefully return him to his senses before it is too late,' he added darkly.

Society, as Gabriel knew only too well, did not, and would not, ever forgive such a social indiscretion as an earl aligning himself in marriage to a woman who had previously been a singer in a gentlemen's gambling club.

'Now I believe it is time I took my leave—before Mrs Wilson returns and has me forcibly ejected from the premises!' He fastidiously straightened the lace cuff of his shirt beneath his superfine.

'Can't see it m'self,' his friend snorted as he rang the bell for one of the servants to escort Gabriel down the stairs. 'My Aunt Gertrude may have me at a disadvantage for the moment, but I very much doubt she would ever have the same effect on you.'

In truth, Gabriel had found Mrs Wilson's polite if cool attitude towards him something of a relief after the years of being shunned by society. Obviously coming into the title of earl did make a difference! 'Think it lucky that you have a relative who feels enough affection for you to bother herself about you,' he said drily. His own family, such as it was, had not troubled themselves to even learn of Gabriel's whereabouts this past eight years, let alone enquire about his health.

As Gabriel travelled in his coach to Westbourne House he considered the possibility, now he was in possession of the old and much respected title of the Earl of Westbourne, with all the wealth, estates and power that title engendered, as to whether there might be a sea change in the attitude of the family that had chosen to banish him from their sight all those years ago. Even if there was, Gabriel thought coldly, he was indifferent to becoming reacquainted with any of *them*.

Gabriel's air of studied indifference suffered a severe blow, however, when he arrived at Westbourne House some minutes later.

The front door was opened by a perfectly liveried butler who, upon enquiry, informed Gabriel, "Lady Diana is not at home at the moment, my lord, but is expected back very shortly."

Lady Diana Copeland? One of the previous Earl of Westbourne's rebellious daughters who was supposedly missing from home? And, if so, exactly how long had she been in residence at Westbourne House?

'The earl requests that you join him in the library immediately upon your return, my lady,' Soames stiffly informed Lady Diana Copeland as he opened the front door to admit her. Instead the butler succeeded in bringing her to an abrupt halt so that she now stood poised upon the threshold.

'The Earl of…?'

'Westbourne, my lady.'

The Earl of Westbourne!

Lord Gabriel Faulkner?

Here?

Now?

And apparently awaiting her in the library…

Well, who had more right than Lord Gabriel Faulkner, the newly titled Earl of Westbourne, to be awaiting Diana in what was, after all, now *his* library, she scolded herself. Besides, had she not been anticipating just such an opportunity in which to personally inform the new earl exactly what she thought of both him, his blanket offer of marriage to herself and her two sisters, and the serious repercussions of that preposterous offer?

Diana stiffened her spine in preparation for that conversation. 'Thank you, Soames.' She continued confidently into the entrance hall before removing her bonnet and handing it and her parasol to the maid who had accompanied her on her morning errands. 'Is my Aunt Humphries still in her rooms?'

'She is, my lady,' the butler confirmed evenly, his expression as unemotionally non-committal as a good butler's should be.

Nevertheless, Diana sensed the man's disapproval that Mrs Humphries had taken to her bed shortly after they had arrived at Westbourne House three days earlier and that she had chosen to remain there during the uproar of Diana's efforts to ensure that the house was cleaned and polished from attic to cellar.

Diana had been unsure as to what she would find when she reached Westbourne House. Neither she, nor her two sisters, had ever been to London before, let alone stayed in what was the family home there. Their father, the previous earl, had chosen not to go there either for all of ten years before his death six months ago.

The air of decay and neglect Diana had encountered when she'd first entered Westbourne House had been every bit as bad as she had feared it might be—as well as confirming that the new earl had not yet arrived from his home in Venice to take up residence here. The few servants who remained had fallen into almost as much decay and neglect as the house in the absence of a master or mistress to keep them about their duties. An occurrence that Diana had dealt with by immediately dispensing with the servants unwilling or unable to work and engaging new ones to take their place, their first task being to restore the house to some of its obvious former glory.

A task well done, Diana noted as she looked about her with an air of satisfaction. Wood now gleamed. Floors were polished. Doors and windows had been left open for many hours each day in order to dispel the last of the musty smell.

The new earl could certainly have no complaints as to the restored comfort of his London home!

And, Diana knew, she had delayed that first meeting with the new earl for quite long enough...

'Bring tea into the library, would you, please, Soames,' she instructed lightly, knowing that all the servants, old as well as new, now worked with a quiet and competent efficiency under the guidance of this newly appointed butler whom she has interviewed and appointed herself.

'Yes, my lady.' He gave a stiff bow. 'Would that be tea for one or two, my lady? His Lordship instructed that a decanter of brandy be brought to him in the library almost an hour ago,' he supplied as Diana looked at him questioningly.

Diana could not help a glance at the grandfather clock in the hallway, noting that the hour was only twelve o'clock—surely much too early in the day for the earl to be imbibing brandy?

But then what did she, who had lived all of her one-and-twenty years in the country, know of London ways? Or, the earl having lived in Venice for so many years, were they Italian ways, perhaps?

Whichever of those it was, a cup of tea would do Lord Gabriel Faulkner far more good at this time of day than a glass or two of brandy. 'For two, thank you, Soames.' She nodded dismissively before drawing in a deep and determined breath and walking in the direction of the library.

'Enter,' Gabriel instructed tersely as a knock sounded on the door of the library. He stood, a glass half-full of brandy in his hand, looking out at what was undoubtedly a garden when properly tended, but at the moment most resembled a riotous jungle. Whoever had seen to the cleaning and polishing of the house—the absent Lady Diana, presumably?—had not as yet had the chance to turn her hand to the ordering of the gardens!

He turned, the sunlight behind him throwing his face into shadow, as the door was opened with a decisive briskness totally in keeping with the fashionably elegant young lady who stepped determinedly into the library and closed the door behind her.

The colour of her hair was the first thing that Gabriel noticed. It was neither gold nor red, but somewhere in between the two, and arranged on her crown in soft, becoming curls, with several of those curls allowed to brush against the smooth whiteness of her nape and brow. A softness completely at odds with the proud angle of her chin. Her eyes, the same deep blue colour of her high-waisted gown, flickered disapprovingly over the glass of brandy he held in his hand before meeting Gabriel's gaze with the same challenge with which she now lifted her pointed chin.

'Lady Diana Copeland, I presume?' Gabriel bowed briefly, giving no indication, by tone or expression, of his surprise at finding her here at all when his last instruction to the three sisters was for them to remain in residence at Shoreley Park in Hampshire and await his arrival in England.

Her curtsy was just as brief. 'My lord.'

Just the two words. And yet Gabriel was aware of a brief *frisson* of awareness down the length of his spine on hearing the husky tone of her voice. A voice surely not meant to belong to a young lady of society at all, but by a mistress as she whispered and cried out words of encouragement to her lover...

His gaze narrowed on the cause of these inappropriate imaginings. 'And which of the three Lady Copelands might you be in regard to age?' In truth, Gabriel had not been interested enough in the three wards that had been foisted on him to bother knowing anything about them apart from the fact they were all of marriageable age! Time enough for that, he had decided arrogantly, once one of them had agreed to become his wife. Except none of them had, he recalled grimly.

'I am the eldest, my lord.' Diana Copeland stepped further into the room, the sunlight immediately making her hair appear more gold than red. 'And I wish to talk with you concerning my sisters.'

'As your two sisters are not in this room at the moment I have absolutely no interest in discussing them.' Gabriel frowned his irritation. 'Whereas *you*—'

'Then might I suggest you endeavour to *make* yourself interested in them?' Diana advised coldly, the narrowness of her shoulders stiff with indignation.

'My dear Diana—I trust, as your guardian, I may call you that?—I suggest that in future,' he continued smoothly without bothering to wait for her answer, 'you do not attempt to tell me what I should and should not interest myself in.' A haughty young miss too used to having her own way presented no verbal or physical challenge for Gabriel after his years spent as an officer in the King's army. 'As such, *I* will be the one who decides what is or is not to be discussed between the two of us. The most immediate being—why it is you have chosen to come to London completely against my instructions?' He stepped forwards into the room.

Whatever sharp reply Diana had been about to make, in answer to this reminder of the arrogance with which she viewed Lord Gabriel Faulkner's "instructions", remained unsaid as he stepped forwards out of the sunlight and she found herself able to see him clearly for the first time.

He was, quite simply…magnificent!

No other word could completely describe the harsh beauty of that arrogantly handsome face. He possessed a strong, square jaw, chiselled lips, high cheekbones either side of a long blade of a nose, and his eyes— oh, those eyes!—of so dark a blue that they were the blue-black of a clear winter's night. His dark hair was fashionably styled so that it fell rakishly upon his brow and curled at his nape, his black jacket fitted smoothly across wide and muscled shoulders, the silver waistcoat beneath of a cut and style equally as fashionable, and his grey pantaloons clung to long, elegantly muscled legs, above black and perfectly polished Hessians.

Yes, Lord Gabriel Faulkner was without doubt the most fashionable and aristocratically handsome gentleman that Diana had ever beheld in all of her one-and-twenty years—

'Diana, I am still waiting to hear your reasons for disobeying me and coming up to town.'

—as well as being the most arrogant!

Having been deprived of her mother when she was but eleven years old, and with two sisters younger than herself, it had fallen to Diana to take on the role of mother to her sisters and mistress at her father's home; as such, she had become more inclined to give instructions than to receive them.

Her chin tilted. 'Mr Johnston merely advised that you would call upon us at Shoreley Park as soon as was convenient after your arrival from Venice. As, at the time, he could not specify precisely when the date for that arrival might be, I took it upon myself to use my own initiative concerning how best to deal with this delicate situation.'

Haughty as well as proud, Gabriel acknowledged with some inner amusement at the return of that challenging tilt to Diana Copeland's delicious chin. She had also, if he was not mistaken, already developed a dislike for him personally as well as for his role as guardian to herself and her sisters.

The latter Gabriel could easily understand; as he understood it from his lawyer, William Johnston, Diana had been mistress of Shoreley Park since the death of her mother, Harriet Copeland, some ten years ago. As such, she would not be accustomed to doing as she was told, least of all by a guardian she had never met.

The former—a dislike of Gabriel personally—was not unprecedented, either, but it usually took a little

longer than a few minutes' acquaintance for that to
happen. Unless, of course, Lady Diana had already
taken that dislike to him before she had even met him?

He quirked one dark, mocking brow. 'And what "delicate situation" might that be?'

A becoming blush entered the pallor of her cheeks,
those blue eyes glittering as she obviously heard the
mockery in his tone. 'The disappearance of my two
sisters, of course.'

'What?' Gabriel gave a start. He had known the
Copeland sisters had chosen to absent themselves from
Shoreley Park, of course, but once he was informed of
Diana's presence at Westbourne House, he had assumed
that her sisters would either be staying with her here, or
that she would at least have some idea of their whereabouts. 'Explain yourself—clearly and precisely, if you
please.' A nerve pulsed in his tightly clenched jaw.

Diana gave him a withering glance. 'Caroline and
Elizabeth, being so…alarmed by your offer of marriage, have both taken it into their heads to leave the
only home they have ever known and run off to heaven
knows where!'

Gabriel drew in a harsh breath as he carefully placed
the glass of brandy down upon the table before turning his back to once again stare out of the window.
While he'd known the three Copeland sisters had
absented themselves from Shoreley Park, to now learn
that his offer of marriage had actually caused the two
younger sisters to run away, without so much as informing their older sister of where they were going, was not

only insulting but, surprisingly, had also succeeded in affecting Gabriel when he had believed himself to be beyond reacting to such slights.

He had been forced to live in disgrace all these years, always knowing that of all the people Gabriel had previously loved or cared about, only his friends Blackstone and Osbourne believed in his innocence. It had meant he hadn't particularly cared, during his five years in the army, as to whether he lived or died. Ironically, it had been that very recklessness and daring that had succeeded in making him appear the hero in the eyes of his fellow officers and men.

Realising that two young, delicately bred ladies had been so averse to even the suggestion of marriage to the infamous Lord Gabriel Faulkner that they had chosen to flee their home rather than contemplate such a fate had laid open a wound Gabriel had believed long since healed, if not forgotten…

'My lord?'

Gabriel breathed in deeply through his nose, hands clenched at his sides as he fought back the demons from his past, knowing they had no place in the here and now.

'My lord, what—?' Diana recoiled from the icy fury she could see in Gabriel's arrogantly handsome features as he turned to glare across the room at her with eyes so dark and glittering they appeared as black as she imagined the devil's might be.

He arched a dark brow over those piercing blue-black eyes. 'You did not feel the same desire to run away?'

In truth, it had not even entered Diana's head to do

so. It was not in her nature to run away from trouble and she had been too busy since discovering her sisters' absence for there to be any time to think of anything else. But if she had thought of it, what would she have done?

Ten years of being the responsible daughter, the practical and sensible one, had taken their toll on the light-hearted and mischievous girl she had once been, until Diana could not recall what it was to behave impetuously or rashly, or to consider her own needs before those of her father and sisters. She would definitely not have left.

'No, I did not,' she stated bluntly.

'And why was that?' An almost predatory look had come over his face.

Diana straightened her shoulders. 'I—'

Quite what she had been about to say to Gabriel she could not be sure as the butler chose that moment to enter with a tray of tea things and place them on the table beside the fireplace. A tray of tea things set for two, Gabriel noted with some amusement; obviously, from that flicker of disdain he had seen on the fair Diana's face a few minutes ago, she did not approve of the imbibing of strong liquor before luncheon, if ever.

To hell with what the Lady Diana approved of!

Gabriel moved with deliberation as he picked up the glass of brandy he had been enjoying earlier and threw the contents to the back of his throat before replacing the empty glass down upon the table beside the tea tray, the smooth yet fiery liquid warming his insides, if not his mood.

He waited until the butler had left the room before speaking again. 'I believe you were about to tell me why it is you did not choose to run away as your sisters have done?' he asked.

'Would you care for tea, my lord?'

His eyes narrowed at this further delay. 'No, I would not.'

Blonde brows rose. 'You do not care for tea?'

'It is certainly not one of the things I have missed in all these years of living abroad,' he said drily.

Diana continued to calmly pour a cup of tea for herself before straightening, her gaze very direct as she looked across at him. 'I trust your journey from Venice was uneventful, my lord?'

He gave an impatient snort. 'If you are intending to distract me with these inanities, Diana, then I believe I should warn you that I am not in the habit of allowing myself to be distracted.'

'I have heard you were considered something of a war hero during your years in the army,' she commented.

She had heard of his time in the army? Had she heard something of those other, much more damaging rumours of his behaviour eight years ago, too?

Gabriel's expression became closed as he observed Diana through narrowed lids. 'And what else have you heard about me?'

Guileless blue eyes met his unblinkingly. 'In what context, my lord?'

Over the years Gabriel had faced down enemies and so-called friends alike, without so much as even the slightest possibility of any of them ever getting the better of him, but this young woman, who had lived all of her life in the country, nevertheless showed no hesitation in challenging him.

'In any context, madam,' he finally replied.

Slender shoulders lifted in a dismissive shrug. 'I make a point of never listening to idle gossip, my lord. But even if I did,' she continued, just as Gabriel felt himself starting to relax, 'I fear I have not been in town long enough, nor is my acquaintance wide enough as yet, to have had the time or opportunity to be made privy to any…confidences.'

If Diana Copeland feared anything, then Gabriel would be interested to learn what that something was. She had certainly shown no hesitation as yet in speaking her mind, clearly and often! And if Gabriel had his way, this young lady would be returning to the country long before she had the opportunity to become "privy to any confidences"…

She raised one delicately arched brow. 'Perhaps you would care to enlighten me?'

She was good, Gabriel recognised admiringly. Very good, in fact. She showed just the right amount of calm uninterest to indicate that the subject on which they spoke was of little or no relevance to her. If Gabriel had been less sensitive to the subject himself, he might even have been fooled by her…

'Not at this moment, no.' His jaw tightened. 'Nor have I forgotten our original subject.'

'Which was…?'

He drew in a deep and controlling breath, even as his hands flexed impatiently at his sides. 'I wish to know why, instead of disappearing before my arrival in England as your sisters have obviously chosen to do, you have come to stay at Westbourne House instead?'

She straightened haughtily. 'Are you, as the new owner of this property, expressing the sentiment that I no longer have that right?'

Gabriel made another attempt to regain control of the conversation. Something he was finding it harder and harder to do the longer it continued! 'No, I am not saying that. As my ward you are, of course, perfectly at liberty to continue using any of the Westbourne homes or estates. It is only that, in this case, you must have been aware that once I had learnt you weren't in Shoreley Park, Westbourne House was sure to be my first choice of residence?'

'I was aware of that, yes.'

'Well?' Gabriel found himself becoming more and more frustrated with this conversation.

She sipped her tea delicately before answering. 'Surely the reason for my being here is obvious, my lord?'

'Perhaps to make enquiries about your two sisters?'

'That was my first concern, yes.'

'And your second?' That nerve was once again pulsing in Gabriel's jaw, and if he was not mistaken, he was developing a twitch in his left eyelid too!

Diana sat forwards to carefully place her empty teacup down upon the silver tray, that slight adjustment in her pose revealing more of the deep swell of her creamy breasts. Full and plump breasts, Gabriel noted admiringly, and slightly at odds with the slenderness of the rest of her revealed by the cut of her gown.. Born and raised in the country or not, Diana Copeland was every inch a lady, he noted as his gaze trailed down her graceful slim arms and her elegant hands in their white-lace gloves. A self-confident and outspoken young lady who—

'My second reason for awaiting your arrival here is, of course, that I have decided to accept your offer of marriage.'

If Gabriel had still been enjoying his brandy at that moment, then he would surely have choked on it!

Chapter Two

Diana remained outwardly calm as she stood up to cross the room with purpose and rearrange the flowers in the vase that stood upon the small table near the window, having averted her face, she hoped, before any of the inner trepidation she felt in having voiced her acceptance of this man's offer of marriage could be revealed.

His lordship's surprise on hearing that acceptance had been all too obvious in the way those midnight-blue eyes had widened incredulously, followed by his stunned silence.

At any other time Diana might have felt a certain satisfaction in having rendered speechless a man of Lord Gabriel Faulkner's obvious arrogance and sophistication. Unfortunately, in this case, and on this particular subject, she would have welcomed almost any other response from him.

Perhaps, as Diana had initially refused his offer, the earl had now decided to withdraw it? In which case, she would not only have caused herself embarrassment, but also placed him in the awkward position of having to extricate himself from an unwanted engagement.

If that incredulity was for another reason, such as now that he had actually met her, the new Earl of West-bourne found either her looks or her character unsuitable in his future countess, then Diana was not sure—following other hurtful events of this past week—that she would be able to withstand the humiliation.

'Correct me if I am wrong, but did you not say you are the eldest of the Copeland sisters?' he finally managed to say.

A frown creased Diana's brow as she turned. 'I did, yes...'

He looked a little bemused. 'My lawyer led me to believe that the eldest of Copeland sisters was already betrothed. Is that not correct?'

Diana drew in a sharp breath even as she felt the warmth colouring her cheeks. 'Then he was misinformed, my lord. I am not, nor have I ever been, formally betrothed. Nor do I have any idea how Mr Johnston could even have heard such a thing,' she added waspishly.

Gabriel studied her closely, noting that high colour in her cheeks, the proud almost defiant tilt to her chin, and the challenging sparkle in those sky-blue eyes. He wondered as to the reason for them. Just as he also questioned the precise and careful way in which she had dismissed the existence of any betrothal...

His mouth firmed. 'I believe Johnston was told of the betrothal by one of your sisters.'

'Indeed?' Blond brows rose haughtily. 'Then it would seem that the man was not misinformed, after all, but merely misunderstood the information given to him.'

Somehow he did not think so... He had inherited William Johnston, along with the title, estates and guardianship of the three Copeland sisters, from their father, Marcus Copeland, the previous Earl of Westbourne. The lawyer was a precise and self-satisfied little man whom Gabriel did not particularly like, but at the same time he believed the lawyer would make it a matter of professional pride never to be misinformed or mistaken concerning information he gave to one of his wealthy and titled clients. So why was this betrothal no more?

Gabriel looked at her directly. 'Was it you or the young gentleman who had a change of heart?'

'I have just told you there was no gentleman!' she protested.

'A young man, then. One who no doubt found the prospect of marriage to a titled young lady whose fortunes now rested on the goodwill of her guardian a far different marriage prospect than the eldest daughter of a wealthy earl?' Gabriel enquired, eyeing her knowingly.

Diana withstood that gaze for as long as she could before turning away abruptly, determined he should not see the tears that now glistened in her eyes and on her lashes.

Damn the man!

No—damn *all* men!

And most especially Malcolm Castle for having the backbone of a jellyfish!

She and Malcolm had grown up together in the village of Shoreley. Had played together as children. Danced together at the local assemblies once they were old enough to attend. They'd taken walks together on crisp winter days and fine summer evenings. Diana had even allowed Malcolm the liberty of stealing her very first kiss after he had declared his love for her.

She had believed herself to be equally as smitten. Her father had shown no disapproval of their deepening friendship. Malcolm's parents, the local squire and his wife, were obviously thrilled at the idea of a possible match between their son and the eldest daughter of the wealthy Earl of Westbourne. All had seemed perfect.

Except, as his lordship had just pointed out so cruelly, the penniless eldest daughter of the previous Earl of Westbourne had not been nearly as appealing as a prospective wife to Malcolm, or to his parents. Diana's father had not expected to die so suddenly and had not set his affairs in order with regard to his daughters. Financially, they were completely at the mercy of the new earl's goodwill—and as he had been away from society for so long, Lord Gabriel Faulkner was an unknown quantity.

Diana had, of course, noted that Malcolm's visits to

Shoreley Park had become less frequent after her father died. There had been no suggestions of their walking out together, let alone the stealing of a kiss or two, and of course there had been no attending the local assemblies because Diana and her sisters were in mourning. But Diana had not been concerned, had believed Malcolm's absence to be out of consideration for her recent bereavement and nothing else.

Until the previous week when Diana had learnt—from inadvertently overhearing two of the housemaids indulging in idle gossip—of the announcement of Malcolm's betrothal to a Miss Vera Douglas, the daughter of a wealthy tradesman who had recently bought a house in the area.

To add insult to injury, Malcolm had called to see Diana that very same afternoon, full of apologies for not having told her of the betrothal himself, and insisting that it was his parents who had pushed for this other marriage rather than himself, and that, in spite of everything, it was still Diana that he loved.

Diana could perhaps have forgiven Malcolm if he had found himself smitten with love for another woman, but to hear from his own lips that he was only marrying this other wealthy young woman because his parents wished it was beyond enduring. A jellyfish, indeed! And one that she knew she could inwardly congratulate herself on being well rid of.

Except Malcolm's defection had left her pride in tatters and made her the object of pitying looks every time she so much as ventured out into the village. So she had decided, with her usual air of practicality, that the perfect way in which to dispel such gossip would be if she were to accept, after all, the offer of marriage from Lord Gabriel Faulkner, seventh Earl of Westbourne. Marriage to any man—even taking into account that past scandal connected to Gabriel, which Diana's neighbours had hinted at, but never openly discussed—surely had to be better than everyone believing she had been passed over for the daughter of a retired tradesman!

'Am I correct in thinking that the dissolution of your previous engagement is the only reason you have now decided to accept my own offer of marriage?' that taunting earl now prompted irritatingly.

How could Diana have known, when she so sensibly made her decision to accept his lordship's offer, how wickedly handsome he was? How tall and muscular? How fashionably elegant?

How irritatingly perceptive to have guessed within minutes of her announcing her acceptance of his offer as to the real reason for her change of mind!

'It was made more than clear that one of us must accept your offer if we wished to continue living at Shoreley Park,' she informed him defensively.

Gabriel frowned darkly. 'Made clear by whom, exactly?'

'Mr Johnston, of course.'

Gabriel could see no 'of course' about it. 'Explain, if you please.'

She gave an impatient huff. 'Your lawyer stated on his last visit to us that, if we all continued to refuse your offer, we might find ourselves not only penniless, but also asked to remove ourselves from our home.'

Gabriel's jaw tensed and he felt that nerve once again pulsing in his cheek. 'Those are the *exact* words he used when speaking with you?'

Diana gave a haughty inclination of her golden-red head. 'I am not in the habit of lying, my lord.'

If that truly were the case—and Gabriel had no reason to believe that it was not—then William Johnston had far exceeded his authority. It was not the fault of the Copeland sisters that they had no brother to inherit the title and estates, or that their father had not seen fit to secure their futures himself in the event of his death.

Damn it, Gabriel had only made his offer of marriage at all out of a sense of fairness, appreciating that, but for fickle fate, one of the Copeland sisters' own cousins would have inherited the title rather than a complete stranger. A cousin, one would hope, who would have treated the previous earl's daughters as fairly as Gabriel was attempting to do.

His mouth thinned. 'I have *no* intention of asking you or your sisters to leave your home, either now or in the future.'

Diana looked confused. 'But Mr Johnston was very precise concerning—'

'Mr Johnston obviously spoke out of turn.' Gabriel's expression was grim as he anticipated his next conversation with the pompous little upstart who had so obviously put the fear of God into the Copeland sisters that they had felt as trapped as cornered animals. 'This is the reason your two sisters have run away?'

'I believe it was…the catalyst, yes.'

Gabriel eyed her curiously. 'But only the catalyst?'

Diana grimaced. 'My sisters have found life at Shoreley Park somewhat limiting these past few years. Do not misunderstand me,' she added hastily as Gabriel raised his brows. 'Caroline and Elizabeth were both dutiful daughters. Accepted the reasons for our father's decision not to give any of us a London Season, or indeed his wish to not introduce us into London society at all—'

'Am I right in thinking your father made that decision based on your mother's behaviour ten years ago?' he interrupted gently.

Blond lashes lowered over those sky-blue eyes. 'Our father certainly blamed the…excesses of London society for my mother having left us, yes.'

Circumstances meant that Gabriel himself had not been part of that society for a number of years, but nevertheless he could understand Copeland's concern for his three no doubt impressionable daughters. 'He did not fear that keeping you and your sisters shut away in Hampshire might result in the opposite of what he intended? That one or all of you might be tempted into doing exactly as your mother had done and run away to London?'

'Certainly not!' Her reply was both quick and indignant. 'As I have said, Caroline and Elizabeth found life in the country somewhat restricting, but they would never have hurt our father by openly disobeying him.'

'They obviously did not feel the same reluctance where I am concerned,' Gabriel pointed out with a rueful grimace. 'Your presence here would seem to imply that you believe your sisters to have finally come to London now.'

In truth, Diana had no idea where her sisters had gone after they'd left Shoreley Park. But having searched extensively locally, with no joy, London, with all its temptations and excitement, had seemed the next logical choice. Except Diana had not realised until she arrived here quite how large and busy a city London was. Or how difficult it would be to locate two particular young ladies amongst its sprawling population.

'I believed it to be a possibility I might find at least one of them here. My sisters did not leave together, you see,' she explained as Gabriel once again raised arrogantly questioning brows. 'Caroline disappeared first, with Elizabeth following two days later. Caroline has always been the more impulsive of the two.' She gave an affectionate if exasperated sigh.

Gabriel's face darkened ominously. 'They had the good sense to bring their maids with them, I hope?'

Diana winced. 'I believe they both thought that a maid might try to hinder their departure—'

'You are telling me that they are both likely somewhere here in London *completely* unprotected?' The earl looked scandalised at the prospect.

Diana was no less alarmed now that she had actu-

ally arrived in London and become aware of some of
the dangers facing a young woman alone here—over-
familiarity and robbery being the least of them. 'I am
hoping that is not the case, and that the two of them had
made some sort of pact to meet up once they were here.'
Rather a large hope, considering Elizabeth had seemed
as surprised as Diana—and resentful—by Caroline's
sudden disappearance. 'In any case, I am sure they will
have come to no harm. That we may even one day all
come to laugh about this adventure.'

Gabriel was not fooled for a moment by Diana's
words of optimism and could clearly see the lines
of worry creasing her creamy brow. It was a worry
he, knowing only too well of the seedy underbelly of
London, now shared. 'I trust *you* did not also come to
London unchaperoned?'

'Oh, no,' she assured him hurriedly. 'My Aunt
Humphries and both our maids accompanied me here.'

'Your Aunt Humphries?'

'My father's younger sister. She was married to a
naval man, but unfortunately he was killed during the
Battle of Trafalgar.'

'And am I right in thinking that she now resides with
you in Hampshire?'

'Since her husband's death, yes.'

Good Lord, it seemed he did not have just three
young, unruly wards to plague him, but an elderly
widow he was also responsible for! 'And where is your
aunt now?'

She looked apologetic. 'She does not care for London and has stayed in her rooms since our arrival.'

Thereby rendering her of absolutely no use whatsoever as a chaperon to her niece! 'So,' Gabriel announced heavily, 'if I am to understand this correctly, your two sisters having run away, you have now decided to offer yourself up as a marital sacrifice in the hopes that, once they learn of our betrothal, they will be encouraged to return home?'

Diana met his gaze steadily. 'It is my hope, yes.'

Gabriel gave a hard and humourless smile. 'Your courage is to be admired, madam.'

She looked startled. 'My courage?'

'I am sure, even in the relative safety of Hampshire, that you cannot have remained unaware of the fact that you are considering marriage to a man that society has wanted nothing to do with this past eight years?'

'I have heard…rumours and innuendo, of course,' she admitted gravely.

Gabriel would wager that she had! 'And this does not concern you?'

Of course it concerned her. But if no one could be persuaded to tell her of this past scandal, what was she expected to do about it? 'Should it have done?' she asked slowly.

He gave a bored shrug. 'Only you can know the answer to that.'

Diana frowned slightly. 'Perhaps if you were to enlighten me as to the nature of the scandal?'

Those sculptured lips twisted bitterly. 'And why on earth would you suppose I'd ever wish to do that?'

Diana stared up at him in frustration. 'Surely it would be better for all concerned if you were to inform me of your supposed misdeeds yourself, rather than have me learn of them from a possibly malicious third party?'

'And if I prefer not to inform you?' he drawled.

She gave him a frustrated look. 'Did you kill someone, perhaps?'

He smiled without humour. 'I have killed too many someones to number.'

'I meant apart from in battle, of course!' Those blue eyes sparkled with rebuke for his levity.

'No, I did not.'

'Have you taken more than one wife at a time?'

'Definitely not!' Gabriel shuddered at the mere suggestion of it; he considered the taking of one wife to be ominous enough—two would be utter madness!

'Been cruel to a child or animal?'

'No and no,' he said drily.

She gave another shrug of those slender shoulders. 'In that case I do not consider what society does or does not believe about you to be of any relevance to my own decision to accept your offer of marriage.'

'You consider murder, bigamy and cruelty to children or animals to be the worst of a man's sins, then?' he asked with a bleak amusement.

'I have no other choice when you insist on remaining silent on the subject. But, perhaps, having now made my own acquaintance,' she suddenly looked less certain of herself, 'you have decided you would no longer find marriage to me acceptable to you?'

Was that anxiety Gabriel could now see in her expression? Had the young fool who had rejected her, no doubt because of that change in her circumstances, also robbed her of a confidence in her own attraction? If he had, then the man was not only a social-climbing fortune-hunter, but blind with it!

Diana Copeland was without doubt beautiful—certainly not 'fat and ugly' as Osbourne had suggested she might be when he'd first learnt of Gabriel's offer for one of the Copeland sisters without even laying eyes on them! Not only were her looks without peer, but she was obviously intelligent, too—and capable. Gabriel was fully aware he had her to thank for having arrived at a house that was not rodent infested and musty smelling, and with servants who were quietly efficient. She was, in fact, everything that an earl could ever want or desire in his countess.

Also, having now 'made her acquaintance', Gabriel had realised another, rather unexpected benefit if he should decide to make her his wife... No doubt that golden-red hair, when released from its pins, would reach down to the slenderness of her waist. Just as those high, full breasts promised to fit snugly into the palms of his hands and the slenderness of her body would benefit from a lengthy exploration with his seeking lips.

Obviously it was an intimacy that Diana's cool haughtiness did not encourage Gabriel to believe she would welcome between the two of them at present—

because she was still in love with the social climbing fortune-hunter, perhaps?—but she would no doubt allow it if she were to become his wife.

Diana felt her nervousness deepening at the earl's continued silence. Nor could she read anything of his thoughts as he continued to look at her with those hooded midnight-blue eyes.

Was she so unattractive, then? Had her role as mistress of her father's estate and mother to her two younger sisters this past ten years rendered her too practical in nature and, as a result, plain? Was Gabriel Faulkner even now formulating the words in which to tell her of his lack of interest in her?

'You realise that any marriage between the two of us would require you to produce the necessary heirs?'

Diana looked up sharply at that softly spoken question and felt that delicate colour once again warming her cheeks as she saw the speculative expression in those dark eyes. She swallowed before speaking. 'I realise that is one of the reasons for your wishing to take a wife, yes.'

'Not one of the reasons, but the *only* reason I would ever contemplate such an alliance,' Gabriel Faulkner bit out, his arrogantly hewn features now cold and withdrawn.

Diana moistened her lips with the tip of her tongue. 'I am fully aware of a wife's duties, my lord.'

That ruthless mouth compressed. 'I find that somewhat surprising, considering your own mother's complete lack of interest in them.'

Her eyes widened at the harshness of his remark. Her chin rose proudly. 'Were you acquainted with my mother, sir?'

'Not personally, no.' His disdainful expression clearly stated he had not wished to be either.

'Then you can have no idea as to why she left her husband and children, can you?'

'Is there any acceptable excuse for such behaviour?' he countered.

As far as Diana and her sisters were concerned? No, there was not. As for their father... Marcus Copeland had never recovered from his wife leaving him for a younger man and had become a shadow of his former robust and cheerful self, shutting himself away in his study for hours at a time, and more often than not taking his meals there, too, when he bothered to eat at all.

No, there was no acceptable explanation for Harriet Copeland's desertion of her family. But Diana did not appreciate having Gabriel Faulkner—a man with an acknowledged, if unspoken, scandal in his own past— point that out to her. 'I am not my mother, sir,' she said coolly.

'Perhaps that is as well...'

She frowned her resentment with his continued needling. 'If, having considered the matter, you have now changed your mind about offering for me, then I wish you would just say so. It is not necessary for you to insult my mother, a woman you admit you did not even know, whilst you are doing so!'

In truth, Gabriel had no interest whatsoever in the

marriage of Marcus and Harriet Copeland; he was well aware that marriages amongst the *ton* were often loveless affairs, with both parties tacitly taking lovers once the necessary heirs had been produced. That Harriet had chosen to leave her family for her young lover, and was later shot and killed by that same lover when he'd found her in the arms of yet another man, was of no real consequence to the present situation.

No, the coolly composed and forthright Diana Copeland, whilst as head-turningly beautiful as the infamous Harriet, was most certainly not the mother!

'Your mother produced only daughters,' he drawled drily.

Those blue eyes once again sparkled with temper. 'And if she had not, then you would not be here now!'

Gabriel gave her an appreciative smile. *'Touché.'*

'Nor is it possible for anyone to predict what children will be born into which marriage,' she argued.

'Also true.' He inclined his head. 'I was merely questioning as to whether or not you are prepared for the physical intimacy necessary to produce those children? If we have girls to begin with, we will keep trying until we have a boy.'

Diana drew in a sharp breath. It had taken several days after Malcolm's defection, accompanied by too many of those pitying looks of neighbours and friends, for her to come around to the idea of seriously considering the offer of marriage from Lord Gabriel Faulkner.

Accepting such an offer would not only salvage some of her own pride, she had assured herself, but would also help to persuade her two sisters to return home now that the possibility of marriage to a man they did not love had been removed.

Both of them were good and practical reasons, she had decided, for her to be the one to accept Gabriel's offer. Except she did not feel in the least practical now that she was faced with the flesh-and-blood man…

She looked at him now beneath lowered lashes, appreciating the way his perfectly tailored clothing emphasised the width of his shoulders, his muscled chest, the narrowness of waist, and his powerful thighs and long legs, before raising her gaze back to that wickedly handsome face, heat suffusing her cheeks as she saw the look in the dark and taunting eyes that stared unblinkingly back at her. A quiver of…something shivered down the length of her spine as she found herself unable to look away from those mesmerising midnight-blue eyes.

Whether it was a shiver of apprehension or anticipation she could not be sure. Although the tingling sensation she suddenly felt in her breasts would seem to indicate the latter.

Diana found that slightly shocking when he had not so much as touched her. She had only ever known a pleasant warmth when Malcolm kissed her, not this blazing heat at just a look from Gabriel… 'As I have stated, I believe I know, and am willing to participate in, all the duties expected of me as a wife,' she said stiffly.

'Perhaps we should test that theory before making any firm decision?' he drawled.

Diana did not at all care for the return of that predatory glint to his navy-blue eyes. 'Test that theory how?'

He raised speculative brows. 'I suggest we try a simple kiss to begin with.'

She gave a start. 'To *begin* with?'

'Exactly.'

Diana swallowed hard, pride and pride alone preventing her from taking a step back as Gabriel crossed the room with a catlike tread until he stood only inches in front of her. So close, in fact, that she was totally aware of the heat of his body and the clean male smell of him that tantalised and roused the senses, her breath catching in her throat when she finally looked up into his compelling face.

Those midnight-blue eyes were hooded by lids fringed with long, dark lashes, his beautiful high cheekbones as sharp as blades on either side of his aristocratic nose, sculptured lips slightly parted, his jaw square and uncompromising.

In contrast, Diana's own lips had gone suddenly dry, her breathing non-existent—in fact, she was starting to feel slightly light-headed from a lack of air in her lungs! She knew instinctively that any kiss she received from this man would be nothing like that chaste meeting of the lips she had infrequently shared with Malcolm Castle.

Diana could feel her pulse start to race and a welling of excitement rising up within her breast as those powerful arms moved firmly about her waist before she was pulled up against the hardness of Gabriel's chest and his head began to lower towards hers.

She was perfectly correct. Being kissed by Gabriel Faulkner was absolutely *nothing* like being kissed by Malcolm…

His arms about her waist crushed her breasts against that hard chest even as he took masterful possession of her lips with his own. His mouth moved over hers in a slow, lingering exploration before the sweep of his tongue parted her lips and he kissed her more intimately still, that skilful tongue seeking entrance in gentle, flickering movements.

Diana's pulse continued to race, to thunder; she felt both hot and shaky as their kiss continued, her hands moving up to Gabriel's chest with the intention of pushing him away, but instead clinging to the width of his shoulders, able to feel the flexing of muscles beneath his jacket as she did so. No doubt he could feel her own trembling, as his hands moved caressingly down the length of her spine before cupping her bottom to pull her thighs up against his muscular ones.

Nothing that had gone before—not Malcolm's kisses, or the talk Aunt Humphries had given concerning the marriage bed on Diana's sixteenth birthday; a talk Diana had dutifully passed on to her two sisters once she'd considered them both old enough to understand— had prepared her for the heat of Gabriel's kisses, or her complete awareness of that hardness that throbbed between his thighs.

Gabriel began to draw the kiss to a close as he sensed Diana's rising panic at the intimacy, knowing by the shyness of her responses that the fool who had passed her over had never even bothered to so much as kiss her properly, let alone introduce her to physical pleasure.

He looked down at her beneath hooded lids, having firmly assured himself of his own willingness to introduce her to every physical pleasure imaginable, before allowing his arms to drop from about the slenderness of her waist. He stepped away from her, his expression deliberately unreadable. 'Perhaps now would be the appropriate time to tell you that you did not ask me the correct question a few minutes ago when you were asking me for details of that past scandal.'

She blinked up at her, her cheeks still flushed. 'No?'

Gabriel's expression was grim. 'No.'

She shook her head as if to clear it. 'Then what should I have asked you?'

'Whether I have ever been accused of taking a young girl's innocence and then refusing to marry her when she found herself with child?'

Diana's throat moved convulsively as she swallowed, knowing that her cheeks were no longer flushed, but deathly pale. 'And have you been accused of that?'

'Oh, yes.' His teeth showed in a humourless smile.

She knew a brief moment's panic, the blood pounding in her veins, the palms of her hands suddenly damp inside her gloves, her legs feeling slightly shaky. There was no possibility of her, or of any decent woman, marrying a man so unfeeling, so without honour— No, wait one moment, she told herself sternly. Gabriel had said he'd been accused of such a heinous crime; he had not admitted to being *guilty* of it...

She looked up at him searchingly. His was a hard and implacable face, the face of a man who would not suffer fools gladly. Those midnight-blue eyes were equally as cold and unyielding. But it was not a sly or malicious face—more one that defied anyone to ever question him or his actions. As he was now daring her to do?

She drew in a shaky breath. 'You said you were accused of it, not that you were guilty.'

Those dark eyes narrowed. 'I did say that, yes,' he allowed softly.

'And so are you indeed innocent of that crime?'

Gabriel gave a small, appreciative smile. Not a single member of his family had bothered to ask him that question eight years ago, choosing instead to believe Jennifer Lindsay's version of events.

His friends Osbourne and Blackstone had not bothered to ask it either, but that was because they both knew him too well to believe he could ever behave in so ungentlemanly a fashion if he were indeed truly guilty of taking a young woman's innocence.

That Diana Copeland, a young woman he had only just met—moreover, a young woman Gabriel had deliberately kissed with passion rather than with any consideration for her own innocence—should have asked that question was beyond belief.

Gabriel looked her straight in the eye. 'I am.' His gaze narrowed to steely slits as she continued to frown.

'Having asked and been answered, you are now doubting my word on the subject?'

'Not at all.' She shook her head. 'I just— What could this young girl, any young girl, possibly hope to gain by telling such a monstrous lie?'

'As an only child I was heir to my father's fortune and lands,' Gabriel explained.

'Was...?'

His mouth firmed. 'That fortune and lands were instead left completely in my mother's care on my father's death six years ago. Fortunately I was not left destitute as my grandfather's estate had been left in trust and could not be taken away from me.'

'And this young girl's lies are the reason your family and society treated you so harshly all those years ago?' she pressed.

'Yes,' he grated.

She gave him a sympathetic look. 'Then I can only imagine it must have been a doubly bitter pill to swallow when you knew yourself to be innocent of the crime.'

'You only have my word for that,' he pointed out grimly.

'And is your word to be doubted?' she asked delicately, eyeing him quizzically.

Gabriel frowned. 'My dear Diana, if I truly were the man almost everyone believes me to be, then I could simply be lying again when I say, no, it is not.'

She smiled gently. 'I do not believe so. You are a

man, I think, who would tell the truth and—excuse me—to the devil with what anyone else chooses to believe!'

Yes, he was. He had always been so, and this past eight years had only deepened that resolve. But, again, it was surprising that this woman already knew him well enough to have realised and accepted that…

'And the—the young girl,' she spoke hesitantly. 'What became of her?'

His mouth tightened. 'My father paid another man to marry her.'

'And the babe?'

That nerve pulsed once again in Gabriel's tightly clenched jaw. 'Lost before it was even born.'

Diana's expression was pained. 'How very sad.'

'Knowing all of this, are you still of the opinion you wish to become my countess?' he asked her directly.

Her cheeks were pale, her hair in slight disarray from their kisses, but there was still that familiar light of resolve in those sky-blue eyes. 'You are no more responsible for what people may wrongly choose to believe of you than I can be held accountable for my mother having left her husband and three daughters.'

Gabriel's mouth quirked. 'The announcement of a betrothal between the two of us would certainly give society much to talk about!'

She smiled a little sadly. 'No doubt. Perhaps, if you hope to become reconciled to society you should not, after all, contemplate taking one of Harriet Copeland's daughters as your countess?'

Gabriel's expression hardened. 'I have absolutely no interest in becoming reconciled to society, or in having society be reconciled to me. Nor do I care what any of them may choose to think of me or the woman I take as my countess.'

'Then we are in agreement?' Diana held her breath as she waited for his answer.

'I will have the announcement of our betrothal appear in the newspapers as soon as is possible.' He gave a sharp inclination of his arrogant head.

This was what Diana had wanted, what she knew was necessary to salvage her own pride after Malcolm's defection, and to encourage her sisters to return home. Yet the reality of being betrothed to the hard and unyielding Lord Gabriel Faulkner, a man beset with a past scandal that rivalled even that of Diana's mother—worse, a man who had kissed her with such passion only minutes ago—caused her to inwardly tremble.

Whether that trembling was caused by apprehension or anticipation she was as yet unsure…

Chapter Three

'I am seriously starting to doubt that your Aunt Humphries exists,' Gabriel commented drily the following morning as he and Diana sat together in the small dining room, eating their breakfast attended by the quietly efficient Soames.

The previous afternoon had been taken up with various visits to the newspaper offices, the Westbourne lawyer, William Johnston, and to an old comrade in connection with Dominic Vaughn's disappearance into the country. But Gabriel had returned home in time to change for dinner before joining Diana downstairs. Only Diana. Mrs Humphries had sent her apologies. Those same apologies had been sent down again in regard to breakfast this morning.

Diana smiled. 'I assure you she does exist, but suffers dreadfully with her nerves. In fact, she did not wish to come to London at all and only did so because I insisted on coming here,' she added affectionately.

Gabriel raised dark brows. 'I am relieved she had enough sense to agree to accompany you, at least. But taking to her rooms the moment you arrived, and remaining there, is certainly not helpful. In fact, it is totally unacceptable now that I am residing here, too.'

She looked enquiringly at him. 'Surely there can be no impropriety when you are my guardian?'

'A guardian who is now, officially, your betrothed.' Gabriel passed the open newspaper he had been reading across the table to her.

Diana's hands trembled slightly as she took possession of it, searching down the appropriate column until she located the relevant announcement. *The betrothal is announced between Lord Gabriel Maxwell Carter Faulkner, seventh Earl of Westbourne, Westbourne House, London, and his ward, the Lady Diana Harriet Beatrice Copeland, of Shoreley Park, Hampshire. The wedding will take place shortly at St George's Church, Hanover Square.*

There was nothing else. No naming of who Gabriel Faulkner's parents were, or her own, just the announcement of their betrothal. Nevertheless, there was something so very real about seeing the betrothal printed in the newspaper and knowing that it would no doubt be read by hundreds of people all over London this morning as they also sat at their breakfast tables.

Not that Diana had even considered changing her mind about the betrothal since they had come to their agreement yesterday. Nor did she baulk at the comment that the marriage was to 'take place shortly'—the sooner the better as far as she was concerned, preferably before Malcolm Castle and Miss Vera Douglas walked down the aisle together!

No, Diana had no regrets about her decision; it was only that seeing the betrothal in print also made Gabriel Faulkner so very real to her too. Not that there could really have been any doubts in her mind about that, either, after being held in his arms and kissed so passionately by him yesterday.

Just thinking about that kiss had kept her awake last night long after she had retired to her bedchamber…

Nothing in Aunt Humphries's talk all those years ago, concerning what took place in the marriage bed, had prepared Diana for the heady sensations that had assailed her body as Gabriel had kissed and held her. The heat. The clamouring excitement. The yearning ache for something more, something she wasn't sure of, but believed that marriage to a man of his experience and sophistication would undoubtedly reveal to her…

Gabriel watched beneath hooded lids as the colour first left Diana's creamy cheeks before coming back again, deeper than ever. That rosy flush was practically the same colour as the gown she wore this morning, accompanied by an almost feverish glitter in those sky-blue eyes as she raised heavily lashed lids to look across the breakfast table at him. 'You are concerned by the word "shortly" in the announcement, perhaps?' he asked.

'Not at all,' she dismissed readily. 'I would like to find my sisters first, of course, but can see no reason why the wedding should not take place immediately after that.'

'No?' Gabriel looked at her wickedly. 'I had imagined that perhaps you might wish to give your young man—I trust he is a young man?—the appropriate time in which to rush to your side and admit to having made a mistake as he proclaims his everlasting love for you?'

Irritated colour now darkened Diana's cheeks at Gabriel's teasing tone. 'He is a young man, yes…as well as a very stupid one. And even if he were to do that, I would not believe or trust such a claim.' Her mouth—that deliciously full and tempting mouth—had firmed with resolve.

Gabriel leant back in his chair to look across at her speculatively. That Diana was beautiful could not be denied. That she had a firmness of will could also be in no doubt. That her nature was unforgiving where this young man was concerned he found surprising. Especially considering she had accepted Gabriel's own claim of innocence the previous day without his having produced so much as a shred of evidence to back up that claim. Except his word…

He set his jaw. 'Perhaps I should know the name of this young man? So that I might send him about his business if he should decide to come calling,' he added as Diana gave him a sharp glance.

'I trust I am perfectly capable of dealing with such

a situation myself if it should ever arise,' she retorted snippily.

Gabriel was well aware of the strength of Diana's character—how could he not be when he knew she had acted as both mistress of her father's house and mother to her two sisters since the age of eleven?

No, his reason for wishing to know who the young fool was who had turned away from Diana when her fortunes had changed was a purely selfish one; having secured her agreement to marry him, he had no intention of now allowing her to be persuaded into changing her mind. Firstly, because they would both be made to look incredibly foolish if the betrothal ended almost before it began. And secondly, because kissing her yesterday had shown him that marriage to her would not be the hardship he had always envisaged matrimony to be…

Beneath the coolness, and that air of practicality and efficiency she had displayed so ably by preparing Westbourne House for habitation, Gabriel had discovered a warm and passionate young woman that he would very much enjoy introducing to physical pleasure. He certainly had no intention of allowing some fortune-hunting young idiot to reappear in her life and steal her away from under his very nose. Or any other part of his anatomy!

Gabriel's mouth compressed. 'Nevertheless, you will refer any such situation to me.'

Diana looked irritated. 'I feel I should warn you, my

lord, that I have become accustomed to dealing with my own affairs as I see fit.'

He gave an acknowledging inclination of his dark head. 'An occurrence that I believe our own betrothal now renders unnecessary.'

It was Diana's first indication of how life was to change for her now that she had agreed to become Gabriel's wife. A change she was not sure she particularly cared for. Ten years of being answerable only to herself had instilled an independence in her that she might find hard to relinquish. Even to a husband. 'I am unused to allowing anyone to make my decisions for me,' she reiterated.

Gabriel did not doubt it; it was because Diana was no simpering miss, no starry-eyed young debutante looking to fall in love and have that man fall equally as in love with her, that he could view their future marriage with any degree of equanimity. 'I am sure that, given time, we will learn to deal suitably with each other.'

Diana gave a knowing smile. 'I think by that you mean, with time, *I* will learn to accede to *your* male superiority!'

Gabriel found himself returning that smile. 'You do not agree?'

She shook her head. 'I do not believe you to be in the least superior to me just because you are a man. Nor is my nature such that it will allow for subservient and unquestioning obedience.'

Since meeting Diana, Gabriel had come to realise that the last thing that he desired in a wife was sub-

servience or obedience. When he had told Osbourne
and Blackstone a week or so ago of his plans to marry,
Gabriel had assured them both that his marriage was
a matter of obligation and expediency. Firstly, because
he needed a wife, and, secondly, because of a sense of
obligation to the Copeland sisters, because they had all
been left without provision for their future when their
father had died so unexpectedly. As such, subservience
and obedience in his future wife had seemed the least
that Gabriel could expect.

Having glimpsed the fire hidden beneath Diana's
cool exterior yesterday, Gabriel knew that in their marriage bed, at least, he required neither of those things!

'My lord…?' Diana gave him a searching glance as
the silence between them lengthened uncomfortably.

Had she said too much? Been too frank about her
character? But surely it was better for him to know the
worst of her before they embarked on a marriage
together, rather than learn of it after the event?

She had certainly believed so. But perhaps she had
been a little too honest? 'I could perhaps attempt to…
quell, some of my more independent inclinations.'

'There is no need to do so on my account, I assure
you,' he said with a twinkle in his eye before turning to dismiss the attentive Soames, waiting until the
butler had left the room before continuing. 'Diana, I had
expected to be bored, at the very least, in any marriage
I undertook; it is something of a relief to know that will
not, after all, be the case.'

Her eyes widened. 'You do not think it preferable to wait and perhaps marry a woman whom you love?'

'Love?' He managed to convey a wealth of loathing in that single word.

'You do not believe in the emotion?' she asked cautiously.

His top lip curled back disdainfully. 'My dear Diana, I have discovered that love comes in many guises—and all of them false.'

She could perhaps understand Gabriel's cynicism towards the emotion when he had been so completely ostracised after being falsely accused of taking advantage of an innocent young lady. Had he loved the young lady before she had played him false?

Yes, Diana could sympathise with him—possibly even shared his cynicism towards love. Malcolm Castle had certainly made nonsense of that emotion when he'd professed to still love Diana, but had every intention of marrying another woman!

She sighed. 'Perhaps you are right and a marriage such as ours, based on nothing so tenuous and fickle as love, but on common sense and honesty instead, is for the best.'

Gabriel frowned as he heard the heaviness in Diana's tone. One and twenty was very young for such a beautiful young lady to have formed such a pragmatic view on love and marriage. But perhaps, with the experience of her parents' marriage, and her young man's recent abandonment of her, she was perfectly justified in forming that opinion. After all, Gabriel had been but twenty years old himself when he learnt that hard lesson.

'Which is not to say…' he stood up slowly to move around the table to take Diana's hand in his before pulling her effortlessly to her feet '…there will not be other…compensations in our marriage to make up for that lack of love.'

She blinked up at him as she obviously realised it was his intention to kiss her once again. 'I—my lord, it is only nine o'clock in the morning!'

Gabriel threw back his head and laughed. 'I trust, my dear, you are not about to put time limitations on when and where I may make love to you?'

Not at all. Indeed, she would dare anyone to put limitations on a man such as Gabriel Faulkner. It was only that his behaviour now deviated drastically from her Aunt Humphries's description of what marriage would be like.

Her aunt had led her to believe that it was usual for a husband and wife to go about their daily lives separately—for the husband that involved dealing with business and correspondence in the morning and visiting his club in the afternoon, for the wife it meant dealing with the household responsibilities, such as menus of the day, answering letters, receiving visitors and returning those visits in turn, along with needlework and reading. Evenings would possibly be spent together, either at home or attending social functions, followed by returning home and retiring to their separate bedchambers.

On one, possibly two nights a week, the husband

might briefly join the wife in her bedchamber, during which time it was the wife's duty to do whatever her husband required of her. Aunt Humphries had been a little sketchy as to what that 'whatever' might entail, with the added advice that a husband had 'needs' a wife must satisfy, 'silently and without complaint'...

Luckily, Diana had some idea as to what those 'needs' might entail; her father had bred deer on the estate in Hampshire—no doubt what took place between a husband and wife in their marriage bed was not so very different from that process. Such an undignified business that it was not surprising her aunt had chosen not to discuss it!

But at no time had Diana's aunt mentioned that a husband—or, in this particular case, a betrothed—was in the habit of stealing kisses throughout the day. Most especially the type of kisses that yesterday had made Diana's toes curl in her satin slippers!

She straightened. 'As I assured you yesterday, I believe I know my duty towards my future husband, my lord.'

Gabriel's brow lowered. Damn it, he did not wish Diana to allow him to kiss her out of a sense of duty; he wanted her to now give freely what he had taken so demandingly yesterday. 'Gabriel,' he encouraged huskily.

That pulse was once again beating intriguingly in the slender column of her throat. 'It would be improper of me to be so familiar until after we are wed, my lord,' she said, her eyes lowered demurely.

His jaw clenched. 'I believe you know me well enough by now to realise that I have no care for what is considered "proper".'

She gave a nervous smile. 'I am not sure—' Her words were cut off abruptly as Gabriel lowered his head and took possession of her lips.

Full and sensuous lips that had tempted him unbearably this past hour as Diana had first sipped her tea and then bit into a slice of buttered toast smothered in honey. He'd found himself imagining heatedly what other uses those deliciously plump lips might be put to…

She tasted of that honey she had spread so liberally over her toast earlier, deliciously sweet, with an underlying heat that encouraged him to kiss her more deeply. His tongue appreciated the honey upon her lips before moving past that plumpness and into the hot, moist cavern of her mouth.

There had been no shortage of women in Gabriel's life during his years spent on the Continent: blondes, redheads, dusky-haired and dusky-skinned Italian women, young and slightly older, all experienced, and all initially intrigued by his scandalous past, but choosing to linger after once sharing his bed in the hopes of being invited to share it again.

He had become an expert lover during those years, able to give satisfaction to even the most demanding and experienced of women. That he had never personally enjoyed anything more than the immediate satisfaction of the flesh was not the fault of any of those women; Gabriel had only allowed his physical emotions to become engaged in those trysts.

Holding Diana in his arms, moulding the soft curves of her body against his, tasting, feeding from her lips and experiencing the sweetness of her instinctive response, brought out a gentleness in Gabriel, a need to protect that he had long thought forgotten, if not completely dead—emotions that he knew from experience could be called incautious at best and dangerous at worst. Slowly introducing Diana to the pleasures of their marriage bed, melting that cool exterior, was one thing, feeling anything more than that physical pleasure himself was something Gabriel did not intend to allow to happen. No matter how tempting the honeypot!

Not liking the trend of his own thoughts one little bit, he swiftly removed his mouth from hers and raised his head before putting her firmly away from him. 'I think we should stop there, don't you, Diana?'

Diana felt too dazed at first to wonder why he'd ended their kiss so abruptly, but as his words penetrated that daze she instantly felt the embarrassed flush that heated her cheeks. Had her enthusiasm in responding to his love-making perhaps been inappropriate in his future countess, after all?

She stepped back, her expression becoming cool despite feeling her legs tremble slightly from the effects of that passionate kiss. 'I believe *you* were the one who initiated that kiss, sir.'

He looked down his arrogant nose at her. 'Are you questioning my right to do so?'

Diana suddenly realised that once she was Gabriel's wife, she would have no right to question him about anything he might choose to demand of her. Could she bear that? Could she stand being nothing more than this man's possession, his to do with whatever he wished?

If it succeeded in salving her wounded pride following Malcolm's betrayal of the love they had professed to feel for each other, then yes, she could, she thought defiantly. 'I apologise if you feel I lacked…decorum just now,' she said stiffly. 'I—I am overset, I believe, and far too emotional, both from Caroline and Elizabeth's disappearance and seeing the announcement of our betrothal this morning.'

Gabriel felt a moment's regret, guilt even, for what Diana evidently believed. But only for a moment—the tender emotions he had briefly felt towards her whilst kissing her were not for someone as disillusioned as he. Far better to keep some distance between them. For as much as he believed he would enjoy introducing her to all the pleasures of the flesh once they were wed, he had no wish to do so if there was any danger she might give in to romantic flights of fancy. It would only result in her knowing a worse disillusionment than she had already suffered at the hands of her fickle young man.

Gabriel stepped away and placed his hands firmly behind his back to withstand the temptation to touch her again. 'No doubt we will receive an avalanche of visiting cards and invitations this morning following the announcement of our betrothal.' His mouth twisted derisively. 'The socially polite and the simply curious, all anxious to claim they were the first to receive Lord Gabriel Faulkner upon his return to London after an eight-year absence. Needless to say, I do not expect you to accept any invitations without first consulting me,' he added.

Diana bristled with obvious indignation. 'I may have lived all my life in the country, but even so I trust I know the correct way to behave. As such, of course I will not receive visitors, or accept any invitations, without first discussing them with you.'

He gave a hard smile. 'My request has little to do with behaving correctly and more to do with the fact that I do not care for most of society.'

Diana was well aware of the reason for Gabriel's dictate— 'request' was not at all a fitting description! She also empathised with it; as the daughter of a notorious countess, Diana would no doubt come in for her own share of curiosity where society was concerned following the announcement of their betrothal. As such, she was more than happy to leave the choice of deciding which invitations they would accept or decline to Gabriel's superior knowledge on the subject; left to her own devices, she might make a social gaffe.

She stifled a sigh. 'I believe I will go upstairs and check upon my aunt.'

'Perhaps whilst there you might suggest it would be a good idea if she were to join us for dinner this evening?'

Diana was aware that this was no more a 'suggestion' than Gabriel's earlier dictate had been a 'request'.

'I will certainly enquire if she is feeling well enough to join us this evening,' she answered coolly. She might as well start as she meant to go on; she had no intention of allowing Gabriel to simply dominate every aspect of her life, however arrogant he was.

He frowned slightly. 'And I suppose that is the best I can hope for?'

'It is.' Diana met his dark gaze unblinkingly.

Gabriel gave her an appreciative smile. One thing he could say for Diana—she did not back down from any of his challenges. 'It is my intention this morning to make discreet enquiries concerning your two sisters. I will obviously need detailed descriptions of them both...' He listened attentively as Diana eagerly supplied him with those details. 'Is there anything else you need to tell me before I go?'

She looked confused. 'Such as?'

His mouth quirked ruefully. 'Such as could either of your sisters have run off to be with a young man?'

'Certainly not!' Diana's denial was immediate.

Gabriel held up his hands defensively. 'I had to ask.'

There were high wings of indignant colour in her creamy cheeks now. 'My sisters may have behaved rashly by running away, but I do not believe they would have been so rash as to have totally ruined their reputations, my lord.'

Gabriel wished he felt the same certainty about that as she did. Unfortunately, even if neither Caroline nor Elizabeth had initially run off to be with a man, he knew that situation could have changed. Caroline had, accord-

ing to Diana, now been missing for over two weeks, and
her sister Elizabeth only two days less than that. Plenty
of time for unscrupulous men to have noted and taken
advantage of two young women alone and unprotected.

'I am glad to hear it,' was all he said, as he didn't
want to distress her further. 'Please pass along my
respects to your aunt.'

Diana watched as he crossed the breakfast room in
long and forceful strides, noting the way his dark-brown
superfine moulded to the width of his shoulders and
narrow waist, his buff-coloured pantaloons doing the
same for his long and muscled thighs. Physical attributes, along with those sensually pleasurable kisses,
which set her pulse racing just to think of them, indi-
cating that the best—and certainly the safest—course
was not to think about them at all!

'I had almost forgotten...' Gabriel suddenly said as
he came to a halt in the doorway to turn and look back
at her standing so elegantly in the centre of the room.
'I realise that Hampshire is a large county, but do you
by any chance know of a family named Morton?' He
had already sent several old comrades into Hampshire
in search of Dominic Vaughn and the woman he had
announced it was his intention to marry, but it would
be negligent on his part not to enquire if Diana knew
of the woman's family. Something he had almost forgotten to do since kissing her earlier.

'Morton?' She looked momentarily startled. 'The
butler at Shoreley Park is named Morton, but, apart
from that, I'm not aware of any family of that name.'

Gabriel's expression became guarded. 'Indeed? And does he possess a family? In particular, a daughter of marriageable age?'

'Not that I am aware of… No, I am sure he does not,' she said firmly. 'Morton has been with us for years. I am sure I would have heard of a daughter if he had one.'

'Hmm,' Gabriel murmured softly. 'Still, it is curious that your butler also possesses that name…'

'Why is it curious, my lord?' Diana looked puzzled.

'I am not sure.' He scowled darkly, the pieces of that particular puzzle becoming more obscure the deeper he delved into it. 'It is a start at least,' he muttered. 'It may be that this butler has a niece of that name.'

'I do not recall him ever mentioning one…' A frown creased Diana's creamy brow. 'What is this woman to you, my lord?'

Gabriel became suddenly still. 'Why should you assume she is anything to me?'

A delicate blush coloured her cheeks. 'I thought, as you asked about her—'

'Did you think that because I said the woman is young I must, either now or some time in the past, have had some personal interest in her?' he queried with a gleam in his eyes she wasn't at all sure of.

Diana had no idea what to think. In fact, this whole conversation was somewhat confusing to her. Indeed, she still felt slightly befuddled by her response to his kiss earlier and its abrupt and slightly hurtful ending.

She suddenly became aware how little she really knew of the man she had agreed to marry. She had

believed him yesterday when he'd told her that he was
not responsible for seducing that young girl and leaving
her pregnant. However, she had to acknowledge that his
past might appear in a somewhat different light to her
if she were to learn that the allegedly wronged woman
from eight years ago, and the one he now sought, were
one and the same...

Chapter Four

Gabriel's lids narrowed over glittering dark blue eyes as he watched the emotions flickering across Diana's expressive face. Puzzlement. Alarm, quickly followed by wariness. 'Well?' he demanded harshly.

Her throat moved as she swallowed before speaking. 'I have no idea what to think, my lord.'

'Then perhaps it would be prudent if you were to remain silent on the subject until you do know,' he rasped angrily. He had taken all the suspicion and accusations he could stand eight years ago. He had no intention of suffering them again from the young woman he intended to make his countess.

Even if that young woman had accepted nothing more than his word on it yesterday when he'd claimed his innocence of that past misdeed? his conscience whispered to him.

He eyed Diana in some frustration, nostrils flared,

jaw clenched. He was not used to explaining himself
to anyone, but…'If you must know, I am seeking this
woman in connection with a friend rather than having
any interest in her myself,' he said tautly.

'A friend, my lord?'

Gabriel gave a humourless smile at her continued uncertainty. 'Believe it or not, I do still possess
some. Men who have remained loyal and true all these
years despite what my family and society may have
chosen to believe of me.'

Diana had not meant to imply otherwise; she had
merely been curious to know who this young lady might
be and exactly what she meant to Gabriel. For instance,
could she be his mistress? When she had so coolly and
practically decided to accept his offer of marriage, she
had done so without consideration for the fact that he
might already be involved with another woman And if
he was, would he want to continue seeing her even after
he married Diana?

Her aunt had mentioned to her how both the married men and women of society, once the heirs had been
born, often chose to go their own way in regard to bed
partners. That Diana's own marriage might become
so sordidly complicated was a situation she found too
unpleasant to even contemplate.

'I am glad to hear it.' She gave an inclination of her
head. 'And you say it is for one of these friends that you
are seeking this lady named Morton?'

'I have said so, yes.'

She looked at him searchingly as she heard the challenge in his tone. A challenge that was reflected in the hard glitter of those midnight-blue eyes as they easily met her gaze. 'Then I hope that your enquiries are successful.'

So did Gabriel. Otherwise Dominic could find himself married to the chit and socially ruined; having experienced that for himself, it was not something Gabriel would wish upon one of his closest friends.

That was not to say he would easily forget Diana's suspicions of him just now…

'You cannot possibly have become betrothed to such a disreputable rake as Gabriel Faulkner!' Aunt Humphries goggled up at her from where she lay resting upon her *chaise* in the sitting room that adjoined her bedchamber.

A room Diana found both cluttered and hot, warmed as it was by both the fire in the hearth and the sun shining in through the huge bay window. 'He is Lord Gabriel Faulkner, seventh Earl of Westbourne, now, Aunt,' she said quietly.

'Well…yes. And his mother was a gracious and lovely woman, to be sure…'

'You were acquainted with Mrs Faulkner?' Diana asked curiously.

'Felicity Campbell-Smythe and I were the greatest of friends thirty years ago.' Her aunt smiled affectionately at the memory of that friendship. 'We lost touch when we both married, of course,' she continued briskly. 'But

I recall that her son was involved in the most dreadful scandal some years ago—'

'His lordship and I have spoken of that.' Her tone was stiffly disapproving; she loved her aunt deeply and she'd helped to fill the place of the mother who had left them all those years ago. But even so, Diana did not intend to discuss Gabriel's past with her or anyone else. He had spoken of the matter to her in confidence, and it was a confidence she would not, could not, break.

Her aunt sat up agitatedly, her greying blond curls bouncing about her thin and lined face. 'But—'

'It is not polite of us to discuss either Mrs Faulkner or the Earl in this way.' Much as Diana might wish to learn more about Felicity Faulkner, she knew that to do so would only lead to more questions and comments about Gabriel from her aunt. 'All that is important for now is that you know I am betrothed to him, and that we will very shortly be married.'

'But—'

'There is nothing more to be said on the subject, Aunt,' she added firmly as she moved away from the *chaise* to stand in front of the window, looking out at the square below.

There was a nursemaid and her small charge in the park across the road and a footman walking a large black dog, with a maid hurrying along the pavement carrying several brown paper-wrapped parcels. All of them such normal, everyday occurrences. It was so very strange when Diana felt as if her own life would never again be what she had considered normal…

She was to be married soon. Was to become the wife of the forceful and arrogant Earl of Westbourne. The changes in her life had started before that, of course. They had begun with the death of her father six and a half months ago. If not for that, Gabriel would not have inherited the title. There would have been no reason for her sisters to have run away from home. No reason for Diana to have agreed to marry a man she did not know and who did not know her either.

How strange fate was. How fickle. A few months ago, Diana's life had seemed settled. Malcolm Castle would become her husband, and after their wedding they would reside in the gatehouse to Castle Manor, only moving into the manor itself after Malcolm's own father had died.

Diana had been able to envisage it all in her mind's eye. Her future, certain and sure, stretching out before her. She would marry Malcolm. They would have several children together, followed by grandchildren. With her two sisters also perhaps married to men who lived locally, the three of them would meet often to gossip and laugh together.

Instead, Diana now found herself in London. Malcolm was to marry another woman and was no longer even a part of her life. Her two sisters were missing, heaven knew where. And she was betrothed to a man of mercurial moods at best, and cold and unapproachable at worst.

A handsome and exciting man, whom she privately admitted caused her pulse to race just by being in the same room with her...

* * *

'Is it bad news, my lord?'

Gabriel scowled as he looked up from the letter he had been reading to see Diana standing in the doorway of the study. It was one of the many letters and visiting cards that had been delivered to the house since the announcement of their betrothal in the newspapers two days ago.

Diana had not been in evidence when he'd returned late that afternoon from yet another fruitless attempt to locate the missing Copeland sisters, an enquiry from Soames eliciting the information that she was with the housekeeper consulting on the menus for the week. Menus that would no doubt have to be changed once he had sifted through the invitations that had arrived these past two days and decided which, if any, of the social engagements they would attend.

For himself, Gabriel had absolutely no interest in attending any social functions, having no wish to place himself in the position of being the visible focus of the *ton*'s gossip. But to refuse them all would be unfair to Diana when he knew she had lived all of her one-and-twenty years shut away from the class of people to which she rightly belonged. Bad enough that she was to become the wife of the scandalous Gabriel Faulkner, without, as her father had already done, denying her the company of her peers.

'It's not news that concerns either of your sisters, if that is your worry.' Gabriel placed the letter he had been reading down upon the desk in front of him as he looked at her with appreciation.

She wore a gown of pale and misty blue, the red lights in her hair seeming more prominent against its muted colour. Her cheeks were slightly flushed, with a bright sparkle to those sky-blue eyes, the whole endowing her with a vibrancy of beauty that was extremely easy on Gabriel's somewhat jaundiced eye.

He raised an eyebrow. 'Perhaps we might begin discussing the arrangements for the wedding? I had thought next week would be—'

'Next week!' she echoed breathlessly, those blue eyes widening.

Gabriel frowned. 'You said you had no objections to it taking place shortly?'

'And I do not,' she explained. 'It is only that I had not thought to be married until after we have found my two sisters.'

Gabriel sighed. 'But we have no idea when that might be.'

Diana looked unhappy. 'You were again unsuccessful in your enquiries?'

He stood up impatiently. 'It would seem that your two sisters have succeeded in appearing to have completely disappeared from the face of the earth—I trust you are not about to faint, Diana?' Gabriel said as he swiftly crossed the room in three long strides to grasp the tops of her arms as she swayed.

He cursed himself for speaking so frankly to her about her sisters. His mood had been terse and irritable

for the past two days as he first went about the business
of retaining a new lawyer after dispensing with William Johnston's services—but not before Gabriel had
first left the other man in no doubts as to his displeasure concerning his treatment of the Copeland sisters.
That had been followed by the seeking out of half a
dozen of the men who had once served with him in his
regiment and instructing them to search every inch of
London for the two missing women.

He had risked having lunch at his old club today too,
not a wise decision as it turned out, as he was forced to
fend off the curiosity of several of the other members
who had obviously been instructed by their wives to
elicit whatever information they could about him and
his bride-to-be.

Returning to another avalanche of invitations and
letters—and one of those letters in particular—had not
improved his temper, with the result that now he had
upset Diana.

She shook her head in denial, her face still very pale.
'My sisters have to be somewhere!'

Gabriel's hands dropped back to his sides as he
stepped away from her. 'Indeed they do,' he reassured
her heartily, although privately he was not sure that
'somewhere' necessarily had to be in London. He had
been thinking that Diana revealing the butler at Shoreley Park was named Morton was surely too much of
a coincidence to actually be one. 'Tell me, Diana, do
either of your sisters sing?'

She looked a little bewildered by the question. 'I—

they both do. Caroline has the finer voice of the two, but they are both perfectly competent. Why do you ask?'

'I merely wish to know as much about them both as possible,' Gabriel said vaguely, storing this piece of information away with the rest of what he now knew of Caroline and Elizabeth Copeland. Information, on Caroline at least, that was leading him to a conclusion he could barely credit!

'Of course,' Diana accepted ruefully. 'I am very grateful for all your help in this delicate matter.'

His mouth compressed grimly. 'Time enough for thanks once they have both been found.'

Something Diana was beginning to doubt might ever happen. She had been in London a week now without any success; it really did seem, as Gabriel had pointed out so succinctly, as if Caroline and Elizabeth had completely disappeared from the face of the earth!

She firmly dismissed such negativity from her mind. Her sisters would both be found, safe and sound. 'You seemed…distracted by your letter, when I first came in, my lord,' she commented.

'Did I?' A shutter seemed to come down over his face before he turned to stroll back to the desk. 'Perhaps it is at the thought of having to reply to all these letters and invitations,' he said drily.

There were indeed a large number of them; Diana had been surprised at just how much correspondence had been delivered this past two days when Gabriel had been ignored for all these years. The sheer volume of post seemed to indicate his past sins had indeed been forgiven, if not totally forgotten, now that he was the wealthy Earl of Westbourne.

She sighed. 'Perhaps we should just refuse them all? With my sisters still missing, I do not feel particularly sociable, and we have the added excuse that I am still in mourning for my father.'

Gabriel leant back against the desk as he regarded Diana through narrowed lids. She was a beautiful and gracious young woman, and would no doubt make something of a stir in society. Amongst the males, especially—the women, old as well as young, would no doubt envy her beauty. A beauty that deserved to be seen, if not touched…

'No, I am afraid we cannot do that, Diana.' He groaned inwardly at the thought of the posing and posturing he would no doubt be forced to endure during these necessary forays into the *ton*'s ballrooms. 'It is over six months since your father died and our betrothal has been announced. We will have to attend some of the quieter social events together, at least.' He stood up to resume his seat behind the desk, his expression becoming grim as he once again glanced at one of the letters he had received today.

Diana moved closer to the desk. 'Will you not share your news with me, my lord?'

Should he show her the letter that had so disturbed him? Perhaps it was better that she have absolutely no illusions about the man that he was and would continue to be once they were married? 'It would appear that the announcement of our betrothal in the newspapers has not just alerted the *ton* to my presence here at West-bourne House.' He held up the letter.

Diana gave him a searching look before taking the single sheet of notepaper from him, able to sense the tension in his lithe and athletic body. She glanced down at the signature at the bottom of the letter she held, but was none the wiser for reading that signature. 'Who is Alice Britton?'

'She was my mother's companion.'

Diana raised one silky brow. 'Was?'

He gave a terse inclination of his head. 'It would seem she retired some months ago and is now living in Eastbourne.'

She quickly read the contents of the letter, very soon realising the reason for Gabriel's tension. 'We must both prepare to travel into Cambridgeshire immediately—'

'No.'

She gave him a startled glance. 'Of course, I will understand if you would prefer that I not accompany you—'

'Diana, whether I would prefer you to accompany me is of absolutely no relevance when I have absolutely no intentions of going anywhere near Cambridgeshire, now or in the future.' Gabriel's expression remained grim as he began to pace the room.

'I—but Miss Britton says that your mother's health was fragile when she last saw her four months ago.'

His eyes glittered as he glared at her. 'Then my rushing into Cambridgeshire to see her would only result in making it even more so.'

Diana realised he believed that statement to be the truth. She just found it hard to accept that his own mother would not want to see him if her health was so poor. 'I am sure you are mistaken, Gabriel—'

'Are you?' Gabriel looked at her bitterly. 'I have not received a single card or letter from any member of my family since I left. And what do you make of the fact,' he continued remorselessly when Diana would have pointed out that his family could not have written to him when they did not know where he was, 'that when I learnt of my father's death six years ago, I wrote to my mother immediately, expressing my sorrow, and with the added request that I might visit her. A letter to which she did not even bother to respond.'

Diana's heart ached at the emotion she so clearly heard in his tone. 'That does seem damning, yes—'

'It is no more than I might have expected,' he rasped harshly. 'Yet my mother's ex-companion now requests that I hasten to visit my mother because her health is "fragile"? I think not.'

'She also states that your mother has longed to see you for some time—'

'Something I find extremely unlikely. Nor will she receive any forgiveness from me to ease her conscience.'

Diana eyed him compassionately. 'It was not concern for your mother's mortal soul I was considering when I suggested we should both go and see her.'

Gabriel's eyes narrowed. 'What then?'

'Your own,' she said gently.

'Mine?' he barked. 'You claimed to believe me when I told you I have done absolutely nothing for which I need feel ashamed.'

Diana had believed him. She still believed him. Indeed, this past two days in his company made her more convinced that Gabriel Faulkner was a man it was impossible not to believe when he claimed something was so! 'Do you not see that, if your mother dies, now or some time in the future, without the two of you having reconciled, then *you* will be the one who is left alive to suffer the torment, possibly for the rest of your life, knowing that you could have set things right between you, but your pride would not allow you to do so?'

He stopped his pacing, his gaze suddenly shrewd as he looked down at her. 'And is that what happened to *you*, Diana? Did your mother ask for your forgiveness for leaving you all and you refused her?'

Diana's heart skipped several beats. 'We were not discussing me or my mother—'

'We are now,' Gabriel cut in. 'Tell me, did your mother come to regret leaving you all for the arms of her young lover? Did you refuse her your forgiveness?' he persisted ruthlessly.

Diana knew that her cheeks had grown pale at the memories that assailed her of that terrible time they had all suffered after her mother had left them: her father a white and ghostly figure as he wandered from room to room in Shoreley Park, as if he might somehow find his wife in one of them if he just looked hard enough;

her two sisters crying constantly at night until they fell into an exhausted sleep, only to wake again screaming or crying, and demanding to know why their mother did not come and comfort them as she'd used to do when they were beset with bad dreams.

And through it all, as Diana had done the best that she could to comfort all of them, she had felt her anger towards her mother growing for having so selfishly hurt them all, until it seemed her heart had become utterly consumed with hatred for her.

Her throat moved convulsively now as she swallowed down the bitter bile that had risen in her throat. 'My mother never wished to return to us or ever asked for our forgiveness, so how could I have refused her?' Her voice was flat, emotionless.

He frowned darkly. 'Diana—'

'If you will excuse me, my lord?' She held her head regally high, her gaze deliberately avoiding his. 'It is time that I go upstairs and change before dinner.' Even if the thought of eating now made her feel ill.

She very rarely thought of her mother any more. There seemed little point.

'You are standing in my way, my lord,' she said stiltedly as Gabriel effectively blocked her escape by moving to stand in the open doorway of the study.

'Will you allow me to apologise, Diana?' Gabriel looked down at her searchingly, knowing by the pallor of her face and the haunted look in those sky-blue eyes that he had hurt her with his taunts about her mother.

Even though he himself was hurting after receiving that letter concerning his own mother, it was not an acceptable reason for his having upset Diana.

He reached up to lightly clasp the tops of her bare arms. 'I am sorry for my churlishness just now,' he said huskily. 'It is only—' His mouth tightened. 'I am sure that Alice Britton meant only to act for the best, but the past is better left alone. By both of us, it would seem,' he added gently.

Diana raised long-lashed lids, those sky-blue eyes over-bright. With unshed tears? Had Gabriel hurt her that much? Had he really become so unfeeling this past eight years? So selfishly absorbed in his own disillusionment that he had ceased to care if, or when, he hurt others with his coldness and cynicism?

'You are forgiven, Gabriel.'

He drew in a sharp breath at Diana's softly spoken absolution, for once in his life not sure what to do or say next. Any more of his arrogance or sarcasm was likely to cause the glitter of tears he could see in her eyes to overflow, and yet to do anything else would be—

'As I hope you will forgive me for my intrusion into something that is so very personal to you.'

It was too much. Diana apologising to *him*, when he was the one who had behaved so churlishly, was too much. He released her arms to pull her into his embrace, the top of her golden-red curls now resting under his chin and smelling of lemons. 'I am a brute for hurting you.'

The warmth of her cheek rested against his chest. 'I should not have attempted to interfere.'

'No one has more right to do so,' Gabriel grated fiercely. 'You are to become my wife. My countess.' And it was only now, holding her in his arms and totally aware of the vulnerability she was usually at such pains to hide behind that veneer of practicality and determination, that he realised the enormity of what his betrothal to this woman meant.

He had renewed his offer of marriage in the belief it was to be an arrangement of mutual expediency, she needing a sop to her injured pride following her young man's defection, and he needing a suitable wife to act as mistress in his homes and provide the necessary heirs. All well and good.

Except he had not expected to actually like the woman whom he married. Or to desire her to the extent that holding her in his arms again like this was a physical torture. But as Gabriel refused to run the risk of his heir perhaps making his appearance only seven or eight months after the wedding and therefore causing even more unwanted gossip for them both, he knew he'd have to continue to suffer the torture a little longer unless he removed the temptation.

He took a firm hold of her arms and moved her away from him, dark eyes hooded by lowered lids as he looked down at her. 'As you say, it is time we both went upstairs and changed for dinner.'

Diana blinked up at him, momentarily stunned by the sudden return of his previous coldness. But what had she expected? That talking of their mutual hurt at their mothers' hands would somehow forge a bond between the two of them? That it would bring about an understanding between them, a closeness that would make their betrothal seem less daunting to her?

If that had indeed been her hope, then one glance at his haughtily remote expression, at the coolness in those dark blue eyes as he looked down at her, was enough to tell her that such a warmth of understanding did not, and never would, or could, exist between them.

Her own expression was as proudly distant as she gave a stiff inclination of her head. 'Until dinner then, my lo—' Diana broke off abruptly, startled into silence as she heard the sound of voices raised outside in the hallway. 'What on earth…?'

'Indeed.' Gabriel's expression was suddenly tense as he heard the commotion.

She frowned. 'Perhaps we should go and see what is wrong?'

'Perhaps we should.' He brushed lightly past her to walk swiftly in the direction of those raised voices.

Diana almost had to run to catch up with those long strides, so intent on doing so that she almost crashed into his broadly muscled back as he came to a sudden halt in front of her to stare across the wide hallway to where there were three people standing in the open doorway.

The butler, Soames.

A tall and handsome dark-haired man, with icy grey eyes and a livid scar down his left cheek that did nothing to detract from that handsomeness, but instead gave him an almost dangerous air.

And standing beside him, her beautiful face animated, was Diana's sister Caroline…

Chapter Five

If there had been any doubts in Gabriel's mind as to the identity of the young woman who stood beside his friend Dominic Vaughn, the Earl of Blackstone, then they were instantly dispelled as Diana gave a choked sob before moving past him to run quickly across the hallway on slippered feet.

She threw herself into the other woman's arms with a loud cry of 'Caroline!', her joy obvious as she began to both laugh and cry at the same time.

Caroline joined in as they held each other tightly, causing Gabriel and Blackstone to exchange a look that involved raised eyebrows and wry smiles, before Gabriel then turned his attention back to studying Lady Caroline Copeland. Seeing how his friend looked at her, no doubt she was none other than "Miss Morton"—the same young woman who until a few days ago had been singing in Dominic's gambling club wearing a jewelled

mask and ebony wig in order to disguise her appearance! He'd started to suspect the truth after learning
the Copelands' butler's name was Morton—truly no
coincidence.

Slender and elegant in a gown of sea-green beneath
her grey cloak, Caroline Copeland's hair was pure
golden rather than the reddish-gold of Diana's, her eyes
that same beguiling sea-green as her gown, her com-
plexion alabaster, her pointed chin bearing the determination of her older sister.

A determination that, in Caroline's case at least, had
led to her both risking her reputation and putting herself
in danger rather than ever marry Lord Gabriel Faulkner,
he thought bleakly. His reputation had much to answer
for.

'How good it is to see you back in England at last,
Westbourne!' Dominic Vaughn came forwards to grasp
the other man's hand. 'Not now, Gabe,' he bent forwards
to murmur softly to his friend before stepping back, the
brightness of his smile lending his usually austere features a boyishness that Gabriel had not seen in him for
some years. 'We travelled all the way to Shoreley Park
in order to see you, only to arrive and find that you had
not gone there, after all.'

'You have come from Shoreley Park, then?'

Gabriel turned to see a somewhat bewildered Diana
standing beside her sister, their arms about each other's
waists as Diana stared across at the two men. Just as
she no doubt wondered what Caroline was doing in the
company of such a dangerous-looking man. Injured in

the Battle of Waterloo, Dominic Vaughn had a scar the length of his left cheek, from his eye down to his arrogant jaw line. A scar that gave him a somewhat sinister appearance.

Gabriel turned to the stony-faced butler. 'Bring tea for the ladies and brandy for the gentlemen to the study, if you please, Soames.'

'Very well, my lord.' The elderly man bowed stiffly before leaving, giving no indication, by word or demeanour, that he had moments ago been involved in a verbal exchange with a man and woman who were obviously known to his employer.

'What—?'

'We will wait until we are in the study to talk further, Diana,' Gabriel instructed before standing back to allow the ladies to precede them, his bride-to-be obviously still dazed by the sudden and unexpected appearance of her sister in the company of Dominic Vaughn and Caroline eyeing Gabriel somewhat challengingly as she walked at her sister's side.

'You are going to have your work cut out with that one, Dom,' he murmured drily to his friend as the two of them fell into step behind the women.

Dominic gave him an unconcerned smile. 'It already is.' He sobered slightly. 'You intend to give us your blessing, then, Gabe?'

'From the little I have already learnt of this business from Nathaniel, I believe I had better!' He gave a rueful shake of his head as he followed the ladies into the study.

As expected, Diana instantly demanded to know
how and why her sister came to be here at all, let alone
accompanied by a man such as the Earl of Blackstone.

What followed, once Soames had delivered the
requested tea and brandy, was almost certainly a trun-
cated version of what Lady Caroline Copeland had been
up to since her arrival in London, totally for Diana's
benefit, so she need not worry about the potential risks
to her sister's reputation, and also to place Dominic in
the most positive light possible.

'It seems I have you to thank for my sister's safe
delivery back to her family, my lord.' Diana's gratitude
to Dominic for ensuring her sister's safety since her
arrival in London was tinged with concern. That he had
been a close friend of Gabriel's for some years had been
made obvious to her during this past conversation, but
grateful as Diana was to have Caroline restored to her,
she could not help but think her sister travelling about
the countryside in the company of such a man as the
earl was highly improper.

She turned to Caroline. 'Why did Elizabeth not travel
back with you?'

Her sister looked surprised. 'With *me*? But I assumed
she had travelled up to London with you and Aunt
Humphries.'

Diana's trepidation grew. 'She left Shoreley Park two
days after you did.' Caroline's face paled.

'You mean she may have been in London alone these
past weeks? Dominic!' Her expression was slightly pan-

icked as she turned to grasp the arm of the stern-faced Earl of Blackstone.

Diana was no less concerned at having her worst fear confirmed—that Elizabeth and Caroline had not, as she had hoped, arranged to meet up in London…

'One of your sisters has been returned to you unharmed, my dear; there is every reason to believe the same will prove true regarding your other sister.'

Diana barely heard Gabriel's words of comfort as he walked into her bedchamber uninvited when she had not responded to his brief knock upon the door.

The initial shock of realising that Elizabeth was still missing had resulted in there being more questions than answers. The hour becoming late, Gabriel had suggested that Lord Vaughn also stay here for the night at least, and that Caroline's and the earl's luggage be taken upstairs, so that they might all retire and change for dinner before resuming the conversation.

Except Diana had been too upset to do more than collapse upon her bed once she'd reached her bedchamber.

She now sat in a ball of misery on the side of that bed, her eyes red and sore from crying, her cheeks still damp with those tears as she looked up at Gabriel. 'I would not call finding Caroline alone in the company of such a man as Dominic Vaughn having her returned to me unharmed.'

Gabriel stiffened. 'Blackstone has been one of my closest friends since childhood. Moreover, he is a man

I would trust with my life. In fact, I believe I have done so on several occasions.'

Diana gave a despairing shake of her head. 'Caroline is but twenty years old—'

'Blackstone is only eight and twenty—'

'In years, perhaps. But anyone looking at him could see that in experience and worldliness he is a man of much greater years.' She gave a delicate shudder. 'That he is—'

'Have a care, Diana.' Gabriel eyed her icily now. 'After you and your sister had left the study earlier, Blackstone formally offered for Caroline and I have given them my blessing.'

Diana stood up abruptly, her eyes wide with shock. 'You cannot be serious!'

He nodded. 'Completely.'

'But—'

'Do not be naïve, Diana, one need only look at the two of them together to see how things stand between them.'

Yes, Diana had felt the undercurrents of heated awareness between her sister and the Earl of Blackstone. Felt them, and at the same time feared for her impetuous sister. 'Caroline has led such a sheltered life—'

'Diana.' Just her name, but spoken in such a reproving tone that it would be unwise to ignore it.

Except she was feeling less than wise at this moment! 'Caroline has always been strong-willed and head-strong, but in this instance she cannot possibly be sure of her feelings. She and the earl haven't known each other for that long—'

'And we had known each other for less than a day when you accepted my own offer of marriage,' he pointed out.

'That is not the same at all!' she said impatiently. 'You know as well as I that the only reason I accepted your offer of marriage was so that neither of my sisters need do so.'

Yes, Gabriel knew of Diana's reasons for accepting him. But knowing them and having Diana state them so bluntly were two entirely different things...

Something she also became aware of as she glanced across at him almost guiltily. 'I did not mean to imply—'

'I am well aware of what you meant, Diana,' Gabriel said frostily. 'But our own reasons for marrying should not reflect on Dominic and Caroline. Whether you like or approve of the match, they are in love with each other and intend to marry.'

And Gabriel's own opinion hadn't mattered either! His conversation with his friend, once the two ladies had retired to their bedchambers, had been brief and to the point; Dominic intended to marry Caroline Copeland as soon as it could be arranged for them to do so. His gruff advice that Gabriel not object to the match or the swiftness of the upcoming nuptials had been enough of an indication to him as to the intimacy of their relationship.

Although Gabriel doubted Diana would welcome

hearing of that…'I had the impression during our conversations about your sisters that you wished only for them to be free to choose who they fell in love with?'

'Yes, of course I do.'

'But you do not accept, because they have not been long acquainted, that Caroline is as deeply in love with Dominic as he is with her?'

Did Diana accept that? Caroline had always been the most stubborn and rebellious of the three sisters, the one always caught out in some mischief or another when they were growing up. Never seeming afraid of seeing a notion through once she had set her mind on it—Caroline's flight to London two-and-a-half weeks ago was evidence of that!

But to accept that Caroline was in love with Dominic Vaughn, the fierce-looking Earl of Blackstone, and that he was in love with her, that the two of them wished to marry, could not be attributed to either mischief or stubbornness. And yet Diana had seen the love shining in Caroline's eyes every time her sister so much as glanced at Dominic, as it was in his when he returned those glances. Indeed, Diana would have to be blind not to see the way the two constantly touched and looked at each other. Or how Caroline, usually so independent, had instantly turned to him for comfort the moment she realised Elizabeth was missing…

Could Diana possibly be jealous of that closeness? Oh, not of the love that so obviously glowed between the couple—having suffered what had proved to be the shallowness of Malcolm Castle's love, Diana had no intention of trusting in a man's declaration of love ever again, hence the expediency of her betrothal to Gabriel.

But could her misgivings now be because she resented the fact that Dominic Vaughn had now taken her place as the stalwart in Caroline's life? Could that possibly be the reason for her doubts about the match? If that was the case, then they were selfish doubts and did not deserve to so much as be acknowledged, let alone voiced!

Besides which, there was that air of intimacy between her sister and the earl that implied her concerns might already be too late…

She drew herself up determinedly. 'I will offer them both my warmest congratulations when we all meet downstairs for dinner.'

Gabriel looked admiringly at her. Whatever doubts and misgivings she still had concerning the sudden-ness of her younger sister's betrothal, she now had them firmly under control. No doubt the same firmness of control that had governed Diana's decision to accept his own offer of marriage. 'Perhaps, once they learn of our own betrothal, they will offer those same warm congratulations to us?' he teased.

'Of course.' It was obvious from the way Diana's cheeks had paled slightly that she had momentarily overlooked her own hasty engagement in her concerns for her sister.

'Then we are agreed that your sister and Blackstone will marry soon?' he asked.

'I did not think you required my agreement to the match,' she replied.

'I do not,' he acknowledged. 'But I am sure that your sister does.' Gabriel straightened and turned to leave.

'My lord, what do you intend to do concerning our earlier conversation?'

Gabriel's eyes narrowed. 'Which earlier conversation would that be, Diana?'

She moistened those pouting and sensuously full lips before speaking. 'I—in regards to the letter you received from Miss Britton about your mother, of course.'

Of course. He should have known, been prepared for the fact that the conscientious Diana could not simply let the subject be. 'Nothing, Diana. I intend doing absolutely nothing in regard to that letter.'

'Perhaps you might travel to Eastbourne first and talk to Miss Britton in person—?'

'I have already written back to Alice Britton informing her that I am far too occupied in town at the moment to spare the time to travel into Cambridgeshire.' He gave an impatient snort as Diana looked less than satisfied with this reply. 'I wish I had never shown you the damned letter!' Indeed, he wished he had never placed the announcement of their betrothal in the newspapers at all, if by doing so he had provided Alice Britton with an address where she might write to him.

Blue eyes widened. 'Miss Britton's letter was so filled with warmth and affection for your mother...'

'Yes, she was with my mother for many years.'

'She also seems most concerned that your mother

is now living alone at Faulkner Manor apart from the servants and a Mr and Mrs Prescott,' she pressed.

With good reason—given a choice Gabriel would not have trusted one of his horses to the care of said Mr and Mrs Prescott! 'My mother's younger brother Charles and his wife,' he told her tersely.

Diana eyed Gabriel curiously, aware of the harshness of his expression and the increase in tension in that tautly muscled body; his wide shoulders were stiffly set back, his arms rigid and his hands clenched at his sides. 'Do you have a large family?' In truth, Gabriel was a man who, by his very nature, gave the impression of complete self-containment; so much so that it had never occurred to her that he might have family other than his mother and deceased father.

'I have no family.' Those midnight-blue eyes were utterly implacable.

'But—'

'At least, none that I care to acknowledge,' he added. 'Nor any who have cared to acknowledge me for the past eight years, either.' There was no missing the dangerous edge of warning in his tone now.

Even so, she found herself curious to know more about the family he dismissed so easily. 'Is Mr Charles Prescott your mother's only brother or—?'

'I have said I do not wish to discuss this with you any further, Diana.' He looked down at her with fierce eyes.

The past few hours had been fraught with emotion, to say the least, and as such she did not feel inclined to humour his usual arrogance. 'Does your desire not to discuss a certain subject usually meet with success?' she came back tartly.

'Invariably, yes.' Gabriel raised amused brows as he saw the light of battle deepen in those sky-blue eyes; whether she realised it or not, Diana was every bit as headstrong and strong-willed as she claimed Caroline was!

'What a pity, then, that it has failed in this instance.' Her chin jutted out stubbornly.

He grinned. 'I trust, Diana, that you are not about to disobey me before our marriage vows have even been made?' He could not resist teasing her.

Those blue eyes sparkled rebelliously. 'Indeed, at this moment it crossed my mind to request that part of the marriage service be omitted altogether, my lord!'

Gabriel gave an appreciative chuckle. 'Personally, I have always preferred the part of the vows that say "with my body I thee worship",' he drawled and instantly had the satisfaction of seeing two wings of colour heat her cheeks. In embarrassment? Or at the memory of the times Gabriel had already taken her in his arms and kissed her?

Something, against his previous better judgement to the contrary, he felt more than inclined to repeat now. Perhaps he might allow himself a little—just a little enjoyment of her graceful, desirable body?

Diana's eyes widened in alarm as he moved stealthily towards her. 'I—what are you doing?' Her voice came out as a breathless squeak as he now stood so close to her she could feel the heat of his body through the thin material of her gown.

He quirked dark brows. 'I thought, following the tensions of the past hour or so, that perhaps a little demonstration of how I intend to worship you with my body once we are married might be beneficial to us both.'

She swallowed hard, at the same time aware that her heart had begun to pound so loudly she was sure that he must hear it too. 'We are alone in my bedchamber, my lord...'

Those sculptured lips curved into a smile that added warmth to the intensity of those compelling midnight-blue eyes. 'The perfect time and place, I would have thought, for such a private demonstration—wouldn't you agree?'

Diana was more than alarmed now—she was light headed, both from his proximity, and the delicious intent reflected in those dark blue eyes fixed so purposefully upon her parted lips. 'That will not be necessary, my lord.'

'I do not recall saying it was necessary, Diana,' he murmured. 'Just something we might both enjoy.'

Diana would only be deceiving herself if she did not admit to having enjoyed the times Gabriel had already taken her in his arms, as she had noticed their absence this past two days. And perhaps the intimacy that so obviously existed between Caroline and Dominic Vaughn was having an effect on her own sensibilities—because she wished for nothing more at that moment than for Gabriel to repeat those earlier kisses.

She moistened her lips with the tip of her tongue. 'I am not sure my guardian would approve.'

Gabriel's grin could only be described as wolfish. 'On the contrary, your guardian is in complete agreement with your participating in the exercise.'

'Then how can I refuse?' She smiled up at him shyly.

As before, Diana felt light and very feminine as Gabriel took her in his arms, with that smell of lemons and flowers, her lips against his soft and yielding, the womanly curves of her body moulded against his much harder ones. Gabriel couldn't help deepening the kiss, becoming more demanding as he parted her lips with a slow sweep of his tongue before dipping into the moist cavern of her mouth to become even more aroused by her heat.

Dear God! He should not have played this dangerous game, should have heeded his earlier warnings and avoided taking her in his arms again at all until they were safely wed. At the very least, he should find the strength to put her away from him now.

Instead he found himself groaning low in his throat as desire surged through him with the speed of a lit taper igniting paper, engorging his shaft until it throbbed with the same rapid heat as his heart pulsed. The kiss became even more passionate as his lips now devoured hers, crushing the full roundness of her breasts against his chest.

Diana's breath caught and her neck arched as Gabriel wrenched his mouth from hers to travel the length of her throat, his tongue a rasping caress as he tasted her, a trembling beginning in her knees and climbing to between her thighs as one of his hands moved restlessly across her back and hips before moving up to cup the softness of her breast.

'Perfection,' he groaned huskily, his hand tightening, fingers seeking, squeezing, plucking at the sensitised tip through the thin material of her gown even as his lips and tongue continued their sensual exploration of her throat.

Diana's fingers moved from the broad width of Gabriel's shoulders to become entangled in the heavy thickness of the hair at his nape, feeling on fire, her skin hot, sensitive to his every touch, every caress. His lips were moist and warm against her heated flesh as he kissed his way down to the bare swell of her breasts above her gown, causing those already aroused nubbins at their tips to pucker and harden and ache even more. For what exactly, Diana was still unsure.

Gabriel tugged down the soft material of her gown to bare one of her breasts, satisfying that ache as he drew the tight tip into the heat of his mouth hungrily, his tongue sweeping across it, making it tingle and burn at the same time.

Diana had never known such pleasure as this existed, a hot and pulsing pleasure that caused a flood of moisture between her thighs so that she now ached there too. An ache that increased as Gabriel's fingers curled about her hips to pull her into the hardness between his thighs, moving rhythmically against her. Each stroke of that hardness sent a fierce pulse of desire deep inside her as he continued to pay attention to her breast, causing that pleasure to build higher and higher until she suddenly felt as if she were about to explode.

'Gabriel?' She was unsure if that gasp was a plea for him to stop or to continue, her fingers curled tightly into his hair as she held him to her at the same time as she wanted to put an end to the torment of emotions that surged throughout her body.

Hearing the uncertainty in her voice was enough to bring Gabriel to his senses and realise exactly what he was doing, and with whom. This was no woman of experience, no woman he could take to his bed, to freely explore and pleasure, then forget all about her. Diana was to become his wife. His countess. The mother of his children. Children he fully intended would be born securely inside the parameters of their marriage so that no breath of scandal could be attached to them. Until Elizabeth was found, Diana wouldn't marry him, and he had no idea how long it would take to find his last runaway ward. He dared not risk bedding her until the knot was securely tied.

He drew in a hissing breath as he pulled away from her and held her at arm's length. Just the sight of her plump and bared breast, slightly reddened from the ministrations of his lips and tongue, was enough to make his thighs throb uncomfortably. 'I believe that is enough enjoyment for one evening,' he said unevenly as a redfaced Diana hastily straightened her gown and looked up at him with bewildered blue eyes.

Gabriel was starting to feel just as bewildered and

unsure of himself whenever he was alone in Diana's company, and he didn't like it one little bit!

'I believe it is time that you changed for dinner,' he said, attempting to regain control of the situation.

'But—'

'Now, please, Diana.'

If she carried on standing there, tempting him, looking at him with her beautiful wide blue eyes, he might just have to take her in his arms again and that would be a disaster. Good sense and experience told him not to allow this woman beneath the guard he had so carefully erected about his emotions this past eight years. But just holding her in his arms was enough to force all those good intentions completely from his mind. What on earth was happening to him?

Chapter Six

'You have seemed somewhat preoccupied, all evening, Gabe.'

Gabriel looked down the length of the dining table to where Dominic was sitting, his expression uncharacteristically inquisitive as he sipped his after-dinner brandy now that the two men were alone in the dining-room.

In actual fact, Gabriel had found his friend's whole demeanour to be out of character this evening, as the four of them had eaten dinner together before the two ladies had retired to leave the men to enjoy their brandy and cigars. Mrs Humphries had once again sent her apologies; apparently she had been rendered prostrate at the sudden reappearance of her niece Caroline in the company of the twelfth Earl of Blackstone!

Dominic was certainly a changed man. For one thing Gabriel had never seen his friend smile as much as he had this evening, let alone indulge in the lovingly teasing banter that seemed to be such a part of his relationship with Caroline Copeland.

It was a sharp contrast to the stilted politeness that now existed between Diana and Gabriel!

To make matters worse, the announcement of the betrothal between the two of them had not been met with warm congratulations at all, but with astonishment from Caroline and concerned silence from Dominic—the same concern with which he still looked at Gabriel now.

'You and Caroline did not seem particularly pleased earlier at the announcement of my betrothal to Diana,' Gabriel commented, sipping his brandy.

The other man grimaced. 'Obviously I have not had chance as yet for private conversation with Caro, but I fear she may believe that her sister has only agreed to the marriage because she and Elizabeth made clear their own reluctance to do so.'

Gabriel raised dark brows. 'And what is your own opinion on the subject?'

Dominic breathed in deeply before answering. 'Recalling your own comments in Venice a little over a week ago, I cannot help but think that may indeed be the case. You said yourself you only offered marriage to one of the Copeland sisters because you felt it was the correct thing to do as they had been left so badly off by their father—as well, of course, as providing you with the necessary heirs.'

Both, Gabriel considered, very sound reasons for his

offer of marriage to the Copeland sisters. Except he had not known Diana when he made that offer. Had not held her in his arms. Kissed her passionately. Caressed her bountiful curves…

He sat back in his seat abruptly. 'And if it is purely a marriage of convenience?'

His friend sighed heavily. 'I completely sympathise with your reasons for wanting to avoid emotional involvement, Gabriel. I should; I felt exactly the same way until I met and fell in love with Caro,' he added ruefully.

'Yes, I would be very interested to hear exactly how that came about…' Gabriel eyed the other man speculatively.

'No doubt you would,' Dominic drawled drily, 'but, as you are well aware, a gentleman does not kiss and tell.'

Gabriel raised dark brows. 'Not even when the lady in question happens to be my own ward?'

'Most especially then!' Dominic grinned. 'I would hate to have to put you in the position of having to call me out. Especially as I should win.'

Gabriel laughed. As, no doubt, he was expected to do; both men knew that of the two them Gabriel was the superior swordsman, as Dominic was the superior shot. Just as both men knew that there were no circumstances under which Gabriel would ever lay such a challenge before one of his two closest friends…

He smiled. 'On the contrary, I wish you and Caroline every happiness together.'

Dominic gave an acknowledging inclination of his head. 'And will you and Diana be as happy together, do you think?'

He glanced away. 'We can only hope.'

'Gabriel—'

'Dominic, no matter what you may or may not think to the contrary, I did not in any way coerce Diana into our betrothal.' He scowled darkly. 'In truth, I was as surprised as you when she decided to accept my offer.'

'Caro led me to believe that Diana was to marry a son of the local Hampshire gentry. What happened to that?'

Caroline was probably also the person who had revealed that fact to William Johnston. 'I believe you will find that it was the gentleman's change of heart that has prompted her to accept my own offer,' Gabriel admitted curtly.

Dominic looked regretful. 'So this really is to be a marriage of convenience for both of you?'

'What else?' he said flippantly.

'Gabe—'

'We have been friends a long time, Dominic, and it is a friendship that I value highly, but in this particular circumstance I will thank you to keep your opinion to yourself,' Gabriel cut in, eyeing his friend warningly.

Dominic returned that gaze for several long seconds before allowing the tension to slowly ease from his wide shoulders. 'You do realise that at this moment Caro is probably engaged in a similar conversation with Diana?'

Gabriel nodded wryly. 'I'm sure Caroline is advising Diana to inform me she has changed her mind and will not marry me after all.'

The other man looked intrigued. 'And your reaction if Diana *were* to do that?'

What would he feel if that should happen? Gabriel wondered. Annoyance, certainly, at having to retract the announcement in the newspapers. But what else would he, personally, feel…?

He would feel nothing else, *nothing*! Diana was no more necessary to his happiness than any woman had been. If she should change her mind about marrying him, then no doubt he would find another quickly enough who would accept; from the mountain of invitations he had received these past two days it would appear that inheriting the earldom of Westbourne had made him as eligible to the ladies of the *ton* as it had assured his place back in society.

Besides…'Diana will not change her mind.'

'You sound very sure of that fact,' Dominic murmured.

Gabriel gave a slight smile. 'When you have come to know your future sister-in-law only a little longer you will realise that Diana is not a woman to go back on her word.' The abruptness with which he stood put an end to that particular conversation and Gabriel moved down the table to replenish both men's glasses before speaking again. 'Dominic, there is something else I would talk to you about…'

The other man's gaze sharpened. 'Yes?'

'I received a letter earlier this today from my mother's companion, Alice Britton.'

'The devil you did!' Dominic burst out incredulously.

'Indeed.' Gabriel made no effort to resume his seat at the table, but instead began to pace the room.

'For what purpose?'

He ran a hand through his hair. 'To inform me that my mother's health has been fragile since my father died.'

'I am sorry for that, Gabe.'

'As am I,' he admitted. 'She also wished me to know that my Uncle Charles and his wife have resided at Faulkner Manor with my mother this past six years.'

'Good God!'

'Yes.'

'What do you intend to do about it?'

'You are the second person this evening to ask me that.' Gabriel sighed.

'Diana?' Dominic said knowingly.

'Exactly.'

'Shall you go into Cambridgeshire, then?'

Gabriel looked at him. 'What do you think?'

His friend snorted. 'I think that you are as likely to return to Faulkner Manor with Charles and Jennifer Prescott in residence as you are to consign yourself to the fires of hell!'

'Exactly,' Gabriel confirmed.

'Does Diana know? Is she conversant with what happened eight years ago?'

'I am not a complete blackguard, Dominic,' Gabriel said. 'I felt it only fair that Diana be made aware of the...basics of that past scandal.'

'But not the details?' Dominic asked shrewdly.

'No.'

'Such as the *name* of the lady you supposedly ruined?' his friend pressed.

'We both know that I never laid so much as a finger on her.' Gabriel's mouth had thinned into a grim line. 'And I dispute the claim that she ever was, or ever could be, considered a lady!'

'Gabriel—'

'No, I have not informed Diana of her name.' His hand was now clasped so tightly about his brandy glass that Gabriel was surprised it did not shatter.

Dominic looked wary. 'Do you not feel that perhaps you should?'

Gabriel shook his head. 'I don't feel it's necessary that I do so at this point in time, no.'

And if he had his way, it never would be...

Caroline was distraught. 'I cannot even bear the thought of you marrying a man you do not love. Even one who has surprised us all by being so sinfully handsome,' she allowed grudgingly.

Diana smiled affectionately at Caroline now as she paced Diana's bedchamber energetically. 'He is rather handsome.'

'Even so—'

'If, like our Aunt Humphries, you are about to raise the subject of the past scandal attached to the earl's name, then I think you should know that he has already discussed it with me.'

Her sister's eyes widened with curiosity. 'He has?'

Diana smiled ruefully. 'If we are to have nothing else between us, then I believe we are to have honesty, at least. But only between the two of us,' she added firmly as she saw Caroline's interest. 'I have no intention of breaking the earl's confidence by discussing the subject with you or anyone else.'

'But to even think of marrying without love—'

'Caroline, I am not looking for love and romance in my marriage.' She sighed.

'Why on earth not?' her sister demanded, outraged.

Diana smiled sadly. 'Possibly because I have good reason to know how fickle those two things can be?'

'I do not understand.' Caroline halted her pacing to shake her head. 'I was sure that you and Malcolm Castle were to be married.'

'Malcolm is no longer a part of my life.' It was Diana's turn to stand up restlessly.

'But why not? What on earth happened?'

'He is to marry another. And that is an end to it, Caroline,' she added decisively as her sister would have demanded to know more. 'Now I am happy to settle for marriage to a man who makes no false declarations of love, but has stated firmly and clearly exactly what he expects of me.'

'He expects you to become nothing but a brood mare,' her sister snorted.

Diana stiffened. 'You are being unfair—'

'Forgive me, Diana!' Caroline stepped forwards to hug her impulsively. 'It is only that to love, and know that I am as deeply loved in return, is the most joyful experience of my life: I simply cannot bear the thought of your settling for less.' The light of rebellion shone in her sea-green eyes.

'I am not like you, Caroline.' She smiled gently. 'I do not require that a man be as wildly in love with me as your earl obviously is with you. A mutual respect and liking will suit me just as well.'

'And do you respect and like Gabriel Faulkner, Diana?' her sister probed softly.

Did she like and respect Gabriel? Diana wondered, her cheeks feeling suddenly warm. She respected his honesty, at least, and he was, as Caroline proclaimed, sinfully handsome. He was certainly not a man to be overlooked under any circumstances. She had also found his kisses and caresses to be thrillingly pleasurable— But did those things all add up to a liking for him?

'I have every confidence that Lord Faulkner and I will deal very well together in our marriage,' she finally said evasively.

Caroline eyed her. 'That does not answer my question.'

No, it did not, because she had no idea whether or not she liked the man she had agreed to marry. Surely liking someone was a comfortable feeling, an easy relationship, and did not involve the knife-edge of awareness that Diana experienced whenever she was in his company?

'It is enough for now that I respect both him and the honesty he has given me,' she reiterated with such finality that even the impulsive Caroline knew not to probe any further.

'We appear to have caused something of a stir when we announced our betrothal to Dominic and Caroline yesterday evening,' Gabriel commented, glancing across the breakfast table at the coolly composed Diana.

Neither Caroline nor Blackstone had made an appearance as yet this morning, causing Gabriel to wonder privately whether the pair were not together in one of their bedchambers indulging in the intimacy that had been so apparent between them yesterday evening. Not that he was overly concerned if they were; Dominic had made it more than plain yesterday that his marriage was to take place at the earliest convenience.

How different, how much more acceptable to Gabriel was Diana's air of capable calmness than her younger sister's obvious fiery and impulsive nature; he certainly did not envy Blackstone his choice of wife. Although he did have doubts as to whether Diana's cool composure was not merely a thin veneer this morning.

'Perhaps, having had opportunity to talk with your sister, you have decided that you do not wish our own betrothal to continue,' he suggested.

'If one more person dares to suggest that to me, then I fear I might actually scream!' Diana pierced him with over-bright blue eyes as she glared across the small table at him.

Somehow Gabriel did not think so. 'Caroline?'

'Yes.'

'And your Aunt Humphries was less than warm to the idea when she was informed, was she?'

Diana lifted that stubbornly pointed chin. 'I have given my word, Gabriel, and I will not break it.'

His mouth quirked as she repeated the claim he had made to Blackstone the previous evening. It seemed his reading of her character was correct. 'No matter what terrible tales you are told about me?'

'Not even then.'

Gabriel looked at her admiringly. 'If we'd had a dozen women like you beside us in the fight against Napoleon, then the war would no doubt have ended much sooner than it did.'

'If that situation had been left in the hands of women, then there would not have been a war at all,' Diana returned waspishly.

Gabriel gave an appreciative smile. 'You are determined to go ahead with our marriage, then?'

Diana's outward confidence wavered slightly at the caution she sensed in Gabriel's manner. 'Unless you are having second thoughts on the matter?'

'Not at all,' he dismissed easily.

She felt somewhat reassured by that ease of manner. 'In that case, I suggest we turn our discussion as to what we are to do about the disappearance of Elizabeth.'

The earl's good humour instantly evaporated. 'Tell me, is she as without fear as Caroline?'

Diana's expression softened with affection. 'Despite appearances, I believe Elizabeth's character to be less headstrong, certainly. Her initial impulses are invariably tempered by caution,' she explained at Gabriel's look of enquiry.

'That is something to be grateful for, at least!'

Diana laughed. 'I only met Lord Vaughn yesterday, but I believe him to be more than capable of curbing the more dangerous of Caroline's excesses.'

'Let us hope so.'

'They are so very much in love, are they not…?'

Gabriel wondered if she was aware of how wistful she both sounded and looked. Probably not—her own foray into romantic love had not had such a happy ending. Any more than a marriage between the two of them would? he wondered.

'They are, yes.' Gabriel resolutely shook off any doubts he might have about Diana becoming the wife of a man who was incapable of feeling love. 'With Blackstone's help I intend to intensify the search for Elizabeth this very morning.'

A frown creased her creamy brow. 'Do you really think it possible she followed Caroline here?'

'I am sure of it.' Just as sure as he was that it would be too much to hope that the youngest of the Copeland sisters had faired as well as Caroline, who had fallen into a safe pair of hands.

She gave him a quizzical glance. 'And you are still

as determined this morning not to travel into Cambridgeshire to see your mother?'

His mouth thinned. 'Oh, yes.'

'Very well.' She gave a cool inclination of her head. 'If you should change your mind—'

'I will not.' Gabriel threw down his napkin and stood, a nerve pulsing in his cheek. He had succeeded in distracting both Diana's attention and his own from this subject the previous evening by taking her in his arms and kissing her. A course of action that had, if anything, backfired on himself. 'The subject is at an end, Diana. I advise you not attempt to discuss it with me again.'

Diana knew, from the ruthless resolve she could see in his expression as he left the room, that she would have little choice but to do as he asked.

Or, at least, Diana *would* have had little choice if a second letter had not arrived from Alice Britton the following morning, care of Westbourne House, and addressed to her this time…

'Caro is becoming most displeased at our lack of progress in regard to our search for Elizabeth.' Dominic grimaced as the two men strode back into the entrance hall of Westbourne House.

Gabriel shot his friend a disbelieving glance after handing his hat and cane to the attentive Soames. 'I cannot believe how quickly you have fallen beneath that young lady's beautiful thumb.'

Dominic gave an unconcerned grin. 'It is not the beauty of Caro's *thumb* under which I have fallen!'

Gabriel snorted with laughter. 'I would find you quite nauseating if it were not for your obvious happiness with the arrangement.' In truth, he had never seen his friend so happy or contented; even these few brief hours Dominic had spent away from Caro's company were chafing the other man's patience.

Dominic grinned unabashedly as he turned from handing over his own hat and cane. 'I cannot recommend the arrangement strongly enough.'

Gabriel looked down the length of his nose. 'I am perfectly content with my own betrothal to Diana, thank you very much.'

'As you please,' Blackstone shrugged.

'I do please,' Gabriel replied before turning to the butler. 'Where are the ladies, Soames?'

'I believe Lady Caroline is upstairs with her aunt, my lord.'

'And Lady Diana?'

'She and her maid departed in the carriage more than an hour ago, my lord.'

'Departed?' Gabriel repeated softly, a terrible sense of foreboding settling over him.

'Yes, my lord.'

'To go where?'

'She did not say, my lord.' The butler placed the two hats and canes upon the stand in the hallway. 'She was in somewhat of a hurry when she left, but she did ask me to keep this note about my person to give to you as soon as you returned.' The butler produced the slightly crumpled missive from the breast pocket of his jacket.

Gabriel took the note before striding into the privacy of the parlour and breaking the seal. It was a letter from Diana, explaining where she was going and why. Along with a second letter tucked inside the first, from Alice Britton and addressed to Diana, entreating her to exert her influence upon Gabriel to encourage him to visit his mother at his earliest convenience.

Gabriel read Diana's letter three times. Disbelievingly. Incredulously. She had gone to Cambridgeshire! The colour drained from his cheeks and a furious glitter entered his eyes, his fingers finally clenching about the paper before he crushed it into the palm of his hand.

Chapter Seven

Diana's nervousness at her decision to travel to Faulkner Manor in Cambridgeshire accompanied only by her maid increased the further they travelled away from London, aware as she was that Gabriel was sure to be most displeased when he returned to Westbourne House and learnt what she had done.

Displeased enough, she hoped, to follow her…

In view of his determination not to even discuss the subject any further, there had seemed no other way in which to ensure that he travelled to see his mother, something she felt even more strongly that he should do upon receipt of that second letter from Alice Britton. The elderly woman was obviously deeply concerned for Felicity Faulkner.

Except Diana had quickly realised the glaring fault with her plan: there was no guarantee Gabriel *would* follow her. Indeed, he had not done so in the almost twenty-four hours since she had departed London. Nor had Diana slept during her overnight stay at a coaching inn, as she instead worried about the force of Gabriel's anger when they next spoke. Yet he still had not arrived.

Diana's decision to travel to Faulkner Manor had not been made lightly, torn as she was between worry over her youngest sister's whereabouts and the obligations she felt were expected of her as the future wife of the Earl of Westbourne. Indeed, she would not have even contemplated such a journey as this had she not been reassured concerning Elizabeth's welfare by the fact that Caroline and Lord Vaughn, now that they were aware Elizabeth was missing, were just as single-minded in their determination to find her.

That particular concern put to rest, Diana was able to concentrate on her duties as Gabriel's future wife; as such, she had made her preparations to leave for Cambridgeshire.

Only now was she beset with such trepidation, both at her temerity in having requested Gabriel's valet pack a trunk of the earl's clothes to travel in the carriage with her, and the anger she knew to expect from Gabriel for her having gone at all. She very much doubted that he would appreciate her explanation that she considered their betrothal to mean that his family was now as much her responsibility as it was his!

It was too late to do anything else now but continue her journey, Diana told herself with a determined straightening of her shoulders. Gabriel might even now—she could only hope—be somewhere on the road behind her, in hot and angry pursuit...

'I trust there is some good reason why you have not already followed Diana?'

Gabriel slowly turned from where he had been standing, watching stony-faced out of the window in his study as what seemed to be an army of gardeners set to work putting order back into the overgrown lawn and tangled flowerbeds; he had no doubts that the work was being carried out under the exact instructions of Lady Diana Copeland...

Lady Caroline Copeland stood imperiously in the open doorway, Gabriel's gaze cool and unemotional as he looked down the length of his nose at her; he had been aware of her brief knock upon the door several seconds ago, but had chosen not to acknowledge it. 'I do not recall giving you leave to enter.'

She stepped fully inside the room and closed the door behind her. 'I do not recall having asked for it.'

No, she had not, Gabriel acknowledged with grudging admiration. Petite and beautiful in a gown of pale grey, aged only twenty, Caroline nevertheless had a determination of will that exceeded both those attributes—was it any wonder that she had managed to bedazzle the arrogant and cynical Earl of Blackstone?

Nevertheless...'I am not in the habit of discussing my movements, or lack of them, with anyone.'

'Indeed?' She gave an inelegant snort. 'Might I suggest, where Diana is concerned at least, that you *become* used to it?'

Gabriel raised arrogant brows. 'You *suggest*?'

'Insist,' she said crisply.

'As I thought.' Gabriel suppressed a small smile as he turned fully into the room, the afternoon sunlight warm upon his back, a warmth that did nothing to dispel the coldness of the anger he felt towards Diana.

He was also, he acknowledged ruefully, still somewhat nonplussed at having learnt of her departure for Faulkner Manor. The years he had spent as an officer in the King's army had resulted in his being used to issuing orders and having them obeyed. That the woman he had been betrothed to for only six days, a beautiful and elegantly composed young woman whom he knew to possess a regard for duty far beyond her years, had none the less completely disregarded his wishes was beyond belief.

Perhaps he should have taken more notice of Diana's previous remark concerning having the word 'obey' removed from their wedding vows!

'Well?'

Gabriel frowned as he refocused his attention on Diana's sister. 'As I have already stated, I see no reason to explain myself, to you or to anyone else.'

She gave an exasperated sigh. 'You are as stubbornly proud as Dominic.'

He raised an eyebrow at her. 'No doubt the reason we have remained friends for so many years.'

'No doubt,' she muttered. 'Your own shortcomings aside, it is Diana who concerns me.'

He looked taken aback at this second insult in as many minutes. 'I fail to understand why?'

Sea-green eyes flashed her impatience as she stepped further into the room. 'Perhaps you are not aware of it, but my sister has always put her own desires and needs aside in favour of others—'

'Considering your own recent actions, I am surprised to hear that you are at all aware of Diana's selflessness!' Gabriel's mouth was tight with disapproval.

Warmth coloured her cheeks at this more-than-obvious rebuke concerning her own recent waywardness. 'How could I not be aware of it when it is obviously the only reason she has agreed to marry you?'

Dark eyes narrowed in warning. 'Have a care, Caroline.' His voice was silkily soft. 'I have deliberately not mentioned your own recent scandalous behaviour in running off and becoming a singer in a gambling club to Diana, because of her deep love for you and my own friendship with Blackstone, but I assure you—both those things will cease to matter if you continue to berate me in this unacceptable way.'

The colour as quickly faded from her cheeks, but she gamely continued. 'I know little or nothing of past happenings, of course, but you cannot seriously mean to leave Diana to face your family alone!'

'I believe I would be perfectly within my rights to do so when she has so blatantly disobeyed my wishes,' Gabriel drawled back. 'But, no,' he relented at Caroline's outraged expression, 'that is not my intention.' He had known from the moment he read her letter earlier that he would have to follow her, that by lingering in London in this way he was only putting off the inevitable.

'Oh?' Caroline now looked less certain of her indignation on her sister's behalf.

Gabriel explained. 'Even as we speak my horse is being saddled in preparation for my own departure.'

Caroline visibly relaxed the tension in her shoulders. 'Why did you not just say so immediately I came in the room?'

Gabriel gave a rueful smile. 'You seemed so determined to be outraged on Diana's behalf that I did not like to disappoint.'

She tossed her head. 'You and Dominic are so much alike you could be brothers!'

He grinned. 'Considering that you and he are shortly to be married, I will take that as a compliment.'

'I should not if I were you,' Caroline said honestly. 'A certain arrogance in one's beloved may be acceptable, but it is not so attractive in the man set to marry one's sister.'

'I will try to bear that in mind,' Gabriel replied, inwardly warmed by Caroline's obvious love for her sister and her open declaration of loving Dominic as much as he loved her; it boded well for a marriage between the two.

She eyed him uncertainly. 'I trust you will not be too displeased with Diana when you see her again?'

He gave her a straight look. 'On the contrary, Caroline—I am very much looking forward to demonstrating the depths of my displeasure to your sister.' He was anticipating that very much indeed!

Diana was cold, tired, and feeling extremely irritable by the time the carriage came to a halt at the end of the long gravel drive in front of Faulkner Manor early on the second evening after her hasty departure from Westbourne House.

The cold and tiredness were explained by the long hours of travelling in the carriage whilst the rain fell steadily outside, that rain dampening her pelisse and bonnet when they risked a brief stop at a reputable roadside inn in order to enjoy a light luncheon.

The reason for the feelings of irritation lay firmly upon Gabriel Faulkner's broad shoulders.

Her initial nervousness at the thought of his anger, once he discovered where she had gone, had first changed to relief when there came no sound of the thundering of horse's hooves in angry pursuit. But that relief had then turned to puzzlement as a day and night passed, and then another day, still with no sign of him. Finally, she had become irritated when she had to accept that he really had decided not to follow her.

She had felt sure he would—so why hadn't he? Obviously their betrothal was a matter of convenience for both of them, but nevertheless she had believed any gentleman's sense of honour would dictate he at least show loyalty to the woman he intended to make his wife.

Apparently in Gabriel's case that sense of honour did not come into play when it might involve seeing any of his family again. What was she to say to them concerning his absence? To his mother?

She came to an abrupt halt as the groom offered his hand to assist her in stepping down from the carriage, her senses suddenly humming as she became aware, alerted, by a feeling of—of something—

It was pure instinct that caused her to turn and look down the length of the gravel drive, her cheeks paling, eyes widening, as she saw the huge black stallion silhouetted there in the last of the sun's evening rays, the rider upon its back equally as huge and daunting and dressed all in black, with his hat pulled low over his brow and his black cloak swirling behind him.

Diana knew with certainty the identity of that rider. Gabriel!

Even as she stood in arrested stillness, a sheet of lightning flashed across the darkening sky behind him and caused the horse to rear up on its back legs, clearly revealing his face, accusing dark eyes visible beneath the brim of his hat, his expression stony as the horse's hooves clattered back down upon the gravel.

The horse galloped towards where she stood, its rider bent low upon its back, giving him the appearance of the archangel of the same name about to swoop down vengefully upon his enemy.

Diana…

It had been Gabriel's hope that he would succeed in meeting up with Diana before she arrived at Faulkner

Manor and, in doing so, prevent either of them going there. Unfortunately his malingering in London meant that was not the case. He easily recognised the black coach that had come to a halt—he should; it was now one of his own and bore the Westbourne crest of an angel and a rampant unicorn upon its doors. A groom wearing the Westbourne livery had opened one of the doors, lowered the steps and was waiting to assist Diana in alighting from the carriage.

She turned a startled face in Gabriel's direction even as she stepped down on to the gravel, blue eyes widening with alarm as she obviously recognised him seated upon the back of the glossy black stallion.

An alarm she would find was well deserved as soon as the two of them were alone together, he thought in grim satisfaction!

It had been a long and uncomfortable ride from London, despite an overnight stay at a mediocre inn, and he was now tired and hungry and very wet; it had been raining for most of the day, but the heavens had opened up completely five miles back, and succeeded in soaking him through to the skin in the process.

But none of those things were as unpleasant to him as finding himself back at Faulkner Manor after all these years. Nor was he in any doubt as to who was to blame for that.

Lady Diana Copeland. The woman to whom he had recently become betrothed. The interfering young lady who would very shortly be made aware of the penalty for disobeying him...

Gabriel pulled Maximilian to a halt mere feet away from her before sliding from the saddle to throw the reins into the hands of the waiting groom. He marched across to where she still stood in transfixed alarm beside the coach, her eyes becoming wider still as he reached out and grasped her arm.

The length of her creamy throat moved convulsively as she swallowed before speaking. 'How good it is to see you, my lord, when I had thought you said that commitments in town would not allow you to join me until tomorrow.' Her voice was smoothly composed, despite her obvious discomfort.

This last was said for the listening servants, Gabriel knew. As far as Diana was aware, he had not intended coming with her at all; indeed, he still wished himself anywhere but here! 'I could not bear to be parted from you for even so short a time,' he replied to save her face. 'Especially when you took it upon yourself to bring most of my clothes with you,' he grated for her ears alone.

Diana knew that his initial words must sound lover-like to those listening, but there was no missing the promise of retribution in his next comment, or those dark and piercing eyes that glittered down at her so intently. 'I am gratified to know you feel that way, my lord.'

'Let us hope that you feel as *gratified* once we are alone together,' he murmured.

Diana's nervousness grew. 'Did you not receive my letter of explanation?'

'I would not be here at all if I had not,' he bit out.

'Then—'

'What on earth is all the fuss about? Good God, is that you, Gabriel?' a female voice said.

Gabriel gave Diana one last quelling glance before a shutter came down over all his emotions as he turned to look at the obviously shocked young woman who was standing at the top of the steps leading up to the house, only the tightening of his fingers upon her arm betraying that he was not as composed as the blank expression on his face meant to imply.

Diana turned slowly to look up at the woman who still gazed at Gabriel with utter disbelief.

She was young, possibly only a few years older than Diana's one and twenty, and possessed of a smooth perfection of beauty: a wide and creamy brow, fine brown eyes, a small and perfect nose, her lips full above a delicately vulnerable jaw. Her hair was a pure raven-black and arranged in fashionable curls and the slenderness of her figure was shown to full advantage in a fashionable gown of pale peach.

'Your powers of perception have not failed you, madam,' Gabriel said smoothly, answering the other woman.

Her cheeks paled even as she fought for composure in the face of his biting sarcasm. 'I see that the years have done little to reduce your unbearable arrogance.'

'Did you expect them to have done?'

'I did not expect to see you at all!' she exclaimed.

'Obviously not,' he murmured.

The woman glared at him. 'If you had bothered to inform us of your visit, then I would have told you that you are not welcome here.'

A nerve pulsed in Gabriel's rigidly clenched jaw. 'For some inexplicable reason I seem to have had several conversations recently concerning my lack of need to inform anyone of my actions.'

Diana knew that was a little dig at her, too...

'If you would not mind?' He now eyed the other woman coldly. 'Diana and I will join you in the house in a moment.' It was unmistakably a dismissal.

The young woman looked as if she were about to continue arguing his right to enter the house at all, but then obviously thought better of it after another glance at his expression, instead satisfying herself with one last glare before turning away to hurry back inside.

Diana could only surmise that the haughty young beauty was another of Gabriel's relatives—perhaps the daughter of Mrs and Mrs Charles Prescott? Her manner towards Gabriel had certainly been familiar— and insulting—enough to be that of a cousin.

'All will shortly be revealed, Diana,' Gabriel assured her as the threatening rain began to fall once again. He took her arm and began to swiftly ascend the steps.

'But—careful, Gabriel!' Diana protested as she hastened to accommodate those steps and instead stumbled over the hem of her gown.

Gabriel's impatience, his anger, was such that he was beyond being reasoned with. Diana had brought them both into this scorpions' den, and he had little sympathy for her if she now found his resentment not to her liking. 'I am already very wet and weary from spending unnecessary hours in the saddle; I would advise you not to add another soaking to my list of discomforts.'

She pulled her now-soiled skirts away from her slippered feet before looking up at him from beneath lowered lashes. 'I can see that you are angry with me, Gabriel, but I assure you I thought only of you when I decided to come here.'

'On the contrary, I believe you to have acted completely *without* regard or consideration towards my feelings when you made that decision,' he corrected her curtly, not so much as sparing her another glance as he pulled her up the last of the steps.

She gasped. 'How can you possibly say that when I abandoned my search for Elizabeth in order to come here?'

'So that I would not be beset with guilt and regret when I one day learn of my mother's demise,' he reminded her witheringly.

'Yes.'

Gabriel's eyes glittered down at her darkly. 'That was *my* decision to make, not yours.'

'But—'

'I will allow you plenty of time later in which to explain yourself.'

She felt the sting of icy coldness in his tone. 'With any intention of actually listening to what I have to say?'

'Probably not.'

'Then I see little point—'

'Will you, for the love of God, just be silent, Diana!' he said, coming to a sudden halt, his breathing harsh as he paused outside the home he had left so ignominiously eight years ago.

The anger he had felt towards Diana had sustained him through the arduous journey into Cambridgeshire, as he'd mentally listed the many and varied ways in which he intended to make her suffer for putting him to the trouble of following her here. To now find himself standing outside the front door of the home he had been so cruelly banished from, the family he had never thought to return to, filled him with a desolation that struck to his very heart.

'Gabriel?' Diana could not help but feel concerned at the bleakness of his expression as he gazed up at the house that had once been his home. Their acquaintance was of such a nature that it had been fraught with tension from the onset, but as she now looked up into the face above her own she knew that this man was not even the arrogant and dictatorial one she had known for the past six days, but one who was a complete stranger to her...

She swallowed hard, knowing in that moment that she should not have forced Gabriel into following her here, that by doing so she had painfully lanced an old and festering wound that would have been better left alone. 'It was never my intention to cause you discomfort, my lord,' she whispered.

'Your apology comes too late and is too little, Diana.'

Gabriel looked down at her with the eyes of the stranger he now seemed to her. 'There is no turning back or away now,' he muttered for her ears alone before taking the step forwards that would take them both inside the house.

As Diana stepped inside the cavernous marble entrance hall, she was instantly struck by a chill that sent rivulets of cold down her spine. It was not a chill of temperature, but of atmosphere, as if the very walls of the house had absorbed a malignance of spirit for so long and so intensely that it now existed in the very fabric of the bricks and mortar of which it was built.

Which was in itself fanciful; bricks and mortar did not absorb emotions, any more than could the opulent statuary and paintings upon the walls, she told herself. It had to be her own tiredness and hunger—and not a little trepidation at the thought of the promised conversation with Gabriel when they once again found themselves alone together—that was to blame for these imaginings.

Nevertheless, Diana found herself holding the folds of her cloak more tightly about her in an effort to ward off that chill.

'Is my mother well?' Gabriel rasped as the dark-haired beauty hurried down the wide and sweeping staircase, her beautiful face slightly flushed from the exertion.

She ignored his question and instead spoke to the waiting butler as she reached the bottom of the staircase. 'Bring tea to the brown salon, if you please, Reeve.'

'Bring tea for the ladies by all means, Reeve, but I would prefer something stronger,' Gabriel turned to address the butler, at the same time noting that the passing of the years had not been kind to the elderly man; he looked twenty years older rather than the eight it had been since Gabriel last saw him.

Nevertheless there was a warmth of welcome in the butler's gaze as he realised Gabriel's identity. 'Very good, my lord.'

'And have the green-and-gold bedchambers prepared for both Lady Diana and myself,' Gabriel added as he handed his hat and cloak to him, along with Diana's cloak and bonnet.

'You cannot just walk in here and issue instruction to the servants as if you owned the place!' the woman exclaimed.

'I believe it is my mother who still owns Faulkner Manor?'

'I—yes.'

'Then do it, please, Reeve,' Gabriel said before once again turning his glacial gaze on the dark-haired beauty, who glared at him so resentfully. 'I suggest, madam, that we continue this conversation where it is warmer.'

'You—'

'Now,' he demanded.

With a flounce of her skirt the young beauty turned and preceded them into a room decorated in browns and golds, the fire burning in the hearth doing little to alleviate the chill in the atmosphere, however.

Gabriel's eyes narrowed to glittering slits. 'I believe I asked after my mother's health.'

The woman's mouth thinned. 'Felicity is as well as can be expected.'

'What exactly does that mean?' he asked.

She shrugged creamy shoulders. 'Felicity has become fragile since your father died. In fact, she retired to her rooms following his funeral. She now rarely, if ever, leaves them.'

'No doubt giving you leave to take over as mistress here?' Gabriel said contemptuously.

'How exactly like you to blame others for what we all know to be the results of your own misdeeds!' she came back waspishly.

Gabriel did not react by so much as a twitch of an eyebrow at the mention of his father's death, or of how his mother's grief at that death had been so extreme that she had retired completely from all society, although both pieces of information managed to pierce the shield he had placed so firmly about his emotions. His father had always been something of a strict adherent of the rules of society, and his mother more of a social butterfly, but it had been an attraction of opposites, their deep and abiding love for each other obvious to all around them.

Was Gabriel to blame? If he had not allowed himself to be banished eight years ago, would things be different now? Would his father still be alive and his mother's joy of life still touch everyone and everything around her?

'Would you care to make the introductions, Gabriel?'

He dragged himself back from those thoughts of the past with effort at this gentle reminder of his manners from Diana, looking first at the woman who eyed him so hostilely from across the room, and then down at his bride-to-be as her hand rested lightly upon his arm.

'Diana, this is Mrs Jennifer Prescott, the wife of my Uncle Charles. Mrs Prescott, I present my betrothed, Lady Diana Copeland.' He made the introductions brief and to the point.

Diana stared at him blankly for several long seconds, before turning to look at the other woman, unable to hide the incredulity in her gaze at the realisation that the young, incredibly beautiful woman standing beside the fireplace was married to his uncle. A woman Gabriel had wished never to see or hear of ever again…

Chapter Eight

'Mrs Prescott.' Diana's curtsy was perfunctory at best as she tried to dismiss her previously formed opinion that Mrs Charles Prescott would be a plump and matronly woman. Had Gabriel not told her that his uncle was his mother's brother; surely implying that he would be a gentleman in his forties at the very least? The beautiful woman who had now been introduced to her as that gentleman's wife was aged only in her mid to late twenties.

'Lady Diana.' Mrs Prescott gave a terse inclination of her head rather than returning her curtsy.

Diana was very aware of Gabriel's tension as her hand rested in the crook of his arm, like that of a wild beast prepared to spring in defence should the need arise. Did he fear that it might? She felt the return of those misgivings she had experienced when first entering this house, knowing she had been wrong to dismiss them; there was something seriously amiss in this household, something that lay quiet and patiently waiting in its darkest corners.

She longed to escape, if only briefly. 'Gabriel, I believe I would prefer to freshen up after our journey rather than take refreshment.'

He appeared not to hear her for several long seconds, his gaze locked in silent battle with that of his beautiful aunt by marriage, then slowly Diana felt some of the tension ease from his arm as he turned to look down at her between hooded lids.

Even so, his jaw remained tightly clenched as he answered her. 'I am sure that Mrs Prescott will be only too happy to excuse us both.'

Irritation flickered across that beautiful face even as she rang for the butler. 'I would be happier if you had never come here at all,' she spat.

'And why is that?'

'You know why.'

'Perhaps,' he allowed. 'I take it my mother still occupies the same suite of rooms?'

'Of course.' Mrs Prescott frowned. 'But I do not advise that you attempt to visit her this evening, Gabriel. Felicity always dines early and she has already been settled for the night—'

'I believe it is for me to decide if and when it is advisable that I visit my mother this evening and not the empty-headed woman married to my uncle,' he said savagely.

'You are insolent, sir!' she said in outrage.

He quirked challenging brows. 'How clever of you to realise that I am not the same idealistic young man you knew so long ago who was forced to have to leave.'

She glared at him. 'It was by your own choice, sir.'

'I found the alternative contemptible,' Gabriel said silkily.

Jennifer Prescott released a hissing breath. 'You—'

'Where is my dear Uncle Charles this evening?' Gabriel interrupted, aware of how unfair it was to Diana to continue this conversation in which she had no part.

Mrs Prescott's chin tilted. 'My husband departed for London yesterday with the intention of spending several days there.'

'For business or pleasure?'

'Business, of course.'

There was no 'of course' about it in Gabriel's eyes; his uncle had always been an inveterate gambler. 'I had not realised that my uncle still had any business interests in town.' Having no interest in accidentally meeting his uncle or his young wife at some *ton*nish affair, Gabriel had made discreet enquiries about Charles since returning to England, unsurprised to learn that he spent most of his time in Cambridgeshire and ventured to town only occasionally. Occasions when he invariably lost at the gambling tables.

'He does not.'

'Then—'

'Charles and I gave up our own home after your father died and your mother took to her rooms; we moved here so that I might take over the running of the house and Charles could manage Felicity's estates and business interests,' Jennifer Prescott informed him haughtily.

Gabriel continued to view her with scorn. There was no doubting that she was more beautiful than ever or that her youthfully slender curves had matured into those of a voluptuous and desirable woman. But it was a beauty that held no appeal for him, however, distrusting as he did every word and gesture the woman made. Yet having made the mistake of underestimating her once, he had no intention of doing so a second time.

'No doubt Charles has taken every opportunity in which to line his own pockets,' Gabriel said drily. It seemed that Alice Britton's politely worded letters concerning the state of affairs at Faulkner Manor had perhaps underestimated the situation, after all.

The colour faded from Jennifer Prescott's cheeks as she gasped. 'You go too far!'

His mouth tightened. 'Do I?' Dark blue eyes warred silently with those liquid brown ones until Reeve's entrance, in answer to her earlier summons, abruptly broke that tension as she was forced to turn away and issue the instruction to take Gabriel and Diana to their bedchambers.

The brief respite allowed Gabriel several seconds in which to regain his now habitual remoteness. He had not wanted to come here. Would not have come here if it were not for Diana's interference.

A fact she no doubt now regretted almost as much as he!

* * *

'There must be a vast number of years between your Uncle Charles and his wife.' It was a statement rather than a question. Diana looked on in concern as Gabriel paced the bedchamber with restless energy.

It had been something of a surprise to Diana to learn that the green-and-gold bedchambers Gabriel had requested be made ready for them were actually adjoining rooms, the door between the two rooms standing open, a fact that he had taken advantage of the moment the butler departed.

There was no doubting that the arrangement was slightly improper, implying as it did an intimacy between them that did not exist. But at the same time, still disturbed by the undercurrents in this household, Diana felt comfortable with the knowledge that Gabriel was but a room's width away if she should need him.

Neither of them had as yet taken advantage of the warm water that had already been brought up to the bedchambers along with their luggage; instead, Diana had dismissed her maid before sitting down heavily upon the bed to watch Gabriel begin that silent pacing.

He glanced at her now. 'Almost thirty, I believe.'

'You do not seem particularly fond of your aunt…'

'How very astute of you to notice!'

She frowned at the sarcasm in Gabriel's tone. 'Why did you not simply explain to me, when we received Miss Britton's first letter, the complexity of the situation here?'

He became suddenly still. 'What situation?'

'To begin with, that your uncle's wife was not the contemporary of your mother that I had thought her to be?' Diana grimaced. She knew it was not so unusual to find elderly men of the *ton* married to much younger women, but even so…

'As I have already stated—to you, to Caroline and to Mrs Prescott—I believe I am not in the habit of explaining myself to anyone.'

Diana could only imagine the circumstances under which he had told the outspoken Caroline that! 'Surely you must have known I would be surprised to find Mrs Prescott so young in years?'

'Perhaps.'

There was no 'perhaps' about it in Diana's eyes. 'And she and your uncle have resided here with your mother since your father died?'

'So it would seem.' His mouth twisted with distaste.

'But surely it was kind of your aunt and uncle to give up their own home in order to live here and care for your mother?' she said uneasily.

'A word of advice, Diana—do not believe everything that you hear here.' Gabriel looked down at her intently. 'Most especially do not believe anything that Mrs Prescott has to say.'

Diana's eyes widened. 'I do not understand…'

'Then permit me to explain,' he said. 'Mr and Mrs Prescott did not give up their home and move here out of concern for my mother. I made it my business to know that their house, along with everything else of value, was reclaimed by the bailiffs in order to pay off Charles's considerable gambling debts.'

Diana blinked. 'And now you believe him to be lining his own pockets with your mother's inheritance?'

'Let us hope not too deeply.' He frowned. 'I believe my father knew his brother-in-law well enough to have left his will in such a way as to make it impossible for anyone but my mother to touch the capital.'

'I realise this situation is not ideal, Gabriel, but perhaps, now that we have come here,' Diana ventured softly, 'we should try to make the best of it.'

'Is there a best of it?' Gabriel came to an abrupt halt in front of her. 'If there is, then I wish you would tell me what it is.'

Diana gave an inward wince, knowing she fully deserved his displeasure when she had flouted his wishes and succeeded in bringing them both to this cold and inhospitable household to which he had once belonged.

Indeed, she could see only one positive aspect to this mess.

'Hopefully, you will be able to make your peace with your mother, at last.'

He sighed. 'How youthfully naïve you are, Diana.'

She looked at him searchingly, sensing a wealth of pain beneath his words. 'May I…would you like me to come with you when you visit with your mother?'

He raised an eyebrow. 'For what purpose?'

'Gabriel—'

'Diana?'

She frowned at the unmistakable mockery in his rebuke. 'If I am to become your wife, then surely my place is at your side?'

He looked down at her between narrowed lids. 'When you are my wife your place will not be at my side, but beneath me in my bed!'

Diana felt the warmth of the colour that darkened her cheeks at his deliberate crudeness. 'I understand the reason for your anger, my lord—'

'Anger?' he repeated incredulously. 'I assure you, what I feel at this moment is far too fierce to be called anything as lukewarm as anger!'

Once again she was aware of a rivulet of sensation down the length of her spine as she looked up into the burning intensity of those indigo-coloured eyes. But it was not just that icy shiver of apprehension she had experienced earlier. She and Malcolm had been friends and then sweethearts for years. Her acquaintance with this man had been only a matter of days, and yet in that brief time Diana had felt more of a sexual awakening than she had ever known in Malcolm's youthfully inexperienced arms. In years Gabriel was not so much older than Malcolm, yet he far outstripped him in sophistication and experience; he had kissed Diana more deeply, touched her more intimately, than anyone else had ever dared to do.

As she gazed at him beneath lowered lashes, Diana knew they were kisses and caresses that she had secretly longed would be repeated and his comment

just now about being in bed together had only intensified that longing...

Instead of retreating from his anger, she instead
raised her hand to lay her fingers lightly against his
clenched cheek. He felt warm to the touch, his cheekbones rapier sharp beneath the skin, his eyes now so
dark they appeared an inky liquid black.

'I am not a cat or a dog you might tame into docil-
ity with a stroke of your fingertips, Diana!' His voice
sounded harsh in the sudden stillness that surrounded
them, a nerve now pulsing in that clenched jaw.

Her gaze softened. 'I am not so foolish as to believe
anyone could ever tame you, Gabriel,' she said huskily.

That nerve continued to pulse. 'Then what is it you
are attempting to do to me?'

What was she doing? Diana questioned herself
silently. She had forced him to follow here against
his will. They were in a household with an unpleasant atmosphere, she was uneasy in the brittle company
of the young and beautiful Mrs Prescott and she had
yet to meet Gabriel's reclusive mother. And yet at this
moment, here and now, only his obvious pain seemed
of any relevance to her.

'I believe I am attempting to show you, no matter
what you may think to the contrary, that I am not your
enemy,' she said.

'I am aware of exactly what you are, Diana.'

'Which is...?'

He snorted. 'A naïve and idealistic young lady who,
despite her own experiences to the contrary, still some-

how believes the situation that exists in this house could have a happy ending.'

Gabriel had set out to wound with his harshness and knew he had succeeded as she gave a pained flinch and her fingers left his cheek to slowly drop back to her side. At the same time, he realised with a frown, removing the warmth he had briefly experienced beneath the concerned compassion of her touch.

Damn it, he did not need anyone's pity, least of all hers.

Sexual passion, however, he knew from experience, allowed for very little thought other than the satisfaction of aroused desire. And he was aroused, Gabriel realised wryly; all of his recent anger and frustration was suddenly channelled into sexual awareness as he looked down at Diana beneath hooded lids. As he admired the slight dishevelment of the red-gold curls that threatened to escape their pins, the paleness of her cheeks, her neck a delicate arch above the light flush that coloured the swell of her breasts, which were visible above the low neckline of the rose-coloured gown she wore. Gabriel could easily imagine her graceful neckline adorned with pearls that bore the same delicate rosy hue as the full and tempting swell of her breasts.

'Gabriel?' Diana asked uncertainly as she obviously sensed, if not completely understood, the sudden sexual tension that had sprung up between them.

He raised a languid gaze, noting there was now a flush to her cheeks and a brightness in her eyes, her tongue moist and pink as it swept nervously across the sensual swell of her bottom lip. 'Are you afraid of me, Diana?' he voiced softly—aware, at this moment, that his raw emotions had stripped away his previous caution in regard to making love to her.

Her breasts quickly rose and fell, her throat moving above them as she swallowed before speaking. 'Should I be?'

He gave a rueful smile. 'Undoubtedly.'

She shook her head, unwittingly releasing several of her curls from the pins keeping them precariously in place. 'I do not believe you would ever hurt me, Gabriel.'

His smile became wolfish. 'I assure you, at this moment, I am more than capable of causing someone harm.'

Her gaze remained unwaveringly on his. 'I did not say you were not capable of harming me, Gabriel, only that I do not believe you would ever choose to do so.'

Then she knew more than he did himself—because at this moment he could envisage nothing he would enjoy more than to pick her up in his arms, throw her down upon the bed and rip the clothes from her body before ravishing her where she lay.

Or, alternatively, laying her down upon the bed before releasing her hair completely and then leisurely removing every item of clothing that she wore before slowly exploring with his lips, tongue and hands every perfect, delectable inch of her.

His hands clenched at his sides as he could almost taste her pleasure. 'You are awakening the beast that exists in myself and every other man,' he warned her, knowing he was seriously in danger of casting all sense aside and kissing her passionately.

For once in her well-ordered life she did not want to behave cautiously, only wished to banish the coldness that existed between herself and Gabriel even as she hungered for the promise of passion she saw in those piercing blue-black eyes as he looked down at her so intensely.

Many years ago her father had shown her a picture in one of the books he kept in his study of a sleek black panther; at this moment Gabriel reminded her of that big cat. Feral and sleek. Predatory. Dangerous.

She reached up once again and this time touched the silky black softness of his hair as it fell rakishly across his forehead. Long seconds passed and she held her breath in anticipation as he looked deep into the depths of her clear and steady blue gaze, down over the delicacy of her nose and across the creamy pallor of her cheeks, before lingering, settling, on the parted swell of her lips.

She felt the intensity of that gaze almost like a caress as her heartbeats quickened and a warmth spread from her breasts down to between her thighs. She wanted, needed, to be close to him, wanted so much to hold him, to banish, even briefly, the pain he was obviously suffering—

'No, damn it!' Gabriel suddenly grasped the tops of her arms and put her firmly away from him, his expression savage as he continued to glare down at her.

Diana stumbled slightly as she felt the coldness of

his rejection, her humiliation complete as he turned his back on her to walk across the room and stand in front of one of the huge bay windows looking out over the stables.

What had she expected? That they would somehow be united by the uncomfortable atmosphere that existed in this household? That she would be the one to whom Gabriel turned for comfort because of the strain he felt at being back here?

If Diana had expected either of those things to occur, then she obviously was as naïvely idealistic as he had just accused her of being; he had made it more than clear that he would not be here at all if not for her interference. Something he was very unlikely to forgive her for...

She straightened her shoulders. 'Perhaps now might be a good time for you to leave me the privacy in which to wash and change for dinner.'

Gabriel drew in a deep and laboured breath as he clearly heard the hurt beneath the coolness of Diana's tone, a hurt he knew had been caused by his rejection of the warmth and comfort she had so freely offered him.

As much as he might long to accept that offer, to just accept the comfort of Diana's body and forget everything but their mutually satisfying physical release, he could not bring himself to do it—and not just because he wished to wait until after they were married.

The mere thought of consummating their relationship for the first time in the oppression of this house was enough to dampen all arousal. No, better by far that she should suffer a little hurt now than that either of them should ever be haunted by that particular memory.

He drew in a ragged breath. 'You still have absolutely no idea what is going on in this house, do you, Diana?'

She looked confused. 'You have told me some of it and I know there is an unpleasantness of atmosphere here.'

Gabriel gave a hard, humourless laugh. 'If only that were all it was.'

'Then talk to me, Gabriel,' Diana encouraged. 'Let me share this with you.'

'So that you can attempt to fix it? Just as you have fixed so many other things for your own family since your mother abandoned you so cruelly?'

She flinched, stepping away from him. 'You are the one who is being deliberately cruel.'

'I'm sorry, Diana. This house and the people in it make me feel like being cruel.' Gabriel ran an agitated hand through the heavy thickness of his hair.

Diana's heart instantly softened again at this explanation. 'I understand—'

'You understand nothing!' He gave a sudden hard bark of derisive laughter. 'God, I have been back in this house only a matter of minutes and already I feel as if I am suffocating!'

'Then confiding in me can surely only help to ease your suffering.' Her hand once again rested on the rigid tension of his arm as she looked up at him pleadingly.

'Do you seriously believe that?'

'It cannot do any harm.'

'You are wrong, Diana. So very wrong.' Gabriel shook his head, at the same time knowing that if they were going to stay here, even if only for tonight, then it would not be fair to leave her in ignorance of the past any longer. There was another person in this household who would be only too delighted to regale her with a different version of events. 'Very well.' He became very still. 'You have asked to know and said that you wish to share this with me.'

Diana could not help but notice how his mouth had become an uncompromising line, his eyes once again like hard onyx. Knowing that he was not in possession of his usual arrogant control at this moment, she thought that his mood was now such that his previous taunt about her mother's abandonment was likely to fade into insignificance under the avalanche of what he was about to tell her.

Gabriel gave a wry smile as he saw the apprehension in her gaze. 'Or perhaps you have changed your mind and would now prefer not to know?'

Diana swallowed hard, a small cowardly part of her wishing to say, yes, she had changed her mind, that she did not want to hear what he was about to tell her, yet at the same time knowing that nothing in this household would make sense until she heard what he had to say...

Her chin rose proudly. 'I trust I have never shied away from hearing the truth, my lord.'

He bared his teeth in a pained grimace. 'I have no doubt you will want to run from this particular truth.'

Her apprehension grew even as she continued to meet

his gaze with steady resolve. 'Nothing you tell me now will change my opinion of you.'

'Which is?' he asked curiously.

She moistened her lips before answering. 'I know you to be a man who feels a deep obligation in regard to your guardianship of my two sisters and myself. That Lord Vaughn, who was an officer and is a gentleman, holds you in high regard.'

'None of what you have said so far is your own opinion of me,' he pointed out.

Perhaps that was because it seemed wiser, with their own acquaintance so new, for Diana to acknowledge how others regarded him. Her own feelings towards the man to whom she was betrothed were still too tenuous to be voiced. That Gabriel was both arrogant, and impatient of the foibles of others, Diana already knew. That he chose to keep his own emotions firmly hidden from prying eyes behind a wall of hauteur, she was also aware—but as to how she *personally* felt towards him?

She found herself drawn to his unmistakable good looks. Quivered when he took her into his strong arms and pressed her body against his hard and muscled one. Trembled when he kissed her with those sensually sculptured lips. Was filled with a yearning desire when he touched and caressed her with assured and yet gentle hands.

Things that she had no wish to share with him right at this moment!

'Do not trouble yourself to look for an answer when it is obviously so difficult for you to find a suitable one,'

Gabriel said bitterly as he saw how Diana was struggling to find an answer that was not too insulting.

She looked uncomfortable. 'Perhaps you should just tell me what you feel it is I need to know?'

'Where to start?' he mused darkly.

'The beginning?'

Gabriel looked at her. 'That would be eight years ago.'

Eight years ago? At the time of the scandal that had ripped Gabriel's life, and that of his family, apart?

His jaw was tightly clenched. 'I have told you of the scandal that resulted in my being disgraced and disinherited.'

'Yes…'

He nodded tersely, no longer looking at her. 'What you also need to know, if you are to make sense of the tensions that now exist in this household, is—' He broke off, suddenly breathing quickly.

'Gabriel, if you would rather not—'

'The fact that you forced us both to come here no longer leaves me any choice in the matter,' he said grimly.

Diana gave a shiver of apprehension. Gabriel had been honest with her from the first; he had not hesitated to tell her the worst of himself as well as the best, but even so she knew from the fierceness of his manner now that what he was about to tell her was so extreme, so immense, that it could destroy her regard for him for ever…

Chapter Nine

'Jennifer Prescott, the wife of my Uncle Charles, is the same woman I was accused of seducing and then later abandoning when she announced she was expecting my child.'

Diana felt as if she had received a heavy blow to her chest as she took an unsteady step backwards, her breath arresting in her throat, all the colour draining from her cheeks as she stared up at Gabriel in dazed incomprehension. Then she stumbled until the backs of her knees hit the bed and she sat down abruptly upon its softness.

It could not be true—could it?

The young and beautiful woman married to Gabriel's uncle was the same woman who had accused Gabriel of seducing her eight years ago? Worse, Charles Prescott was the man his father had paid handsomely to marry her in Gabriel's stead because he believed that woman was expecting his son's child?

It was too incredible.

Unbelievable.

And yet, was it really so unbelievable a solution? By marrying Charles Prescott, that young woman had still married into Gabriel's family, thereby resulting in her child being born into the family, too. Except the child had not survived...

Besides which, this knowledge now made perfect sense of the open hostility between an icily scathing Gabriel and the outraged Jennifer Prescott.

She raised startled lids to find Gabriel looking across at her with a watchful and narrow-eyed intensity, his jaw arrogantly challenging, his shoulders stiff and his hands tense at his sides.

That wary tension told her more clearly than anything else could have done that the words she spoke next were crucial, not just to the here and now, but to any continuing relationship between them.

But imagining Gabriel and the beautiful Jennifer Prescott engaged together in intimacy was—

No!

Having seen the other woman for herself, and acknowledged her beauty, did not mean Diana should now not believe Gabriel's claim of innocence. Admittedly, it was difficult to imagine any man being immune to that dark and exotic beauty, but if he said he was, then once again she had no reason to doubt his word. Just as she had assured Caroline two days ago, if there could not be love between herself and Gabriel, then surely they must at least have honesty?

Diana either trusted and believed in the word of the man to whom she was now betrothed, or she did not. It was that simple. She stood up to cross the room and stand in front of the window that looked out over the stables and extensive grounds, her thoughts racing as she attempted to come to terms with what she'd been told.

Gabriel's insistence that he was innocent of that past scandal had not changed. It would, she was sure, never change; he was a man who stated the truth, and be damned with whether anyone chose to believe him or not.

She chose to believe him. She must!

Her gaze was very clear and direct when she finally looked across at him still tensely waiting for her response. 'I believe I owe you an apology, Gabriel.'

'What?'

Diana gave a slight nod at his shocked explosion. 'I should have realised that you had another reason other than the past tensions between your mother and your-self for refusing to visit Faulkner Manor.'

Gabriel stared at her wordlessly. For such a coolly composed and self-contained young lady, Diana succeeded in surprising him far more often than he would have wished. He had expected her initial shock at his disclosure concerning Jennifer Prescott, and in that he had not been disappointed. However, he had expected either tears or angry accusations to follow, not that she would apologise to him!

In acting so maturely, she had made a mockery of his own anger and resentment at once again finding himself at Faulkner Manor…'My uncle's marriage to Jennifer Lindsay, as she was then, is not a subject on which I have ever wished to dwell,' he told her.

She looked at him sympathetically. 'I can understand that.'

'Can you?'

'But of course,' she said. 'Not only were you not believed eight years ago, but the woman who made the accusation was accepted into your family whilst you were banished. That must have seemed doubly cruel.'

Cruel to the point that Gabriel had left, vowing never to step foot inside the Manor again. And yet here he was, not only back in his childhood home, but welcomed back—if Jennifer Prescott's obvious shock and dismay at his reappearance could be called a welcome—by the very woman who had once set out to completely destroy his life.

'Yes, it was,' he agreed.

'Were your uncle and aunt acquainted before your father arranged their marriage?'

'I presume so,' he said.

'But you do not know for sure?'

'I don't see how that's important, to be honest,' Gabriel said. 'Charles has always been a frequent visitor to Faulkner Manor and Jennifer's family lived nearby. Usually he came to ask my father to make him a loan they both knew would never be repaid. But what could my father do? Charles was always in debt to the loan sharks, but he was my mother's brother and her only living relative.'

'Those circumstances would have made it difficult for your father to refuse him, certainly.'

'Impossible,' he reiterated.

'And is your uncle a handsome man?' she asked pensively.

Gabriel frowned. 'I fail to see what my uncle's looks have to do with anything.'

Diana shrugged creamy shoulders. 'I was merely curious as to whether or not there is a family resemblance between you and him.'

'Why?' Gabriel's impatience with her questions was barely contained.

Why, indeed? Diana mused. Things were so much more complicated than she could ever have realised before coming here. Jennifer Prescott was an undoubted beauty. The fact that both she and her husband resided at Faulkner Manor, running the house and estates whilst Gabriel's mother remained in her rooms did, as Gabriel had accused earlier, make his aunt the mistress of this household. And the other woman's obvious shock and dismay when she realised Gabriel had come here had been plain to see.

But as well as all of those things was a question that no one seemed to have provided an answer to as yet...

Now that Diana had met Jennifer Prescott—and, she admitted uncomfortably, taken an instant dislike to her—it was a question that greatly intrigued her. Namely, if Jennifer Lindsay had not been expecting Gabriel's child eight years ago, then whose child had it been?

She smiled at the enormity of her imaginings. 'No doubt your uncle is a portly gentleman of middle years—'

'On the contrary, he's an extremely handsome rogue of middle years,' Gabriel drawled drily. 'In fact, I believe Charles was considered something of a catch until his penchant for gambling put him beyond the pale as far as the marriage-minded mamas of society were concerned.'

'I see...'

He gave her a frustrated look. 'What exactly do you see?'

Diana was not entirely sure; she needed to spend more time here, to observe Mrs Prescott—and perhaps her husband if he should return to Faulkner Manor whilst they were still here—to fully put into words what was at this moment only the beginnings of a suspicion.

She shook her head. 'Perhaps we have spoken of this enough for now. There is still some time before we are expected downstairs for dinner—would this not be a good time for you to visit your mother?'

'It would, yes.' In truth, whilst Gabriel now wished very much to see his mother again, he also admitted to an inner feeling of reluctance to do so. His relationship with his mother had always been closer than the one with his father, but it was a closeness that had ceased to exist the moment he'd left home. Not a word or a letter had been exchanged between the two of them in all that time. As such, and in spite of Alice Britton's assurances in her letter that his mother longed to see him again, he still had his doubts.

'I shall be perfectly content in your absence, Gabriel,' Diana assured him briskly. 'Indeed, I would welcome the time in which to wash and change before dinner. After all…' her lips curved in anticipation '… Mrs Prescott must not be allowed to think you are to marry an unfashionable young lady!'

Gabriel scowled. 'Mrs Prescott can go hang herself for all I care about her opinion on anything, least of all the woman I am to marry.'

Diana's smile was rueful. 'This is something between us two ladies, I believe, Gabriel.'

'Have a care, Diana.' He looked troubled. 'She is a woman whom I have learnt at my cost it is dangerous to cross.'

'I may have lived all of my life in the country, Gabriel, but I assure you that I am not without a certain knowledge of my own sex. As such, I believe Mrs Prescott will quickly learn that I am not a woman without thoughts and ideas of my own.'

Gabriel looked at her admiringly. He could not help but be aware of the steely determination in her manner, the same strength of character that had stood her in such good stead during all those years of caring for her father and two sisters and had encouraged her to accept his own marriage proposal. The same force of will that had enabled Diana to travel into Cambridgeshire completely against his wishes.

To his surprise, he suddenly found that he could no longer feel any anger towards her in that regard, accepting the explanation that she had believed she was acting in his best interests. And perhaps she had...

And perhaps Gabriel had delayed his visit to his mother for long enough! 'Your fortitude is to be admired, my dear.'

She gave him a confident smile. 'We may be marrying for convenience rather than love, my lord, but that does not make me any less loyal to you and our betrothal.'

He had no doubts about that when he acknowledged that Diana had travelled into Cambridgeshire alone, but for her maid, simply because she considered it was the right thing to do. Just as she showed every indication of remaining here, despite now knowing of the true unpleasantness of the situation that existed here.

Gabriel could not help but feel scornful of the young man who had so recently rejected the love and regard in which Diana had so obviously held him, even more so because his own respect for her was growing by the minute.

'I am not sure I deserve such loyalty, Diana,' he murmured huskily as he reached down to take her hand in his before lifting it to his lips and placing a kiss upon her lace-covered palm, folding her fingers about that kiss before releasing her hand.

'I live in the hopes that you may eventually do so!' Her eyes sparkled up at him mischievously.

He found himself returning the warmth of her smile. That smile fading again as he grimly considered the task in front of him. 'As you suggest, I will visit my mother now and leave you to change for dinner.'

Diana had not even realised she had stopped breathing until Gabriel left the bedchamber and she felt that breath released in a shaky sigh. Simply because he had taken her hand in his and kissed it? Ridiculous. Dozens of men, young as well as old, had kissed her hand in the past—but it had always been the back of her hand, never her palm...

There had been an unmistakable intimacy in Gabriel having placed that kiss in her palm before then folding her fingers about it. Diana could still feel the warmth of his lips through the lace of her glove. She was just so totally aware of everything about him, from his dishevelled black hair to his rain-spattered Hessians. There was no doubting that, perfectly groomed and tailored, Gabriel was one of the most devilishly handsome men she had ever met. But he was even more so slightly dishevelled and less than his usual arrogant and assured self.

None of which was in the least relevant to their present dilemma! Well...it was mostly Gabriel's dilemma, Diana admitted, but one to which she had assured him she had no intentions of abandoning him.

Alice Britton's concerns for Felicity Faulkner, for the strangeness of the situation here, had, Diana con-

sidered, been completely justified. There was indeed
something bizarre about this household.

'Gabriel?'

Having only seconds ago entered his bedchamber,
Gabriel now looked up to see Diana standing in the open
doorway between their two rooms, the heavy weight he
felt pressing down upon him momentarily dissipating
as he took in the beauty of her appearance.

As she had intended, she had obviously taken advantage of his hour's absence in which to wash and change
before dinner, her cream silk-and-lace gown perfectly
complimenting the magnolia of her skin, her eyes a clear
blue, her lips a full and strawberry blush, and her red-
gold curls kept in place by two pearl-encrusted combs.

The picture she looked was breathtakingly beautiful.

His expression softened somewhat. 'You look…very
lovely, Diana.'

'As intended.' Her manner was brisk as she stepped
into his bedchamber. 'How was your mother?'

Gabriel sobered instantly. 'It is difficult to tell when
she remained asleep the whole time I was in the room.'
Nevertheless, he had been shocked at how much older
his mother looked; her face was much thinner and paler
than it used to be, and there was an abundance of grey
amongst the darkness of her hair as it lay in loose curls
about her shoulders.

Diana frowned. 'She was not aware of your presence
at all?'

'No.'

'Did you attempt to make her aware?'

'Of course I did!' Gabriel said. 'I both held my mother's hand and talked to her, but she remained completely oblivious to my presence.'

Diana could see by the harshness of his expression how much it pained him to admit it. No doubt, having prepared himself for the meeting, it had been something of a disappointment that she had not even woken long enough to acknowledge that her only son was in the room with her.

She moved forwards to place her hand lightly on his jacket-clad arm, at once able to feel his tension beneath her fingertips. 'No doubt you will have better luck in the morning.'

'Let us hope so.' In truth, he had been very disturbed by his mother's condition and wished he had not remained away as long as he had. A fact he must needs relay to Alice Britton at the earliest opportunity, along with his apology for having written back to her so tersely two days ago. If anything, his mother's old companion had understated the situation that existed here, so much so that Gabriel felt inclined to remove his mother as soon as she felt well enough to travel. Always supposing that Felicity would agree to leave with him, that was…

'I am sure, when she wakes, that your mother will be overjoyed to see you again, Gabriel,' Diana said, smiling at him encouragingly.

His answering smile was less assured. 'Let us hope so.'

'Were you and your mother close once?'

'Very.' Gabriel's father had already been aged one and thirty when he and the twenty-year-old Felicity had married thirty years ago. He'd been a man very set in his ways and not inclined to visit the nursery much after his son was born. He'd only really taken an interest in Gabriel once he reached an age where it was possible to put him up on a horse or teach him how to shoot a gun.

Not so Gabriel's mother, who had spent much of her day in the nursery with her only child. Consequently, Gabriel's relationship with his mother had always been that much closer; to now see her looking old and frail was hard indeed for him to bear.

Diana nodded. 'Then I cannot doubt you will become so again.'

Gabriel eyed her ruefully. 'It is as well that one of us is an optimist.'

'Not only that, but I have laid your evening clothes out ready on the bed for you!'

Gabriel turned to look at where his evening clothes were indeed laid out ready for him to change into once he had washed and tidied his appearance.

'I felt it was the least I could do considering I am the one responsible for depriving you of your valet.' Her smile became impish.

He eyed her quizzically after noting that even his shirt studs lay neatly beside his necktie. 'Most women would have no idea what was required.'

Her expression saddened. 'My father decided to dispense with the services of his valet two years before he died, so it was left to me to see that he did not appear downstairs every morning and evening dressed in his nightclothes.'

Gabriel frowned as she avoided meeting his searching gaze by removing her hand from his arm to turn away and look out of the window. She was so young to have needed to take upon her own shoulders the responsibility of her increasingly reclusive father and two younger, impulsive sisters. Even so, he could detect no resentment towards her family in her tone or expression—only love and acceptance.

Diana was like no other woman Gabriel had ever met.

Like no other woman he was ever likely to meet.

And she was very shortly to become his wife.

He seriously doubted that he was deserving of such luck, considering the haphazard way in which he had chosen that wife. He would be nothing but a fool if he were to take that luck for granted.

Gabriel looked admiringly at the fragile arch of Diana's nape. The softness of the hair that fell in enticing curls against her skin. The creamy softness of her shoulders and arms revealed by the wide neckline and short sleeves of her cream-silk gown. The delicate length of her spine. The implied curves of her body beneath the drape of that silk.

And he knew that he no longer cared about where they were and why they were here.

He wanted—no, needed—this connection with Diana like he'd never needed anything before in his life.

Chapter Ten

From the weighty and lengthy silence behind her, Diana believed that she had somehow displeased Gabriel. By putting his evening clothes out ready for him to change into once he returned from visiting his mother? Or perhaps she was mistaken, and it was not she who had displeased him, but the unsatisfactory visit to his mother that still troubled him?

'My lord—oh!' She came to a startled halt as she turned to find him standing just behind her.

So close she could now feel the heat of his body through the thin material of her gown. So close that as she slowly raised her gaze to look at him, she could see the black ring that encircled the dark indigo of his eyes, giving them the appearance of that intriguing and mesmerising midnight-blue.

Her own eyes dropped from the intensity of his stare, only to come to rest on the sensual curve of his mouth, firm and sculptured lips that she knew would feel soft and compelling against her own.

She suddenly pulled herself up short. These were not thoughts, memories, she should be having when they were alone together in his bedchamber!

'Diana?'

She raised heavy lids as a quiver of awareness ran the length of her spine at the husky compulsion in his tone. It seemed she had been mistaken, that Gabriel was not displeased with her at all, that his emotions were something else entirely...

She moistened her lips with the tip of her tongue before attempting to speak. 'It really is time you considered changing for dinner.'

His own lids dropped, the expression in his eyes hidden by long, dark lashes. 'Gladly—if you would care to continue to act as my valet?'

She swallowed hard, her mouth having suddenly become dry as even the air seemed filled with heated expectation. 'Of course I will help if you feel it necessary.'

He smiled slightly. 'Not necessary, exactly, but I believe we might perhaps enjoy the intimacy?'

Betraying heat suffused her body as she responded to the lazy sensuality in Gabriel's voice. Everything else, everyone else, receded to the back of her mind, as she could see and feel only him. 'If you would care to turn around?'

He held her gaze with his own for long, timeless seconds before he gave the slightest of nods and turned the broad width of his back towards her. Something, she believed, that he did not choose to do with many people…

Gabriel could feel how Diana's hands trembled slightly as she raised them to the neckline of his jacket, her fingers lightly brushing against the soft darkness of his hair as it curled on to the high collar, causing him to almost groan in response.

The visit to his mother's bedchamber had been totally unproductive: he had not so much as been able to speak with her, let alone gauge how she felt about him being here. Returning to find Diana waiting for him had filled him with a strange and unfamiliar feeling of gladness. Of unaccustomed warmth.

It was the oddest sensation for a man who had spent the past eight years coldly shunning friends as well as enemies.

Gabriel was so much taller than Diana that it was not easy to slide the perfectly tailored jacket from his shoulders and down the length of his arms. She was very aware of everything about him as she inadvertently touched the width of his shoulders, his muscled arms and finally the bare skin of his long and elegant hands.

She felt decidedly hot—and very bothered—by the time he turned to face her, obviously intending her to now unbutton his waistcoat. Evidence, if she should need it, that this had very little to do with her acting as his valet and everything to do with the intimacy he had mentioned earlier.

She was so aware of his gaze upon her that she fumbled slightly with unfastening the buttons on the silver-brocade waistcoat, her fingers coming into contact with his shirt-covered chest as she slipped this garment down his arms before discarding it on .to the bed beside his jacket.

She hesitated, then asked, 'Would you like me to remove your necktie and shirt, too, or do wish to do that for yourself?'

'Which would you prefer?' he growled softly.

Diana's heart leapt in her chest at the mere thought of unbuttoning and removing his shirt and, in doing so, laying bare the wide expanse of firm and muscled flesh beneath. Her gaze flickered up before as quickly moving away again as she saw how focused his own gaze was on the rapid rise and fall of her breasts. 'Is this altogether wise, Gabriel?' she murmured huskily.

'Does everything between us have to be wise?' he countered.

She raised startled lids. 'We will be expected downstairs for dinner shortly.'

'It is not my dinner for which I feel hungry.' There was an incredible heat in his gaze as he continued to look down at her.

Diana found she could no longer look away from the intensity of those dark and compelling eyes, instead becoming lost in the warm invitation he made no effort to hide. Despite all the recent conflict, they had found a closeness here at Faulkner Manor that was very precious. Alone in his bedchamber there existed only the two of them, so close, so very aware of each other.

Assisting him to undress did not feel at all like it did when she helped her father—

'I would hope not.'

'Surely I did not say that aloud?' Hot colour suffused her cheeks as he teasingly answered the comment she had believed existed only inside her head, but which she had obviously voiced aloud.

'You did,' he confirmed, liking those bright wings of colour in her cheeks, her eyes a bright and sparkling blue as she looked up at him. 'How does it feel then, Diana?' he asked gruffly.

'I—different. So very different.' Her voice was soft and breathy and almost made him shiver in response.

'But not unpleasant?' he pressed.

'I—no, not at all.'

'Then I see no reason why we should not continue...' Gabriel reached out to take both of her hands before lifting them and placing them flat against his shirt-covered chest.

Touching him, able to feel the muscled hardness of his chest through the fine silk material of his shirt, the firm beating of his heart and his warmth, Diana saw every reason why they should not continue.

And every reason why they should!

Her trembling fingers moved to unfasten the meticulous knot of his necktie before placing it on the bed with his jacket and waistcoat, aware of his intense regard as she slowly released the four buttons at the throat of his silk shirt.

The two sides of the shirt fell apart to reveal that the skin beneath was indeed firm and lightly tanned; there was a light dusting of dark hair upon his chest.

'Would you scream in protest if I were to remove my travel-worn shirt completely?'

Diana raised blonde brows. 'I never scream, my lord.'

There were several scenarios in which Gabriel could imagine that she might—scenarios in which his lips and hands were upon the most intimate parts of her body.

He reached up to pull the shirt over his head before discarding it untidily to the floor. 'Leave it,' he instructed as she would have picked it up. 'For God's sake, Diana, would you just touch me?' His jaw was tightly clenched as he steeled himself for the first sensation of those slender fingers upon his naked flesh.

He watched as the moist tip of her tongue moved nervously across her lips even as she raised those hands and placed her fingers lightly against his skin, hesitantly at first, and then more assuredly as she slowly traced the firm contours of his chest. Gabriel sucked in his breath and held it there as her fingernails scraped lightly across the hardened nubs nestled amongst the dark dusting of hair.

Diana stilled, eyes wide as she looked up at him. 'You seem to like that as much as—' She broke off with a self-conscious gasp.

'As you did?' Gabriel finished throatily. 'Oh, yes!'

'I had no idea.' She touched him again, delight now

warming her cheeks as she saw the way those hard nubbins became harder in response, the tension in his shoulders and clenched hands also revealing the intense pleasure he felt from the caress of her fingertips.

As a child Diana had used to love sitting in her father's library, looking through the hundreds of books he had there, and Gabriel's wide and muscled chest, the flat contours of his stomach, were so very much like the drawings of the Greek gods in one of those books.

It was also exhilarating, she discovered, to be able to return some of the pleasure she'd experienced when Gabriel touched her and placed his mouth on her. Ah, yes…

'Diana, what are you doing?'

Her lips and tongue were now against the tautness of Gabriel's flesh, her mouth curving into a smile of satisfaction at she both heard and felt his arousal. She glanced up at him beneath lowered lashes, noting the tension in his jaw and the nerve pulsing in his throat. 'Do you wish me to stop?'

'Dear God, no!' he groaned and one of his hands moved up to become entangled in the curls at her nape as he held her to him.

She needed no further invitation to continue to place open-mouthed kisses on his chest even as her hands moved lower, lightly caressing the muscled flatness of his stomach above the hardness of his arousal pressing against his pantaloons.

It surprised her that there was an answering warmth between her own thighs, her breasts becoming full and aching, the hardened tips chafing against the soft material of her shift.

It was a revelation to Diana that she received as much satisfaction in giving Gabriel physical pleasure as she did in receiving it—

'You might have considered locking the bedchamber door if you had intended bedding your future wife, Gabriel!' There was absolutely no apology in the scornful voice that sliced coldly through their intimacy.

Diana had sprung guiltily away from Gabriel at the first sound of that horribly familiar voice, her face paling as she saw Jennifer Prescott standing in the doorway that adjoined the two bedchambers. Humiliated colour brightened Diana's cheeks as the other woman looked across at her in utter contempt.

'And perhaps *you* should have considered knocking before entering,' Gabriel rasped into the chilling silence, Diana able to feel the blazing heat of his body against her spine as he held her firmly in front of him.

His aunt's mouth sneered at them. 'You may rest assured I will make a point of doing so in future.'

'A better idea would be for you not to come to either of these bedchambers again whilst Diana and I are staying here,' Gabriel bit out. 'Now that you are here, perhaps you might like to tell us what it is you wanted?'

'You had been up here so long I thought it best to come and tell you both that dinner is ready to be served.'

'I had no idea that Faulkner Manor was so depleted of servants that you needed to behave as one yourself,' he jeered.

Jennifer gasped in outrage. 'You are so insulting, Gabriel!'

'I have not even begun to be insulting as yet,' he drawled.

There was an angry glitter in the other woman's eyes as her gaze first raked over Diana's dishevelled appearance before moving to his obvious state of undress, her dark gaze lingering avidly on the bare expanse of his muscled chest.

Gabriel's stomach roiled with distaste as he recognised the avaricious heat in her lingering gaze. 'You have satisfied your curiosity, now get out,' he ordered.

Her dark eyes blazed with fury. 'You will go too far one day,' she warned him.

He eyed her dismissively. 'Your threats hold no interest for me, madam.'

'Indeed?' Her dark gaze settled very briefly on the young woman who stood so still and silent in front of Gabriel. 'Does the same hold true for Lady Diana?'

Gabriel pulled Diana more firmly against the warmth of his chest. 'Be warned, madam, that I will view any attempt on your part to hurt Diana—by word or deed—as a personal attack on me. And I will respond accordingly.'

'Whoever would have thought you would become so sickeningly love-struck, Gabriel?' she openly mocked him now.

His gaze was positively glacial. 'I believe just knowing you has soured me to such tender feelings.'

Diana was now fully recovered from her embarrassment at being discovered in such an intimate situation with Gabriel; in fact, she felt emboldened, by both his responses and the protectiveness he now showed towards her. Or, rather, it was an illusion of protectiveness that would surely be rendered useless if he were to continue in his present vein. 'Was there something you wished to say to me, Mrs Prescott?' Her gaze was unwavering as she looked across the bedchamber at the other woman. 'Something I do not already know, that is,' she added caustically.

'Nothing that I am sure cannot wait until a more… convenient time, no,' his aunt said.

'Which this almost certainly is not,' Gabriel bit out.

Those brown eyes narrowed on him speculatively. 'I have no idea why you are in such a lather, Gabriel. After all, it is far from the first time I have seen you unclothed.' Triumph shone in her face as Diana was unable to repress her startled gasp. 'Admittedly you are more muscular than you used to be, but no doubt the brown birthmark upon your left thigh remains unchanged?'

'Get. Out.' Gabriel said through gritted teeth.

'A word of advice, Lady Diana,' the other woman ignored him to drawl mockingly. 'I believe you will come to realise that Gabriel has something of a selective memory.'

'When it comes to you it is very selective indeed,' Gabriel snarled. 'In fact, it is non-existent.'

Jennifer smiled tauntingly. 'Choosing not to remember something does not mean it did not happen.'

'And imagining something does not mean that it did,' he retorted.

Her smile remained triumphant. 'No doubt I will see you both downstairs shortly.' She turned back into the adjoining bedchamber, the sound of the outer door closing quietly behind her seconds later, evidence that she had gone.

Diana remained standing stiff and unmoving within the circle of Gabriel's arms, her earlier confidence shaken in the face of that barrage of scornful comments, her head awhirl. Admittedly the woman had meant to wound—where Diana was concerned, she had undoubtedly succeeded!—but that did not mean there was not some truth in her remarks, did it?

Jennifer Prescott claimed to have seen Gabriel unclothed in the past and had remarked how he was more muscular than he used to be. Even more damning, she'd revealed that he possessed a birthmark upon his left thigh. How did she know that piece of damning information when Diana herself did not?

'What are you thinking?'

Diana was very aware of how his body remained pressed so firmly against the length of her spine. But the earlier euphoria she had felt had very definitely faded! Gabriel's closeness now made her aware of the shallowness of his breathing and of the hardness in his body as he waited for her answer.

She drew in a ragged breath. 'Is it true that you have a birthmark upon your left thigh, my lord?'

'Damn it!' he snarled.

'Do you?'

'Yes!'

'Dear God…' She pulled out of his arms and moved away from him, uncaring if she upset him, just needing to distance herself from him. To be allowed to think.

Gabriel gave her no time in which to do that. 'Diana, this is not what it seems.'

'Then tell me what it is!' She looked up at him with bewilderment. 'I trusted you, Gabriel, I put my faith in you…'

He immediately became aloof and distant. 'Nothing that has happened here should prevent you from continuing to do so.'

'Then please explain to me why it is that woman knows of a birthmark upon your thigh which you admit does exist?' A small part of her brain realised she was acting very illogically, but the jealousy that was rushing through her was making her ignore rationality and go straight to heated accusation!

Gabriel ran a frustrated hand through the heavy darkness of his hair. He was not accustomed to being questioned in this way. In fact, he had sworn long ago that he would never try to explain himself to anyone ever again.

Except…Jennifer's taunt had sounded so very damning and he realised that Diana had already accepted so much on his word alone. She had absolutely no reason to trust him so blindly, beyond the belief that Gabriel had no reason to lie to her…

Damn Jennifer Prescott! Damn her to hell and back!

His jaw clenched. 'Did you never escape the confines of the schoolroom when you were a child to swim in the local river in your underclothes with the children from the village?'

'No.'

Somehow Gabriel had known that would be Diana's answer; she had been far too occupied, from a very young age, with the care of her father and sisters, to have the time or inclination to behave like a child herself.

'I did,' he said evenly. 'Often.'

'And your uncle's wife was one of the children from the village who also swam there?'

'She was Jennifer Lindsay then, of course, but, yes, she was one of the children who came from the village to swim.' Gabriel's tone was challenging rather than apologetic.

As if he expected Diana to immediately doubt him...

She was still too shaken by her own wildly see-sawing emotions to know what to think. What to believe.

Until she came to Faulkner Manor the young woman from Gabriel's past had been faceless and nameless. To discover that woman was now married to Gabriel's uncle was disturbing enough. To now learn that Gabriel had shared much of his childhood with the youthful Jennifer Lindsay was even more unnerving.

He would have been aged only twenty when the scandal occurred. A young buck, no doubt eager for adventure and physical conquest. Jennifer Prescott was an incredibly beautiful and sensual woman now, and there was no reason to suppose she had been any less so eight years ago. How could the younger, virile and more adventurous Gabriel have possibly resisted her?

Diana had been so certain earlier that his word was to be trusted. That he had no reason to be untruthful. Indeed, that he was not a man who cared enough about anyone or anything enough to ever feel the need to lie or prevaricate.

But she could not deny that Mrs Prescott's taunts had shaken her confidence somewhat concerning Gabriel's version of past events. She desperately wanted to believe him. She needed to do so if there was to be any future for the two of them.

Yet, at the same time, she had to admit to the fact that a few seeds of doubt had been sown in her mind…

She shook of her head in an attempt to rid herself of unwanted thoughts, her gaze no longer able to meet Gabriel's. 'We can talk of this later—'

'We will talk of it *now*, Diana, or never.' He appeared a complete stranger to her, even the bare expanse of his chest and arms doing little to lessen the chasm widening between them.

Diana frowned. 'There is so much more now for me to consider…'

'Such as?'

'Mrs Prescott's beauty is undeniable…'

He scowled darkly. 'I have no interest in that woman. I never did, nor will I ever have any interest in her. You either accept my word on that or you do not.'

Diana looked at him closely. His expression was

totally uncompromising: his eyes glacial, cheekbones drawn tight, his mouth a hard and unforgiving line above the arrogance of his jutting jaw.

Yes, totally uncompromising, and if Diana should doubt him, she knew he would be unforgiving.

She sighed. 'It is most unfair of you to pressure me in this way when so much has already happened since our arrival here.'

Was it unfair? Gabriel considered. Diana had learnt so much more about the past since arriving at Faulkner Manor. Was it too much for her to simply take his word this time that something was so, simply because he said that it was?

Perhaps, he acknowledged grudgingly.

But Gabriel had not sought, or wanted, anyone's good opinion of him for the past eight years. Pride dictated that he could not ask for it now, even from the courageous young woman who had agreed to become his wife.

'Will you not consider, Gabriel,' Diana continued huskily, 'how you would feel if the roles were reversed? If, perhaps, Malcolm Castle was to reveal to you his knowledge of a mole upon my left breast?'

'I am already acquainted with that mole myself,' Gabriel pointed out tautly.

Her cheeks warmed delicately. 'Yes, you are…'

His eyes narrowed. 'And if that gentleman and I *were* to converse on the subject, would he indeed be able to reveal his own knowledge of such an item?'

'Certainly not!' Her cheeks were now awash with colour.

'Then I fail to see the significance of such a comparison,' Gabriel said, hiding his relief at the news he was the first to gaze upon the beauty of Diana's naked breast.

He had not cared for hearing that Castle might have beaten him to it. He had not liked in the slightest even the thought of another being so intimately acquainted with the tender curves of her body. His violent feelings on the subject seemed to indicate an engaging of emotions that was completely unacceptable to him.

He straightened swiftly. 'I believe it is time you left now and allowed me to wash and change in preparation for dinner.'

Diana was no longer sure she even wished to go downstairs for dinner. Untrue! She knew that she had absolutely no desire at all to sit through a meal that promised to be uncomfortable at best and unpleasant at worst! But to make her excuses now would not only make her appear weak in the eyes of Jennifer Prescott, but unsupportive of Gabriel too.

Of course, Diana knew that the other woman had deliberately set out to cause dissention between herself and Gabriel, and she had undoubtedly succeeded; the earlier closeness that had existed between them had been badly shaken by the seeds of doubt that had been deliberately and maliciously put into Diana's mind. Doubts she dearly wished that she could dismiss as easily as she had everything else

Gabriel had told her. But with the unreasoning jealousy still raging through her, she felt unable to do so.

That her feelings had been warming towards Gabriel she could not deny—how could she when she melted into his arms every time he so much as touched her! Yet it seemed that every tentative step they made towards a closeness, a regard for each other, was immediately nullified by something, or someone, which then resulted in a complete lack of understanding between them.

She had so enjoyed being given the freedom to touch and kiss him earlier, his masculine beauty so very exciting, his skin beneath her fingertips having the texture of steel encased in velvet—

'Diana!'

She gave a start as Gabriel's rebuke cut through her remembered enjoyment of those earlier caresses. 'As you suggest, I will leave you now.' She was deliberately dignified as she walked to the adjoining doorway.

'Perhaps you would like to wait for me in your bedchamber and we can go downstairs together?' he suggested. 'Unless you would prefer to go down alone and see whether my uncle's wife does not have some other remembered anecdotes of our idealistic childhood that she wishes to share with you?' he added caustically.

Diana barely repressed a shudder at the thought of any private conversation, on any subject, taking place between herself and that woman. 'I will wait in my bedchamber for you.'

'I thought perhaps you might.' Gabriel's soft taunt followed her from the room.

Her head remained high, her composure only deserting her once she had closed the door behind her and crossed the room to sink gracefully down upon the side of the bed.

She should not have come to Faulkner Manor!

Would she have preferred to remain in ignorance, then? To have married Gabriel, only to learn later of Mrs Charles Prescott's identity as the woman from his past?

She just didn't know the answer to that question yet…

Chapter Eleven

'What on earth are you doing, Gabriel?' A frowning Jennifer Prescott, attired in a silk gown the same deep brown as her eyes, halted in the doorway of the dining room.

Gabriel barely glanced at her. 'What does it look as if I am doing?'

'I am sure that the table was perfectly set as it was!'

She glared her irritation at him, but he was unconcerned. He had requested Reeve to remove his place setting from the head of the table to the middle, so that he would now sit opposite a pale-faced Diana rather than down the length of the table at his uncle's wife.

He had been aware of her scheme as soon as he entered the dining room with a quietly composed Diana upon his arm. The obvious intention had been to make it appear that Jennifer and Gabriel were the host and hostess and Diana a mere guest.

'If I am to look across the table at anyone, then I would prefer it to be my fiancée.' He pulled Diana's chair back and saw her comfortably seated before strolling around the table to wait to take his place once the attentive butler had seen to the seating of Mrs Prescott.

Gabriel was completely aware of Diana's continued silence and how her cheeks still retained their earlier pallor. He had reluctantly accepted that it was he, even more than the vindictive Jennifer Prescott, who was to blame for her distress. The time it had taken him to wash and change before coming downstairs for dinner had also given him the opportunity to rid himself of his anger and consider things from Diana's viewpoint. He had behaved badly earlier, when he'd continued his stubborn stance that she could believe him or not about Jennifer Prescott's knowledge of his birthmark. It was no excuse for his arrogance that he had reacted out of habitual self-defence after eight years of keeping his own counsel.

He also admitted to feeling disquieted by Diana's mention of the man from her past. The more he considered Malcolm Castle, the less he liked him. He certainly had not appreciated hearing even the suggestion that he might have such intimate acquaintance with her body! So, much as he might still baulk at any further need to explain himself, he knew that, having realised his errors, he should have apologised to Diana before they came down for dinner. It was an apology that would now have to wait until this interminable dinner was over. He sighed inwardly.

'I realise that you have been…busy with other things this evening, Gabriel,' Jennifer said, waiting until after the soup course had been served and the butler had left the room before attempting to engage him in conversation. 'Too busy, I am sure, to have found the time in which to visit your mother?' Her smile appeared smugly complacent.

Gabriel glanced at her with distaste. 'Then you would be wrong, madam.'

'Oh?'

He frowned at the unmistakable sharpness in her tone. 'I was with my mother for some time earlier.'

'And how was Felicity this evening?'

He had not imagined it; there was now a definite defensive edge to her manner. 'Sleeping, as you said she might be,' Gabriel answered slowly, aware of Diana's frown as she glanced across the table at him. Because she, too, realised there was something strange about his aunt's behaviour?

'No doubt you found her much changed in appearance?' Jennifer continued to probe.

Gabriel's jaw clenched. 'No doubt.' He gave up all pretence of eating as he instead turned in his chair to face his uncle's wife. 'What interested me more was why, when my mother is so obviously not well, there was no nurse in attendance in her bedchamber?'

'Charles dismissed both the nurse and doctor some months ago. Felicity is so much better now that they were both deemed an unnecessary expense,' she explained airily as he glowered.

His eyes narrowed. 'Deemed unnecessary by whom?'

'By Charles, of course.'

'I was not aware he was a medical expert?'

'Do not be ridiculous, Gabriel—'

'I do not consider it in the least ridiculous to be concerned as to the lack of care my mother has been receiving these past few months.'

'Exactly what are you implying?' Angry colour now mottled Jennifer's cheeks. 'That Charles and I are somehow responsible for your mother's retreat from society?' She gave a disgusted snort. 'You know as well as I do the reason for Felicity's malaise is that her only son was forced to leave the country in disgrace, thereby causing her husband to sicken and die only two years later.'

One of Gabriel's hands clenched on his thigh beneath the table. He had to fight to stop himself getting up, placing his hands about Jennifer Prescott's throat and then squeezing the very life out of her! No one had ever before dared to even hint at what she just had openly stated.

Was he to blame? He could believe past events might have affected his mother that way, but he remembered his father's rigid, emotionless stance only too well to be convinced his own departure for the Continent could have had anything to do with his premature death.

'But perhaps you would prefer to discuss this matter later and in private?' Jennifer suggested. 'I am sure it is not necessary that Lady Diana be made privy to all the family scandals in one evening.'

It was impossible for Diana not to detect the note of

triumph in the older woman's tone at Gabriel's pallor at being accused of causing his parents' suffering. But Diana did not believe it for a moment; her own father had been deeply in love with her mother and been broken-hearted when she left him. However, it had not killed him and neither had Gabriel's absence killed his father. It was deliberately cruel of his aunt to imply that he was at fault.

She also realised she had been thrown temporarily off balance earlier by Mrs Prescott's spiteful remarks about Gabriel's birthmark, but just this past few minutes spent in her vindictive company had finally enabled Diana to see it for exactly what it was; a means of hurting Gabriel, as well as driving a wedge of misunderstanding between the betrothed couple.

And she had so nearly succeeded...

Her gaze was cool as she looked down the length of the table at the other woman. 'I am sure that every family has its secrets and scandals, Mrs Prescott. Including my own,' she added drily. 'But our relationship is such that Gabriel and I do not have secrets between us.' She reached across the table to lightly touch the back of his hand, her heart aching as she saw the agony of emotion in the depths of his eyes as his gaze flickered across to her.

'I somehow find that very hard to believe,' Jennifer said scornfully.

'Perhaps that is because you have always found dishonesty so much easier to understand?' Gabriel rallied to toss the insult at her.

He had foolishly allowed himself to be momentarily shaken by his aunt's taunts—a loss of his normal control that Diana had not only masked by deflecting Jennifer's attention with her own conversation, but acknowledged privately by offering him her tacit and gentle support with that light touch upon his hand. Considering how disagreeably he had behaved towards her earlier, that support was breathtaking. He was fast discovering she was indeed a diamond amongst women.

He turned his hand and captured the slenderness of her fingers within his grasp, the intensity of his gaze holding hers when she looked across at him in shy enquiry. He gave her fingers a reassuring squeeze as he reiterated his resolve to apologise to her as soon as possible for his earlier bad temper.

'Might I remind you *I* am not the one who was disowned by my own family!'

He should have known that Jennifer would not have allowed his insult to go unchallenged. 'There is only your father, the rector, and he was ever blind to your faults.' Gabriel eyed her disdainfully. 'Can my uncle be equally as blind, I wonder?'

She bristled defensively. 'Charles and I are very happy with our marriage.'

'Indeed?'

Angry colour once again darkened those creamy cheeks. 'You will see for yourself when he returns from town.'

Gabriel snorted. 'I have absolutely no intention of still being in Cambridgeshire when my uncle returns.'

'No?'

'No.'

'Because you are too much the coward to face my husband, perhaps?'

Gabriel's eyes glittered fiercely at this slur upon his honour. 'If you were a man, I would call you out for such an insult!'

'If I were a man, there would be no reason for the insult!'

'*You*—'

'Gabriel.' It was Diana's softly spoken warning that brought an end to what was rapidly becoming an intolerable heated row.

He drew in a deep, controlling breath and forced himself to calm down. 'Diana is quite correct; we are digressing from the point.'

'And what point was that?'

His mouth tightened ominously at Jennifer's obvious sarcasm. 'That there was not so much as a maid present when I visited my mother's rooms earlier and I am not satisfied with the level of her care.'

'I have told you—'

'I would also be interested to learn why and by whom my mother's companion was pensioned off four months ago. Perhaps it was another of those decisions Charles made so arbitrarily?'

'How on earth do you know about Alice Britton?' she gasped.

'I believe I asked why and by whom, not how I happen to know of it.'

Dark brows rose haughtily. 'Charles decided she had become too old to perform her duties any longer and sent her away.'

'But did not replace her?' he pressed.

'There's was no need when I am here to keep dear Felicity company,' his uncle's wife simpered.

Gabriel would as soon see his mother in the daily company of a venomous viper! 'And when Charles decided to dismiss Miss Britton, did he also provide her with a suitable pension?' As Gabriel was well aware, Alice Britton had been with his mother since Felicity was a small child, first in the nursery, then as lady's maid and latterly as her companion. Not only was it doubtful that the elderly woman would have the means to keep herself in retirement, but now that he had seen the situation here for himself, he could not believe that his mother would ever have agreed to her companion's dismissal.

Jennifer gave a derisive smile. 'As you know, what happens in this household ceased to be any of your business long ago—'

'I will take that to mean he did not.' Gabriel's jaw was tight with disapproval.

'Take it as you wish,' she shot back as the butler returned to remove their soup dishes.

The more he learnt of the happenings in this household the past four months, the more he began to fear that Miss Britton's concerns for his mother were fully justified.

'I can see how concerned you are for your mother,

Gabriel.' Once again it was the softly spoken Diana who took charge of the conversation after the butler had left the room. 'As such, I am sure that my own maid will be only too happy to sit with your mother until other, more permanent arrangements can be made.'

'That is not necessary, Lady Diana—'

'I do not wish to seem rude, Mrs Prescott…' Diana's voice became firm as she turned to address the older woman; she had suffered quite enough of this woman's opinions for one evening! '…but I believe you will find my remark was actually addressed to Gabriel.'

She flushed at the obvious put-down. 'Even so, I am sure it is completely unnecessary for you be inconvenienced like that.'

'My dear Mrs Prescott, I assure you I do not consider it in the least an *inconvenience* to relinquish my maid to the comfort of my future mother-in-law.' She steadily met the older woman's gaze.

Diana had become firmly convinced during dinner that the atmosphere she had sensed in Faulkner Manor since their arrival was caused by the malice of Jennifer Prescott. Admittedly, having Gabriel return so unexpectedly must have been something of a shock, but that still did not explain why she was so determined to ruin any chance of happiness for him, especially as Diana was now utterly sure that Gabriel had not been guilty of any past seduction of her.

The other woman did not appear to be unhappy in her marriage; on the contrary, her earlier claim that her marriage to Charles Prescott was a happy one, despite its unusual beginnings, seemed to indicate the opposite was true, spoken as it was so convincingly. So what had happened eight years ago and why had Jennifer Prescott lied about it?

Diana turned to look across the table at Gabriel. 'Perhaps we might consider taking your mother back to London with us when we leave? I am sure that a change of scenery might help—'

'Felicity's health is far too precarious for such a long and arduous journey!' Jennifer protested sharply.

'Again, I do not wish to sound rude.' Diana unblinkingly returned the older woman's resentful gaze. 'But I believe it is for Gabriel to decide whether or not his mother is well enough to travel back to London with us.'

'My husband is now the master of this household, not Gabriel.'

'Forgive me. I was led to believe it was Mrs Faulkner's home, and that you and your husband were but guests in her household,' Diana remarked.

Jennifer gave up all pretence of politeness as she rose angrily to her feet. 'How dare you question me in this way?' The skirts of her dress swished as she stalked around the table towards Diana. 'Just because you have a title and a grand manner does not mean—'

'That is *quite* enough.' Gabriel rose to his feet to step in between Diana and the rapidly approaching harpy. 'I advise you to regain control of your emotions forthwith, madam, or I will be forced to do it for you,' he warned her.

It took several moments for his aunt to regain her composure. 'I apologise for my outburst, Lady Diana. I was merely…concerned that you do not seem to understand the fragility of Mrs Faulkner's condition.' This condescending adage completely negated her apology. 'I am sure it would be most inadvisable to even think of moving her at this time.'

Gabriel had to admit—in view of his mother's lack of consciousness when he'd visited her earlier—to being somewhat surprised himself at Diana's suggestion that they remove his mother to London. He watched his wife-to-be stand up and move gracefully to his side, her fingers resting lightly in the crook of his arm as she turned to answer the other woman smoothly. 'I apologise for speaking out of turn, Mrs Prescott.' She turned to him. 'I am sure your aunt is wise to advise caution in regard to your mother, my dear. And no doubt she is also correct in her opinion that your mother does not need the services of my maid, either.'

Remarks that were very odd, considering that Diana had been the one to make both the suggestion that her maid sit with his mother and that they should take her to London in the first place. What was going on here?

Jennifer visibly relaxed. 'Now that tempers have cooled, I suggest we all sit down and resume eating our dinner.'

'An excellent idea.' Diana smiled brightly as she removed her hand from Gabriel's arm and retook her seat at the table. 'One always develops such an appetite when one is in the country.' She placed her napkin lightly across her silk-covered knees before looking up to smile at the now-seated Jennifer Prescott.

Gabriel resumed his own seat at the table far more cautiously. His uncle's wife had just seriously insulted Diana, in both word and deed, and yet the smile that curved his fiancée's delectable lips could not have been sweeter. Not because she was not fully aware of the personal nature of the attack, he felt sure; as he had learnt to his cost, it was most unwise to underestimate the woman he was betrothed to.

Undoubtedly something was seriously amiss with Diana's contradictory behaviour, but Gabriel had no idea what it was. He intended to find out at the earliest possible opportunity, though.

He was none the wiser by the time the meal finally came to an end almost two hours later. An excruciating and long two hours for Gabriel, although the ladies appeared to suffer no such discomfort as they conversed on such subjects as London fashions and the difficulty of acquiring the correct silks and lace. The capabilities of the cook at Faulkner Manor were also extolled as each delicious course was served to them. Diana had briefly excused herself from the table to go off in search of a handkerchief after the main course was finished, leaving Gabriel and Mrs Prescott to enjoy an uncomfortable silence. Diana had resumed control of the inane conversation upon her return, this time asking about the comfort and size of the congregation that attended the church in the village of which Jennifer's father was still rector.

All of them innocuous subjects—and so totally boring Gabriel found himself in danger of falling asleep over his dessert.

'That is two hours of my life that I hope never to live through again,' he muttered as he and Diana ascended the wide staircase together. Gabriel had requested that his after-dinner brandy be delivered to the privacy of his bedchamber rather than run the risk of having to suffer any more of his uncle's wife's company.

Diana could not help but laugh at his disgruntled expression. She agreed; it had been a most tedious evening. Worse than tedious, in fact. 'Never mind, Gabriel.' She patted his hand sympathetically. 'This evening has served one purpose at least—I now completely accept your explanation as to how Mrs Prescott has knowledge of your birthmark.'

He raised surprised brows. 'You do?'

'Oh, yes.' Diana snorted. 'I am sure that even at a very young age you would have required at least some intelligence in the women you bedded.'

Gabriel stiffened. 'I am not at all sure this is a correct conversation—'

'Oh, don't be so pompous.'

He scowled. 'I have just suffered the most agonisingly boring evening of my entire life and now you dare to call me pompous?'

She turned to eye him teasingly as they reached the

top of the staircase. 'It is not in the least flattering that you include the apparently boring company of your future wife in that sweeping statement.'

'Damn it, I was not referring to you!'

'Now you are swearing in front of your future wife, too.'

'I shall do a lot more than that if you do not soon explain your previous remark,' he vowed as she continued to walk along the hallway to their bedchambers, leaving him no choice but to follow her, as he carried the candle to light her way. 'In fact, I wish you would explain the whole of this peculiar evening to me. I would be interested to learn, for example, at what point in the evening you became convinced that Jennifer Prescott has, and always did have, the intellect of a pea?'

'I believe you may be insulting the pea!' Diana laughed. 'And I believe it became apparent to me when she first described your mother's health as being nothing more than a simple malaise that did not require the attendance of a doctor or nurse, before only minutes later claiming your mother was far too fragile in health to be removed to London.' She pursed her lips. 'It has always been my belief that one is in need of a certain amount of intellect in order to be a successful liar.'

'But—' Gabriel was left standing outside in the hallway as Diana entered her bedchamber without so much as a backward glance, meaning he had to follow her if he wished to continue this conversation. 'Are you tell-

ing me you had decided over two hours ago that she is
an unmitigated liar?'

She remained completely composed as she removed
her long lace gloves. 'Oh, no, Gabriel, I decided that
several days ago. Before I had even met her. Think,
Gabriel,' she urged as he looked totally dumbfounded
by her admission. 'I could hardly claim to believe your
own version of past events without at the same time
acknowledging that the young woman involved must
therefore be a liar. As Jennifer Prescott is that young
woman, ergo Jennifer Prescott must be a liar. Once
I had that firmly established in my mind—and, once
again, I apologise for my slight wobble over doubting
your word earlier—'

'It is I who should apologise to you for behaving so
boorishly,' he inserted swiftly.

'Let us not now argue about who should apologise
to whom,' she dismissed with her usual briskness.
'In regard to Mrs Prescott's lack of honesty… Once I
remembered that she *is* inherently dishonest, it became
so much easier for me to realise I must disbelieve anything she had to say. She has also been very cunning,
of course—'

'You just claimed that she lacks intellect!' Gabriel
eyed her with some considerable exasperation.

'Really, Gabriel, I am sure you must be aware that
true intelligence and the slyness of a cunning vixen
are not at all the same thing.' Diana shot him a chiding
glance.

'I must?'

'But of course,' she said. 'You are, I am glad to say, the most intelligent gentleman—apart from my father— that I have ever met.'

Gabriel was not feeling particularly intelligent at this moment; in fact, this whole conversation seemed to have run away from his understanding!

Diana, on the other hand, seemed cheerfully satisfied with her evening. And in her happy state of contentment, she was even more desirable to him. He suddenly realised that, although he still did not want to make love to her properly for the first time under this roof and before they were legally married, there *were* other ways he could satisfy the desire that ignited between them every time they touched. And he was pretty sure he knew them all...

Diana was so caught up in thoughts of the positive results of her evening that she did not even notice as Gabriel placed the lighted candle upon the dressing table before locking the bedchamber doors, only becoming aware once he stood very close to her, the warmth in his eyes unmistakable as his arms moved about her waist and he pulled her gently but determinedly into the heat of his body.

Her eyes widened. 'What are you doing, Gabriel?'

'I am sure you, at least, are far too intelligent a woman for me to need to explain.' His head lowered, his lips nuzzling against the rapidly beating pulse in her throat.

She was undeniably flustered by the warmth of those lips against her flesh. 'But—'

'I have decided that this evening does not have to be a complete waste of time.' Those lips now moved the length of her throat, slowly, pleasurably. 'I also admit the only thing that made this evening at all bearable for me was the thought of reacquainting myself with the mole upon your left breast once we were finally alone together...' His hands were at her back as he began to unfasten the buttons of her gown that ran the length of her spine.

A quiver of anticipation travelled down that spine at the mere thought of his previous familiarity with her breasts; breasts that now tingled in awareness beneath the silk of her gown, the now familiar warmth growing between her thighs. 'And is it also your intention to acquaint me with the birthmark upon your thigh?'

His husky laugh reverberated throughout her body. 'It might be, yes. With your agreement, my dear?'

She lifted her head to look up at him and saw the desire that burned in the dark-blue depths of his eyes and the laughter lines fanning out from the corners. The slant of his cheekbones seemed less severe than usual, too, and his lips, those firm and sculptured lips, were curved up into a lazily amused smile.

This was a question to which Diana could have only one answer...

Chapter Twelve

It was the very gentleness in Gabriel's expression—an emotion so at odds with his usual uncompromising arrogance—which succeeded in melting the very bones in Diana's body. 'I believe I should enjoy that very much,' she responded huskily.

'I am much relieved to hear it.' He had finished unfastening the buttons at the back of her gown and now allowed that garment to slide down the slenderness of her arms before dropping it softly to the floor to pool silkily at her slippered feet, leaving her clothed only in her short shift and a pair of white stockings held in place by pretty white garters decorated with tiny pink rosebuds.

Gabriel's breath caught in his throat as he looked down at her, the fullness of her breasts visible beneath the thin material of her shift, the tips of those breasts already aroused and pouting as they pressed invitingly against it, a darker vee of golden curls also visible between her silky thighs.

His gaze glowed hotly as it moved back up to her face. 'So much has happened since coming into this household, I have discovered that it is only your beauty and honesty which seems real to me.'

Diana felt a wealth of emotion growing, swelling, inside her chest. Gabriel had stated clearly at the time of their betrothal that he did not love her and that he never would, but to have won the regard and the respect of a man as jaded as he was, was a pearl beyond price.

The joy of that lit her eyes as she reached up to begin unfastening the buttons of his waistcoat. 'In that case, allow me to act as your valet again, my lord…'

There was no slow and agonisingly pleasurable removal of his clothes this time, as he aided her in their removal before throwing them on to the carpeted floor beside the bed.

Diana smiled in satisfaction as the small brown birthmark was revealed only several inches above his knee after he had sat down on the bed to remove his boots and then peel off his pantaloons. 'Most respectable, my lord.'

Gabriel grimaced. 'That woman is a vindictive witch—'

He was silenced from further comment as Diana placed her fingertips lightly across his lips. She gave a gentle shake of her head. 'She has no place here with us now.'

'No.' He was completely unconcerned by his nakedness as he stood up before reaching to remove the pins from Diana's hair.

Gabriel drew in a sharp breath as those tresses were finally released to fall, as he had once imagined they might, in a warmth of reddish-gold curls that reached down to the tender curve of her waist, several of those delicate curls framing the creamy warmth of her flushed cheeks and brow.

His hands shook slightly as he raised them to cradle each side of her face before gazing deeply into her eyes. 'You are beauty incarnate, Diana. A veritable goddess come to earth.'

Diana felt almost overwhelmed by their intimacy, the nakedness of his body more perfect, more wonderfully masculine than she could ever have imagined; the muscled hardness of his shoulders and chest was beautifully, gloriously sculptured in the glow of candlelight, and tapered down to the flatness of his stomach and leanly muscled thighs. Those drawings in the book of the Greek gods in her father's library, which Diana had once looked at so admiringly, had not prepared her for the physical evidence of the arousal of a flesh-and-blood man—but then, in all fairness to those Greek gods, none of them had been drawn fully and magnificently aroused!

Diana was unable to stop staring at Gabriel's arousal, steel encased in velvet. What would it be like, she wondered, to kneel down in front of him and place her lips about that—?

She stopped, stunned at herself and her fantasies. She

had no idea where they had even come from! Except she knew it was something that she felt compelled to do; she was sure he would enjoy it as much, if not more, than she would...

'Your turn will come later, little goddess.' Gabriel reached out to grasp her arms before she could sink to her knees in front of him, having seen the direction of her hungry graze. Experienced as he was, perhaps even jaded from the women he had bedded this past eight years, if she so much as touched his aching and throbbing shaft with her mouth at this moment, then he would lose all control. And he wanted to please her first.

'I wish to give you pleasure, Diana.' He slipped one thin strap from her shoulder, then the other, allowing her shift to fall softly down about her hips revealing the deliciously full, naked thrust of her breasts. 'Ah, my familiar friend.' He ran the tip of his finger across the tiny mole now visible just slightly above her left nipple.

She trembled from the pleasure of that single caress, her legs beginning to shake almost uncontrollably as he lowered his head to run the tip of his tongue across that mole before he moved lower, his tongue now a moist rasp across the aching crest of her breast, the nipple standing erect even as his lips parted, his breath hot against her skin before he took that rosy tip fully into the heat of his mouth.

Pleasure coursed from her breast down to between her thighs. She reached out to grasp on to the flexing muscles of his shoulders as she felt her core burning as he drew harder on her nipple even as his other hand cupped its twin and the soft pad of his thumb moved across its tip with the same delectable rhythm.

Diana was so lost in wonder, in pleasure, that she barely noticed as he discarded her shift altogether, only becoming aware that he had done so as he moved his hand to caress a path from her breast, over the slight curve of her stomach, before cupping her lower, the press of his palm sending quivers of pleasure coursing through her even as his fingers began a skilful caress of her moist and sensitive opening.

She gasped, her hands moving up and allowing her own fingers to become entangled in the dark thickness of Gabriel's hair as ecstasy unlike anything she had ever known before claimed and rocked her in a crescendo of ever-increasing waves.

She groaned achingly at her release before collapsing weakly against him.

He released her breast slowly before raising his head to see that Diana had not just collapsed but truly fainted, her lashes resting long and silkily upon her flushed and creamy cheeks, her breathing soft and shallow.

Gabriel frowned with concern even as he swung her up into his arms and carried her towards the bed. He had, he realised, made love with women too numerous to count, but none of them had ever fainted away after climaxing. Had he hurt her? Perhaps she was too delicate, too ladylike to enjoy such pleasures? That had to be it! What a fool he was!

'Gabriel?'

His gaze sharpened on her face, his expression softening in relief as he saw that she was looking up at him with dreamy satisfaction rather than horrified accusation.

She frowned slightly at his continued silence, one of her hands lifting to cradle the side of his sharply etched jaw. 'I had no idea that lovemaking would be so—so gloriously overwhelming.'

'Neither did I,' he assured her huskily as he knelt on the bed to lay her gently down upon the bedcovers.

'But you are a man of experience,' she said wonderingly.

'I would rather not talk about that now, my dear,' he said uncomfortably. He realised the women he had bedded in the past had all ceased to matter, been forgotten, had faded into insignificance after holding Diana in his arms and making love with her. Why that should be he had no idea.

'I believe it is now my turn to—explore,' she said shyly.

Gabriel's heart leapt in his chest at Diana's reminder that he had brought a halt to her caresses earlier. 'Perhaps we have explored enough for one night,' he said gently, recalling how overwhelmed she has just been. This was, after all, her first experience of lovemaking.

'Oh, no, Gabriel.' Diana sat up, the long length of her golden hair falling silkily about her shoulders, the naked pout of her breasts peeping through those curls, the nipples as full and ripe as the berries they resembled.

His breath caught in his throat at the sight of those

juicy orbs, his shaft aching as he imagined feasting on them once again. 'Diana—'

'You will lie still, please,' she instructed as she moved up on to her knees to push him down on to the pillows, appearing not at all abashed that she wore only her stockings and garters as she knelt between his parted legs.

'Lie still,' she said—and how in the blazes was he supposed to do that when she first bent to place a soft kiss against that damned birthmark before straightening to run her tiny hands the length of his thighs? His head fell back on to the pillows as he finally felt the warmth of her lips closing about his hard and throbbing arousal and her hair fell about her like a golden curtain before spilling softly down on to his thighs.

Diana was encouraged in her caresses by Gabriel's throaty groans and the hot leaping of his arousal as she took him deeper into the heat of her mouth. She had never tasted anything so succulently addictive in her life before.

'Diana!' Gabriel sounded short of breath, his voice a low and fervent appeal.

She raised her head to look at him, concerned to see an agonised expression on his face. 'Am I hurting you?'

'Dear God, no, not at all! It is too much pleasure, Diana. Much more of it and I shall disgrace myself completely,' he explained even as he reached down for her.

She evaded his grasp, emboldened by his admission. 'How so? You must tell me, Gabriel, else how will I ever learn how I am to please you?' she pleaded.

He looked rueful. 'If you please me any more than you already have, then I shall lose control and spill myself like some callow youth.'

'Ah.' She nodded in understanding, even as her avid gaze returned to the long, hard shaft she still cradled in her hand. There was a tiny bead of moisture on its glistening tip and she bent slightly and licked it with the slow rasp of her tongue before once again taking him fully into her mouth.

'Diana…' His hands were clenched at his sides, his body completely taut.

Only minutes ago he had introduced her to undreamt-of pleasure, one she now wished to give back to him.

'Dear God!' Gabriel's groans became a litany as— almost against his will, it seemed—his hips began to rise and fall in a distinctive rhythm. Previously innocent of such intimacy, she nevertheless knew the exact moment that he lost all control and became utterly consumed in his own ecstasy.

Minutes passed; all Gabriel could hear was the sound of his own ragged breathing as he lay completely boneless, sprawled back upon the bedcovers, one of his hands still lightly entangled in the gold of Diana's curls as they cascaded across him in wild disarray, her breath a warm caress against his thighs.

Somehow he had found heaven in a place he had come to think of as hell. Somehow this woman had lifted him out of the dark and taken him into a golden paradise. It was as if—

A knock sounded softly on the bedchamber door to

halt his wandering thoughts, followed by an enquiring whisper. 'Miss? Miss, you told me I should call you if—well, if I should need you?'

'What the—?' Gabriel was too satiated, too physically replete, to do more than turn and frown in the direction of the locked door.

Diana's response was much more immediate as she sat up quickly to push back the wildness of her hair from her face before running across the room to pull on and belt her robe. 'Dear Lord, how could I have allowed myself to forget?' she muttered wildly.

'Diana?' Gabriel eyed her sharply as the fog of his physical repletion began to abate.

She shook her head. 'I meant to go immediately after dinner— oh, I should not have allowed myself to become so distracted!' she told herself crossly as she hurried to unlock the door and open it just enough so that she could talk with the person outside in the hall-way, but whoever it was could not see inside the bed-chamber to where Gabriel still lay naked upon the bed.

He sat up, a dark and heavy scowl on his brow as he watched her at the doorway. He had just been transported to some hitherto-unknown plateau of pleasure and she had just referred to their intimacy as being a distraction from some more important purpose!

She had no experience with which to compare their lovemaking, of course, and could have no idea how rare and beautiful it had been. But he was fully aware of it.

She was utterly incapable of artifice. She was the most honest and forthright young woman he had—

'We must both dress immediately.' Diana appeared flustered as, her conversation concluded, she closed and relocked the door, not sparing him so much as a glance as she hurried across the room to fling open the wardrobe doors and began searching through the array of gowns that hung there. She halted as she turned back into the room, blue woollen gown in hand, and found that he had not moved. 'Did you not hear me, Gabriel?' She frowned her impatience with his inactivity as she removed her robe and replaced it with her shift. 'You must dress. We cannot dally here a moment longer.' She stepped lithely into her gown.

Gabriel looked taken aback at her increasing agitation. What on earth was going on? 'I have no intention of dressing or going anywhere until I know exactly where it is I am going and why,' he said with some annoyance.

Of course he had no idea where they were going or why, Diana admonished herself as she finished pulling on her gown. How could he possibly know when she had found no opportunity—had been too lost to the wonder of what had just happened—to tell him what actions she had put into play earlier this evening?

It was far from an ideal end to the ecstasy of their earlier intimacy, but no doubt Gabriel would thank her once he knew what she had done.

'My maid has been sitting with your mother for several hours now, with instructions to come for me should she receive any visitors,' she started to explain hurriedly.

'Your maid has been sitting with my mother?' he repeated slowly.

Diana nodded. 'Do you recall that I left the dining table earlier in search of a handkerchief?'

'Yes.' Of course he remembered that, and a damned long time she had taken about it too. Over ten minutes of absolute silence between himself and Jennifer, as they glared their glittering dislike at each other, knowing that if he said one word to the witch then an avalanche of them would follow, all of them unpleasant. She had seemed to know that too and for once in her life had remained silent.

'I had no real need of a handkerchief.' Diana smiled triumphantly. 'It was merely a ruse to allow me the time in which to arrange for my maid to go to your mother's rooms.'

Gabriel raised an eyebrow. 'I thought you had agreed with Jennifer that there was no need for your maid to sit with my mother?'

'I only gave the appearance of agreeing,' Diana corrected, moving to stand in front of the mirror on the dressing table in order to study her reflection as she pinned her hair neatly into place.

'Did you?' he asked, thoroughly confused.

She turned to eye him impatiently. 'Really, Gabriel, I am sure I am making myself perfectly clear. I lied when I appeared to take Mrs Prescott's word for it that your mother didn't need my maid's company.'

Gabriel became very still. 'I was led to believe you were incapable of lying.'

'The very reason it is easier to be believed when one is left with no other choice but to do so!'

Gabriel stared across at her wordlessly. He had just been mentally praising Diana for her honesty, for her utter lack of artifice, and all the time she was as skilful at deception as the next woman.

No doubt she had a good reason for it, he told himself. She had good reason for most things she did. Even so, it was unsettling to realise she was as capable of lying as anyone else. 'Would you care to tell me why it was you felt the need to lie on this occasion?'

'Surely that is obvious?' she said incredulously.

'Not completely, no,' he said through gritted teeth. 'Explain, if you please.' He stood up and began to gather up his clothes.

Diana blinked. She was not sure how she was supposed to even think, let alone explain, when Gabriel stood before her in all his naked glory! Their lovemaking had been a revelation to her. A wonder. A joy beyond imagining. And just looking at the magnificence of his unclothed body was enough to bring the warmth back into her cheeks. And other places too. Private, intimate places of her body that he now knew more intimately than she did herself.

Gabriel had been beautiful in his arousal, and he was no less so now, the candlelight giving his flesh a golden hue as it caressed the hard planes of his body and revealed that thatch of black hair surrounding his now-softened shaft. Even in repose it was far more impressive than those sketches of the Greek gods in that book—

'Diana!'

She gave a slightly dazed shake of her head, closing her eyes briefly before lifting her gaze to concentrate Gabriel's scowling face rather than the magnificence of his body; she might perhaps be able to concentrate on the matter in hand if she did not look at all that male beauty! 'Could you dress whilst I explain?'

'Willingly, if it is going to speed up the proceedings,' he said. He turned his back on her to sort through the clothes he had amassed on the bed.

Even his sculptured back was beautiful, Diana acknowledged achingly, longing to reach out and touch those wide and muscled shoulders, which tapered down to a narrow waist, to fondle his nicely curved buttocks—

'You do not appear to be explaining anything as yet, Diana,' Gabriel reminded her impatiently, his back still towards her as he pulled his shirt on over his head and instantly covered at least part of his nakedness.

But still not enough for her to focus on coherent thought, the intimacy of the situation rendering her temporarily speechless.

'I swear I will come over there and shake you if you do not begin this explanation in the next ten seconds!'

Diana gave a guilty start as she heard the savagery in Gabriel's tone. It was understandable—she needed to pull herself together. 'When I left the dining room earlier in search of a handkerchief, I first visited your mother's rooms—I wished to satisfy my curiosity before taking any further action,' she explained as he stared at her incredulously.

'And did you? Satisfy your curiosity!' he rasped as Diana looked at him blankly.

'Your mother was still sleeping,' she said.

'Perhaps that is as well when she would have had absolutely no idea who you were if she had been awake.' Gabriel was dressed in his pantaloons and boots now, as well as his shirt, although he had left the latter unfastened, and the darkness of his hair was dishevelled as he looked across at her with accusing eyes. 'I had intended to introduce the two of you tomorrow.'

'Obviously, as she was asleep when I entered her bedchamber, you are still free to do so—'

'How kind!'

She crossed the room to stand before him. 'Gabriel, I believe you are missing the point…'

'Perhaps that is because you have not told me the point, as yet.' His increasing frustration with this situation was obvious in the dangerous glitter of his eyes.

Diana sighed. 'Despite her alleged malaise, I do not believe that a lady who must not yet be fifty should be asleep as much as Mrs Prescott claims your mother has been in recent months.'

'And?'

'And so when I entered her rooms earlier I took it upon myself to check the contents of the medicine bottle, which stood upon her dressing table. Amongst other, less innocuous substances, I discovered—as I suspected that I might—that it contained laudanum. It is a substance I am familiar with because my father took it in the last years of his life in order to help him sleep,' she said.

'Are you saying that all this time my mother has been taking a sleeping draught?' Gabriel asked slowly. That made absolutely no sense to him when his mother's problem seemed to be an over-abundance of sleep, not a lack of it. Unless, of course, her life was now so hellish that she preferred to sleep most of the time rather than live in that hell?

'I am afraid there is no more time for me to explain this situation just now.' Diana moved hurriedly across the room to pick up the lighted candle. 'I had meant to go immediately to your mother's rooms as soon as dinner was over.' Her cheeks became flushed as she obviously recalled exactly why she had not done so. 'May—my maid—came to tell me that Mrs Prescott had attempted to visit your mother's rooms only a few minutes ago.'

'And?' he pressed.

'When she couldn't gain entry through the locked door, she knocked upon it. May ignored that, of course, as I had instructed her to do should the need arise. Mrs Prescott has now gone back down the stairs to collect a second key from the housekeeper.' She grimaced. 'May took advantage of her absence to leave your mother's rooms to quickly come and inform me of events.'

'Considering you are a visitor, newly come into this house, you appear to have taken rather a lot upon yourself,' Gabriel commented. To him, at least, things were still incomprehensible; fortunately, Diana gave every appearance of knowing exactly what she was doing and why.

'I would have preferred to discuss it with you first, of course—'

'Of course,' Gabriel muttered somewhat sarcastically.

'But as we were seated at dinner all together there was obviously no opportunity for me to do so,' she continued. 'As I have already explained, there really is no time to lose,' she added firmly as Gabriel would have pressed her for more details. 'May has been with me for years and is very loyal, but it would be unfair to expect her to deal with Mrs Prescott's unpleasantness twice in one evening.' She turned upon her heel with the obvious intention of leaving.

Gabriel reached out and took hold of her arm. 'Not so fast! First, at least tell me the purpose of keeping Mrs Prescott from entering my mother's rooms?'

'Surely that is obvious?'

His mouth tightened. 'Humour me.'

She glared at him. 'For the purpose of allowing your mother to awaken, of course, and so enabling her to speak to the son she has not seen in eight years.'

Gabriel was so surprised by this explanation that he relaxed his grip on her arm. A fact she did not hesitate to take advantage of as she rushed from the bedchamber.

Chapter Thirteen

By the time Gabriel had collected his addled wits enough to hurry from the now-darkened bedchamber in pursuit, he was just in time to see Diana's skirts disappearing round the end of the hallway in the direction of his mother's rooms, the candle disappearing with her and once again plunging him into darkness.

A darkness that was not only physical, but also emotional.

The depth of their lovemaking had been so consuming that even now he found it difficult to comprehend exactly what she was about from the little she had told him—not an altogether pleasant experience for a man who had always prided himself on his mental and emotional acuity!

Outside his mother's suite of rooms, Diana had placed the lit candle on the hallstand and was standing in front of the door, her arms extended and her expression defiant as Jennifer used every means she could to dislodge her from that protective stance.

One of which was to now reach out and grasp a handful of Diana's hair. 'How dare you?' his uncle's wife ranted shrilly as she tugged viciously on those golden curls. 'You have absolutely no authority to stop me from entering my sister-in-law's rooms—'

'Diana may not—but I certainly do,' he announced.

Diana turned gratefully to look at Gabriel as he approached them quickly, once again looking every inch as vengeful as his angelic namesake with his unfastened shirt billowing about him. Although, thankfully, this time the cold fury glittering in his eyes was not directed at her, but at the young woman married to his uncle.

'Release Diana immediately.' He towered over both women, but it was Jennifer who remained the focus of his ruthless gaze. 'Do not put me to the trouble of having to repeat the instruction, madam,' he warned in an intimidating voice that sent a shiver of apprehension down Diana's spine.

An apprehension that Jennifer also felt, if the suddenness with which she released her grip upon Diana's hair was any indication, although the defiance in her expression remained as she looked up at him, hands now resting challengingly upon her hips. 'Perhaps you should see to restricting the behaviour of your fiancée rather than remonstrating with me.'

Gabriel raised dark brows. 'Diana is more than capable of deciding for herself what she will and will not do.'

The dryness underlying his tone gave Diana the courage to state exactly what she intended doing at this moment. 'I have just informed Mrs Prescott that the two of us will sit with your mother tonight, thus leaving her free to enjoy an untroubled sleep.'

He looked at her searchingly for several long seconds, a shutter coming down over his expression before he turned back to Jennifer. 'I can see no reason why you would have any objection to that?'

Jennifer's beautiful face became flushed with her displeasure. '*I* have seen to Felicity's care this past four months—'

'And a right mess—'

'And now you are deserving of an unbroken night's sleep,' Diana smoothly interrupted his angry outburst; a justified outburst, she felt sure, but one guaranteed to further inflame this already heated situation. 'I assure you,' she continued firmly, 'Gabriel and I are more than happy to sit with Mrs Faulkner tonight.'

'And if I object?' Those brown eyes flashed Jennifer's displeasure with the proposal.

'It is not a matter open for discussion, madam.' Gabriel looked down the long length of his nose at her. 'Nor do I expect to ever witness you treating Diana in that disgraceful manner ever again.'

'But—'

'If you have nothing of interest to say, then I would appreciate it if you would remove yourself from this vicinity altogether.' His expression was full of his undisguised disgust.

Diana knew that she would cringe in mortification if Gabriel should ever look at her in that way and Jennifer Prescott was not proof against it either; she looked less than her usual defiant self. 'Charles shall hear of your highhandedness the moment he returns.'

Gabriel's top lip curled back disdainfully. 'I shall look forward to it,' was all he said.

Brown eyes flashed furiously. 'You have no right—'

'If nothing else, I have the right of being my mother's son,' he said harshly. 'You, on the other hand, are no more than a guest in my mother's house, with no authority to say who shall or shall not visit with her.' He looked down at her scornfully. 'Now, if you would kindly remove yourself, Diana and I wish to go inside and sit with my mother.'

Jennifer bristled with rage. 'If I chose, I could make life so uncomfortable for you that you would wish you had never been born.'

'Madam, if such an occurrence meant I never had to set eyes upon you again, then I would be happy for you to try!'

'You liked me well enough once,' she sneered.

'You are mistaken, madam.' Gabriel's tone was one of boredom now. 'That I succeeded in tolerating your presence when we were both children would be a more apt description.'

Jennifer's cheeks now become deathly pale. 'How I have always hated you,' she spat. 'With your "Lord of the Manor" attitude and your oh-so-superior manner!'

He eyed her mockingly. 'At last we are in agreement

on something, madam—our heartfelt dislike of each other.'

If Diana had needed any further confirmation—which she did not—that Jennifer Prescott had lied about the happenings of the past, then the other woman had just given it to her. So she had always hated Gabriel, had she? That was very interesting…

'It is late and tempers are becoming fractious.' Diana spoke calmly as she turned to the other woman. 'Please do not trouble yourself any further concerning Mrs Faulkner. I assure you, having nursed my father for the last few years of his life, I am more than up to the task of caring for Gabriel's mother.' Having—hopefully—left Jennifer with absolutely no further argument to make, Diana put an end to their conversation by knocking softly on the door of the bedchamber and requesting that May unlock the door and admit her.

Gabriel continued in a silent battle of wills with Jennifer for several seconds after Diana had entered his mother's bedchamber, before finally his uncle's wife gave a frustrated snort and flounced off down the hallway, leaving him to slowly follow his fiancée into the muted illumination of his mother's rooms.

Diana stood beside the bed in whispered conversation with her maid, who then dropped them a light curtsy before she vacated the bedchamber, and Gabriel crossed the room to stand beside his mother's bed.

He had spoken the truth earlier when he admitted to finding his mother much changed from when he had last seen her. Well…perhaps when Gabriel had last seen her was not a good comparison to make; his mother had been distraught the day he'd left Faulkner Manor, her face deathly pale, her eyes red from hours of crying in the face of his father's implacability regarding Jennifer Lindsay's accusations.

But his mother had always been a beauty, a glowing ever-young beauty it had always seemed to him. Now she looked every one of her two-and-fifty years, the darkness of her hair showing strands of grey, her face so white and thin and lifeless it was much like one of the masks worn during the time of carnival in Venice.

'I am sure the changes you see in your mother are only superficial, Gabriel.'

He glanced across the bed to where Diana looked back at him so compassionately. A compassion he found it hard to accept, even from the woman he had so recently been intimate with.

He looked away. 'Perhaps, having now dispatched my uncle's wife, you might care to give me an explanation as to why we have done so?'

'Of course.' She smiled briefly. 'But perhaps we should go through to your mother's private parlour so that we do not disturb her?' She indicated the adjoining room, the door standing open to reveal that it was furnished comfortably. 'We can leave the door open so that we will still hear her if she should stir.'

Gabriel looked at her through narrowed lids. 'From what you already said to me in your bedchamber, I thought disturbing my mother enough so that she awakens is our main purpose for being here?'

Diana felt her cheeks warm at this reference to when they had been in her bedchamber such a short time ago, when Gabriel had touched her with an intimacy and a skill that still took her breath away. When she had returned those caresses in a way that shocked her to even think of it…

Her gaze avoided meeting his. 'I have every hope that your mother will wake very soon,' she said abruptly. 'I simply think it would be better if this conversation were not the first thing she hears when she does so.'

He raised dark brows. 'Why not?'

Diana looked pained. 'Gabriel, when I came to your mother's rooms earlier this evening—'

'You mean when you *said* you were fetching a hand-kerchief?'

'Yes.' Diana squirmed at this pointed reminder of her duplicity—her only excuse was that she had done what she thought was for the best. 'The laudanum in your mother's medicine really is of a very high dosage, much more than it needs to be if it is only taken as an aid to help her sleep. Besides,' she added, 'Mrs Prescott has several times confirmed that she alone has been responsible for your mother's nursing care this past four months. And that care will have no doubt have included administering her medicine.' Diana chose her words carefully, but purposefully.

Gabriel stared at her levelly for several seconds before nodding. 'You are right, Diana—this conversation would be much better taking place in the privacy of my mother's parlour.' He left the room without waiting to see if she followed him.

Which she did, of course; if Diana's suspicions proved to be correct, then this was not going to be a particularly pleasant conversation, even if it was a necessary one.

Gabriel delayed continuing this conversation with her for some minutes by putting a taper to the fire laid in the hearth, staring down at the flames that quickly caught the kindling alight before then bending down to add some of the coal from the bucket beside the fireplace. And all the time his thoughts were racing. Mulling over the things Diana had already said. The suspicions arising from those observations.

It took him several minutes to regain control of his emotions enough to draw in a deep breath before turning to face her, his hands tightly gripped together behind his back. 'Very well,' he said stiltedly. 'You may continue your explanation now.'

She grimaced. 'You understand it is only a theory as yet?'

'At this point in time a theory is more than sufficient.' His jaw was so tightly clenched he felt as if the bones might crack. Dinner had been hellish, the time in Diana's bedchamber had been paradise; only God knew what the next few minutes were going to be like.

She began to pace the parlour. 'I have found Mrs Prescott's behaviour most unusual, since our arrival earlier today. Do you recall that she was not waiting for us in the hallway when we finally entered the house, but was in fact hurrying down the staircase, her face flushed from exertion? As if she were returning from some urgent errand?'

'Yes, I do.'

'I had thought, once you told me of your…past connection—'

'There's *no* past connection!'

'No. Well. Just so.' Diana felt slightly unnerved by the force of Gabriel's protest. 'I believed at first that might be a possible explanation for Mrs Prescott's flustered behaviour, but I have had a chance to rethink her actions since and now believe that she hurried back into the house in order to go up to your mother's room and administer another dose of her medication.'

'Perhaps my mother's medication was due?'

'Then Mrs Prescott's dedication to her patient, at a time when she was in such an obvious state of personal turmoil, would indeed be admirable.' Diana found it impossible to keep the derision out of her tone; she was usually a forbearing woman, usually only too happy to see the good in others, but she simply could not find a single thing about Mrs Prescott to like.

His eyes narrowed. 'Then we are to take it there was another reason for the administration of my mother's medication at that particular time?'

'I believe so, yes.'

'I am sure you are about to tell me what that reason was?' he drawled as she hesitated.

Then, 'None of Mrs Prescott's behaviour would have struck me as odd if it were not for the strangeness of her conversation at dinner. After first assuring us that your mother was not ill enough to require the care of a doctor or a nurse,' she explained at his questioning glance, 'she then went on to claim that your mother was too frail to sustain the strain of a coach journey back to London with us. Those two statements were in complete contradiction of each other. Rather than simply allowing my imagination to run riot at the possible reasons for that, I excused myself with the intention of checking your mother's health for myself.' She pursed her lips. 'You will recall, no doubt, that Mrs Prescott showed the first signs of agitation at dinner after you had told you that you had found the time to visit your mother's rooms earlier?'

'I do recall that, yes,' he admitted.

'I now believe that your mother did not wake during that visit for the simple reason that she was too deeply drugged by the laudanum in her medicine.'

'For what purpose?' he asked curiously.

'I believe to ensure that your mother was not awake to converse with you if you were to visit her this evening.'

Gabriel felt himself blanch as the full import of her suspicions began to take root in his own imaginings. One of them being that his uncle and his wife would already have been in residence here six years ago when he'd written to his mother and requested that he be allowed to visit her following his father's death. A letter he now wondered if his mother had ever received... Alice Britton's letter three days ago had certainly claimed that it was his mother's dearest wish to see him again, and had been for some time. The dismissal of his mother's doctor, nurse, and companion by Charles in the past four months was also suspect, leaving his mother completely alone and at the far-from-tender mercies of the Prescotts.

Diana's heart ached as she saw from the bleakness of his expression exactly how her disclosures were affecting him. 'I am so sorry, Gabriel—'

'You have done absolutely nothing for which you need to apologise,' he assured her.

Maybe not, but she was not enjoying saying any of these things to him. Especially as it had resulted in a return of that cold, emotionally closed-off man from their first meeting.

'If ensuring that your mother remained asleep truly was Mrs Prescott's intention earlier, then I knew from experience that another dose of laudanum would need to be administered some time this evening to maintain that unconscious state,' she continued gently. 'I placed my maid in here, with the door firmly locked, in order to prevent such an occurrence.'

Gabriel drew in a ragged breath. 'Jennifer cannot have seriously believed she could keep my mother asleep for the whole of my visit here.'

'Surely it needed only to succeed until such time as your uncle returned from London?' she suggested. 'At which time Mrs Prescott no doubt intended to pass the responsibility for the delicacy of this situation on to him.'

He snorted. 'Charles is no match for me, I assure you.'

She could well believe that. Just as she knew Gabriel would have succeeded in seeing the danger of the unusual situation that existed at Faulkner Manor for himself if he were not so emotionally close to it all. If his displeasure at seeing Jennifer Prescott again had not clouded his powers of deduction...

She gave a rueful smile. 'I doubt it matters either way now.'

His gaze sharpened. 'How so?'

She shrugged slender shoulders. 'If my suspicions are correct, and the lack of further medication succeeds in reviving your mother, then Mrs Prescott must know that we will quickly learn all about your mother's life these past six years.'

His expression was suddenly anguished. 'You seriously believe it is possible my mother has been lied to and deceived all that time? That she may have been kept as a virtual prisoner in her own home these past four months?'

'I think it is a possibility, yes,' Diana answered carefully.

'With what purpose in mind?' Gabriel shifted restlessly. 'What happened four months ago to bring about such a sudden change?'

'That is something only your uncle and his wife can answer...'

'Do you not have some other "theory" about that, too?'

She flinched as she heard the bitterness in his tone. 'I do, yes.'

'I thought that you might,' he sighed heavily.

'Obviously Charles and Jennifer have become accustomed to living here as your mother's guests for six years, a comfortable and privileged existence that I am sure they greatly enjoy. You have also mentioned to me that your uncle is a man who likes to gamble and that he lost his own home because of it.'

'He did, yes.'

'So perhaps the answer lies there? Even larger gambling debts than in the past would mean they needed a tighter control of the estate? I really do not know the reasons why things changed four months ago, Gabriel.' She spread her hands in apology. 'I can only say what I suspect. If I am wrong, then I shall apologise to all concerned.'

'You are not wrong.' He spoke with flat finality, the bleakness of his expression now absolute.

'We cannot be *sure*—'

'Damn it, I can!' His expression was savage. 'And the worst of it is that none of this would have occurred at all if I had persevered in visiting my mother after my father died.'

'Self-recrimination serves no purpose now, Gabriel—'

'It serves the purpose of easing some of my frustration with this situation.' He began to pace the parlour. 'If all of this is true, and I have every reason to believe that it is, then I will strangle the Prescotts with my own bare hands.'

'Having her only son consigned to prison for the

murder of his uncle and aunt will not aid in your mother's recovery one little bit,' she murmured.

Gabriel's eyes glittered vengefully. 'It would be worth it.'

She crossed the room to lay her hand gently upon his arm. 'You know it would not.' She smiled up at him gently. 'You love your mother very much, do you not?'

He tensed. 'Always.' His chin rose as if to challenge anyone who might dare him to make such a claim after the heartache his family had suffered on his behalf eight years ago.

But it was a heartache Diana believed had never been of his making. 'I think, when you next speak to Mrs Prescott—'

'I do not intend doing anything so banal as *speaking* to her—'

'When you next speak to her,' she repeated firmly, 'you might also like to ask her who the father of her babe really was.'

Gabriel became very still as he stared down at her, his expression changing from puzzlement, to shock, to total disbelief in the matter of only a few seconds. 'You cannot be suggesting—? You do not suppose it was *Charles*?'

She raised her eyebrows at him. 'It is a thought, is it not? I am aware that it is not unusual for an arranged marriage such as the Prescotts' was to find a measure of success, a mutual respect between them, at least.' As Diana hoped that her own marriage to Gabriel would one day achieve. 'But I believe your uncle's wife talks of her husband with more than just respect; I think that she is deeply in love with him. And she claimed earlier, very convincingly, that their marriage was a happy one.'

'I have every reason to believe that it is,' he said thoughtfully.

She gave a slight inclination of her head. 'My Aunt Humphries—who incidentally met both your mother and your Uncle Charles during her London Season almost thirty years ago—told me that he was then something of a charming rogue. Nowhere near the class of his disreputable nephew, of course,' she teased. 'But a rogue, none the less.'

Gabriel's expression lightened only slightly. 'I can see that it is past time your aunt and I made each other's acquaintance.'

She laughed briefly. 'I doubt that would reassure her in the slightest!'

'Possibly not,' he accepted drily, and just as quickly sobered. 'Do you really think it possible that Charles and Jennifer were intimately involved eight years ago and that the babe she carried was his all the time? Even worse, that they planned my disgrace together, knowing I would refuse to take responsibility for a child that categorically was not mine and so end up being disinherited by my father whilst Charles was paid handsomely to marry Jennifer?'

Diana looked sad. 'I cannot answer those questions with any finality. But I do think all these matters are worth investigating further.'

'I really *will* strangle the pair of them if it should turn out to be the truth of it—'

'Gabriel…? Gabriel, is that you, my dearest boy?'

He froze as if struck at the first sound of that soft and quavery voice calling from the adjoining room, his eyes widening with disbelief and his face becoming even paler as he registered his mother's endearment.

'Go to her, Gabriel,' Diana urged huskily, squeezing his arm briefly in encouragement before she stepped away from him.

'Come with me,' he pleaded.

She shook her head. 'I shall be waiting for you in my bedchamber when you and your mother have had a chance to talk together.' She smiled up at him. 'No matter what time it is.' Diana knew she would be unable to go to bed, let alone sleep, until she had heard whether or not he and his mother had managed to resolve their lengthy and, she suspected, completely unnecessary estrangement. Although the love she had heard in Felicity Faulkner's voice as she spoke her son's name certainly gave Diana hope that this would indeed be the case…

Chapter Fourteen

'I am sure you will not be at all surprised to learn that Jennifer has availed herself of one of the carriages and fled Faulkner Manor as if the devil himself were at her heels!' Gabriel stormed into Diana's bedchamber completely without warning some two hours later, still dressed in only his loosened shirt, pantaloons and boots, his hair in even more disarray, as if he had been running troubled fingers through it for some time.

Diana had tried to occupy herself profitably in Gabriel's absence, as her aunt had taught her to do during moments of idleness. First by reading a book. Then by taking out her embroidery when none of the favourite books she had brought with her succeeded in holding her attention or her interest. After unpicking the untidiness of her stitches for the fourth time, she had laid her embroidery aside too, her thoughts and emotions in too much turmoil for her to be able to settle to any worthwhile occupation.

So she had begun to pace instead. And when she tired of that she simply sat down in the chair by the fire, staring into the flames. Wondering. Hoping. So very much hoping that Gabriel's relationship with the mother he so dearly loved would once again be the loving one it had been. For his sake. For his widowed mother's sake.

Yet at the same time, she could not help but wonder how that reconciliation with his mother would affect her own betrothal to him. Gabriel had been completely honest with her from the first. He was now the Earl of Westbourne, and as such he felt he was in need of a wife, primarily as mistress of his homes, and eventually to bear his children. Diana was the daughter of the previous earl, therefore she, or one of her sisters, had been an obvious choice for the role of the new earl's wife. But if Gabriel truly had become reconciled with his mother, and the ice about his emotions melted, he might no longer be of the same cynical frame of mind. He could even decide that he no longer required a wife at all at this moment; his widowed mother could run his homes for him and, at only eight and twenty, there was no rush for him to produce his heirs.

Diana stood up slowly, keeping her expression deliberately calm and composed, even though her doubts as to her own future as Gabriel's wife meant she inwardly felt neither of those things. 'No, I cannot claim to be in the least surprised.'

In truth, if his visit with his mother had proven

her theories concerning Jennifer Prescott to be true, then she had been able to see no other solution to the other woman's dilemma; Jennifer would need to leave Faulkner Manor immediately, no doubt with the intention of joining her husband in London, or risk facing Gabriel's considerable wrath on her own. The devil himself, indeed—and Jennifer, whilst defensive and shrill, did not give the appearance of being quite that brave!

'I trust your mother is feeling more herself now?' she enquired.

His expression instantly became less fierce, the lines beside his nose and mouth smoothing out, his eyes a deep and compassionate blue. 'She fell asleep a few minutes ago as we were still talking,' he revealed huskily.

Diana nodded. 'It will take several days for the complete effects of the laudanum to wear off. I—did the two of you manage to untangle some of your differences?'

'We did,' he said.

'I am so glad.'

Gabriel suddenly looked murderous. 'You might also be pleased to know that it would seem most of your theories might well prove to be correct.'

'I'm not exactly *pleased* to hear that, Gabriel,' she protested.

He gave an impatient shake of his head before crossing the bedchamber restlessly to stand beside the fireplace looking down at the flames. 'At Charles's request, my mother apparently put her brother in charge of the estate accounts after my father died. She did it, she says, because at the time she felt quite unable to cope with the intricacies of managing the estate and fortune herself, and in the hopes that the responsibility would sober Charles somewhat.'

'It did not?'

'No.' Gabriel frowned darkly. 'Oh, he was very clever about his machinations for several years, the amounts that he took for himself apparently quite negligible within the grand scheme of things. Then, four months ago, my mother had to bring him to task when she discovered that a very large sum of money indeed was missing from the estate account.' His face hardened. 'My mother has absolutely no recollection of things since then. She has been kept asleep for so much of that time she was not even aware that Alice Britton had been dismissed.'

Diana drew in a sharp breath. 'That is truly *monstrous*.'

'Nor did she receive my letter following my father's death, when I requested that I might visit her and my father's graveside. And I did not receive any of the letters she wrote to me during the last six years, when she asked if I would visit her. Letters she apparently entrusted to *Charles* for safe delivery.' The loathing in Gabriel's expression promised retribution for that alone, let alone any of the other crimes his uncle might have committed in that time.

'I am sorry—'

'Do not pity me, Diana.' His face was savage in the firelight as he turned to glare at her. 'Pity is for the weak. And I assure you, at this moment my emotions towards my uncle and his wife are very strong indeed!'

She had no doubts that they were. Just as there could no longer be any doubt that Jennifer fleeing into the night was tantamount to an admission of the Prescotts' guilt. 'Then I will reserve my compassion for your mother. For what she has suffered.'

He drew in a steadying breath before making her a formal bow, a gesture that lost none of its sincerity because of his lack of formal attire. 'I should be down on my knees to you in gratitude, not taking my temper out on you.'

In a similar situation she knew she might feel equally as violent in her emotions. 'What will you do now?'

'Despite Jennifer's flight, I feel it best if I remain at my mother's side for tonight at least.'

It was obvious from this statement that Gabriel did not intend to spend the rest of the night in Diana's own bed—but had she really expected that he might? The horror of the Prescotts' treatment of his mother must be very disturbing for him; although she might still be quivering with remembered pleasure at the depth of their earlier intimacy, it had been far from the first time that he had known such physical satisfaction and it could not possibly have had the same impact upon his own emotions. In fact, it seemed to have had so little effect that he gave no indication of remembering it at all.

She gave a slight smile. 'I was not referring to your immediate plans, Gabriel...'

'As soon as my mother is well enough to travel we

will do as you suggested at dinner and travel to London. Once my mother is safely and comfortably settled at Westbourne House I have every intention of seeking out my uncle and his wife, of chasing them down to the ends of the earth if necessary, and ensuring that they pay for what has been done here,' he vowed.

Perhaps it was selfish of Diana, but she could not help but notice that neither she, nor their betrothal, was mentioned in his plans, either with regard to his immediate or his long-term future.

Gabriel had still been reeling, both emotionally and mentally, when he entered Diana's bedchamber a few minutes ago. He could never have imagined the depths to which Charles and his wife had succumbed since moving to Faulkner Manor to live with his newly widowed mother. Beginning, it would seem, with the appropriation of the letters sent between mother and son over the years...

No doubt once Gabriel had chance to check the estate accounts for himself he would find that Charles had been supplementing his gambling habit from those funds for most, if not all, of the past six years. He believed the large sum his mother had brought Charles to task over some four months ago, and which, with his renowned lack of luck at the gaming tables, he would have no hopes of repaying, would indeed prove to be the reason for the dismissal of all the people close to his mother and for the use of heavy doses of laudanum to ensure that she had remained in a haze of sleep for most of the time since.

As for the true events of that supposed scandal eight years ago…

If Gabriel had thought at all about the real identity of the father of Jennifer Lindsay's baby, then he had assumed it must be one of the men from the village. It had never even occurred to him, until Diana had made the suggestion earlier, that it might have been his roguish and disreputable Uncle Charles all the time.

Perhaps it should have done. Even then Charles had been more often than not down on his luck from gambling, and often spent months at a time at Faulkner Manor, sponging on the generosity of Gabriel's father, as much as avoiding his creditors. And no doubt enjoying the favours of the local women as often as possible, too.

Yes, the more Gabriel considered the possibility of Charles being the father of Jennifer's baby, the more inclined he was to believe that the whole course of events had been contrived in order to disinherit Gabriel, and at the same time provide Charles with a generous amount of money to marry the woman who was already his mistress.

It had taken Diana, with her cool detachment, to stand back and see the possible true course of events. Gabriel felt foolish, even ridiculous, for not having seen those things for himself at the time. Not only that, but through his own pride and arrogance in refusing to visit

Faulkner Manor, he had subjected his mother to months of hell.

What must Diana think of him now? For not having seen the happenings here for what they were eight years ago? For allowing his prideful arrogance to leave his mother to suffer for years at the hands of the Prescotts? He knew that Diana, with her no-nonsense attitude, and her very definite views on what was right and what was wrong, would never have allowed that to happen to a member of her own family.

Gabriel looked across at her now between narrowed lids, but was unable to read anything of her thoughts or emotions from the calm composure with which she gazed back at him. Was that deliberate?

No doubt she would need some time in which to digest and accept all they had discovered here. To decide how she felt about those discoveries. And perhaps how, or if, those things affected their betrothal and the regard that had been tentatively growing between the two of them. He would not want her to go through with their marriage if he had given her a disgust of him. Yes, in the circumstances, he accepted that time to think those things over was the least that he could give her.

He drew himself up to his full height, his expression deliberately lacking all emotion. 'Between being with my mother and looking into estate business, I will no doubt find myself very busy during the next few days as we wait for her health to strengthen enough to travel.'

Her eyes were suddenly very blue in the pallor of her face as she steadily returned his gaze. 'Of course.'

'Thank you.' He bowed elegantly. 'You are, as ever, unfailingly generous in your understanding.'

Was she? At this moment she felt an uncharacteristic inclination to scream and wail at the cold remoteness of his expression and manner, when all she wanted to do was throw herself into his strong arms and have him make love to her; she felt in dire need of that evidence of his unchanged desire for her, at least.

She would do none of those things, of course. She had learnt long ago never to ask for, or to expect, the consideration of others in regard to her own emotions, but to keep her own needs to herself and her emotions firmly under her control. Except when she and Gabriel made love…

'I shall endeavour to help in any way that I can to see that your mother's return to full health is a smooth and untroubled one.' Her demeanour was as cool as his own.

He inclined his head. 'I am most appreciative of any kindness you might show her.'

That urge inside her to wail and cry became almost overwhelming as he continued to speak to her with the politeness of a stranger. They had been so wonderfully intimate earlier, which still made her blush to think of it, and yet he was now treating her as if she were nothing more than a kind and considerate friend!

Whereas she now thought of Gabriel as—as what?

Diana frowned, knowing now was not the time to search her own emotions for answers to how she felt towards him. 'Of course. Please do not delay here any longer,' she said. 'Your mother may have reawakened in your absence and wondered if you being there at all was nothing but a dream.'

'Indeed.' Gabriel's jaw was rigidly set as he continued to look down at her for several long seconds. Seconds when he could still read nothing from the calmness of her expression, when he wished for nothing more than to once again take her in his arms and—

'I will wish you a good night, then, my lord,' she added, her tone and demeanour obviously a dismissal.

Gabriel drew himself up proudly. He had felt so close to her when they'd made love earlier, had felt as if they were on the brink of—of what? Feeling real affection for each other, perhaps? An affection that might have deepened over the years, thereby making their marriage of convenience more bearable for them both.

There was no affection in Diana's manner now. None of that earlier warmth and teasing. Instead it seemed as if there was a wall standing between them.

An insurmountable wall?

'I cannot recall the last time I visited London...' Mrs Felicity Faulkner's expression was rapt as she gazed out of the carriage window at the rush and bustle, the noise, the smells, that was the capital of England; the streets were crowded with other carriages, with children dodging in between the horses, dogs barking, voices raised as women sold flowers on street corners, and men stood behind stands with hot pies and ale for sale.

None of which succeeded in impressing itself upon Diana's inner misery in the slightest.

It had taken two further days at Faulkner Manor

for Felicity to recover her wits and to have strength enough to be able to make this slow, three-day journey to London. The two days lingering at the Manor had been excruciating ones for Diana, as she saw little or nothing of Gabriel, and was treated with cool politeness by him whenever they did chance to meet over the breakfast or dinner table. He had been, as he had predicted, excessively busy with estate business, his expression becoming grimmer by the hour, it seemed, as he obviously found further discrepancies in his mother's account books.

Felicity was as delightful as Gabriel had led Diana to believe; a beautiful and vivacious woman who, although sorely tried emotionally for so many years, had quickly recovered her full spirits once she was no longer being plagued with heavy doses of laudanum and could enjoy the return of her son. She was also overjoyed to learn of his inheritance of the title and estates of the Earl of Westbourne.

Forbidden by Gabriel to so much as mention either of the Prescotts to his mother, Diana often took refuge in discussing Shoreley Park with the older woman as a means of avoiding talking about more personal subjects. Something that had not proved too difficult to do when it emerged that Gabriel, no doubt for reasons of his own, had so far not told Felicity of their betrothal; as far as his mother was concerned, Diana was only the eldest of her son's wards.

Perhaps he had every intention of being asked to be released from that betrothal once they were back in London? She couldn't help wondering miserably. If that were to happen then not one, but two men would have passed her over as their choice for a wife; Malcolm because he had met and wooed a woman who could bring wealth rather than a title to their marriage, and Gabriel because their betrothal had only ever been a matter of convenience to him from the first. A betrothal he obviously no longer found convenient or necessary.

The more Diana's thoughts dwelt on those two rejections the angrier she became. How dare they? How dare those men discard her as if she were no more than a pair of boots that no longer fit them comfortably? Quite when Gabriel intended to ask her officially to release him from their betrothal she had no idea, but the past five days, spent in an agony of emotions, meant that she now had plenty of things she wished to say to him once he did decide to do so. So many, in fact, that she had no idea whether she would be able to stop that flow of words once they had begun.

'You seem pensive, my dear?'

Diana turned from gazing out of the window to look across the carriage at Felicity. 'I am sorry if I am being less than companionable, but there is a slight family… disturbance, which occupies all of my thoughts at present.' Not completely true, when what she wished to say to Gabriel kept her so mentally exhausted, but the nearer they came to London the more her thoughts returned to her missing sister Elizabeth. They had received no news at Faulkner Manor on that subject, from either Caroline or Lord Vaughn, and so Diana could only assume that Elizabeth was still missing. Lost and alone somewhere in this noisy, smelly metropolis…

More than anything she now wished to return to Shoreley Park, if only to lick her wounds in private; something she could not do until they had found and returned Elizabeth to the safety of their family.

Felicity's kind face softened in understanding. 'Gabriel has explained to me the…situation—' she glanced at Diana's maid also seated in the carriage with them, '—concerning your sister.'

Her eyes widened. 'He has?'

'Oh, yes.' The older woman smiled. 'Gabriel takes his role as guardian to you and your sisters very seriously indeed.'

His role as her guardian…

When Diana wanted so much more from him! She wanted a return of the man who had made such beautiful love to her five nights ago and she still wanted to become his wife, in the hopes that he might one day come to truly care for her.

As she truly cared for him…

Her feelings for Gabriel were something she had not questioned too often these past few days. Love, once acknowledged, even to oneself, could no longer be ignored, so she refused to look deeply enough into her feelings to know whether or not it was love she felt for him. Besides, surely if she *were* in love with him, she would not also feel this overwhelming urge to pummel her fists upon his chest whilst calling him a long list of names that would no doubt be more suited to coming from the lips of a fisherman's wife?

'I appreciate his concern,' she replied tightly.

His mother looked wistful. 'I wish you could have known him before any of this unpleasantness occurred. He was so much kinder then, so generous with his affections.' She shook her head sadly.

And in return for that kindness and generosity of affection, he had been disinherited and banished by his family and society. Was it any wonder that he had become the hard and cynical man he was today? she thought. 'He is still kind and generous in his affections towards you,' Diana pointed out.

'Oh, he is.' Deep-blue eyes, so like her son's, became awash with unshed tears. 'I only wish… My husband was not really such a hard or unforgiving man, Diana. It pained him so much to be that way with Gabriel. I am sure, if Neville had lived longer, that he and Gabriel would have eventually made their peace with each other.'

Diana knew that mother and son had visited his father's grave together before they'd departed. Gabriel's expression had been one of such grim emotion on his return to the house that Diana had not dared to so much as speak to him before he'd disappeared into his father's study and had not reappeared again until it was time for dinner two hours later, his demeanour then still so remote that she had felt it best to leave him to his own reflections.

She reached across the carriage now to squeeze the other woman's hand. 'I am sure of it, too.'

Felicity shook off her sadness. 'Now I am come to London and am to become reacquainted with your Aunt

Humphries. Dorothea and I were such firm friends in our youth, you know,' she confided warmly.

Diana smiled. 'So she has told me.'

'Not all, I am sure.' Felicity looked far less than her fifty-two years as she smiled mischievously. 'Dorothea was considered something of an Original, you know.'

'Aunt Humphries was?' Diana could not hide her surprise at this disclosure; her aunt had always given the impression of being just a little shy of prudish.

'Oh, yes,' Felicity said. 'In truth, all of the *ton* was surprised when she accepted the offer of Captain Humphries, not only a man so much older than her, but one who could also be very stern on occasion.'

'I believe they were very happy in their marriage.'

'Oh, I do so hope they were!' Felicity's concern for her old friend's happiness was sincere. 'I truly cannot wait to see Dorothea again and catch up on all that has happened in her life these past thirty years.'

And Diana would be just as happy to be relieved of the company; the nearer they had come to London the more difficult it had become for her to hide her true feelings towards Gabriel from his mother. Especially when she did not understand that confusing mix of anger, warmth and despair herself!

Gabriel was tired, stiff and not a little bad-tempered as he stepped down from Maximilian's broad back before handing the reins to one of the grooms who had hurried round from the stables of Westbourne House to greet them.

The first of two discomforts was caused from the many hours he had spent in the saddle, and the latter from an ever-increasing frustration with Diana's recent avoidance of even making polite conversation with him on the few occasions they had been together.

He had hoped—a complete arrogance on his part, no doubt—that with time she might come to feel more warmly towards him again; instead her manner had become cooler with each day that had passed, to the point she now seemed to avoid his company altogether whenever possible.

The stigma of his past so-called scandal had not deterred her from agreeing to marry him—no doubt the kindness of her nature meant she had seen him as a lost soul in need of saving. Learning that the wife of his uncle was the woman from his past had not shaken her composure for too long, either. No, it seemed that discovering Gabriel's pride and arrogance had resulted in his mother's misery and incarceration had finally been too much for the sensitive and kind-hearted Diana to bear. After all, he thought unhappily, it was that very same arrogance that had initially prompted him to propose to whichever of the Copeland sisters would have him.

'You are returned at last, Diana!'

The two ladies barely had time to step down from the carriage before the front door of Westbourne House was thrown open and an excited Caroline ran lightly down the steps to greet her sister with an enthusiasm that attested to their deep affection for each other.

'Mrs Faulkner.' Caroline curtsied politely once Diana had made the introductions. 'My lord.' Caroline's tone cooled slightly as she turned to give him a brief nod of acknowledgement.

No change there, then, Gabriel acknowledged ruefully as he joined the ladies and returned her nod. Even Dominic's championing of Gabriel could not change Caroline's opinion that he was not in the least good enough for her beloved sister.

An opinion Gabriel now shared.

'It is so good to have you back with us in London.' Caroline linked her arm through her sister's as the three ladies preceded Gabriel up the steps to the house. 'And you will never guess who else has come to town?' Her eyes sparkled a deep sea-green as she looked at Diana excitedly.

'I am sure I do not need to guess when you are obviously in such a lather to tell me,' she returned drily.

'Malcolm Castle!' Caroline did exactly that, her face aglow with the enormity of the announcement. 'He called for the first time four days ago, and he has been back every day since in the hopes of learning that you are returned from Cambridgeshire!'

Gabriel's step faltered as he overheard this news, his heart sinking as he realised the significance of this information. Had that young man now realised his mistake and come in search of Diana in the hopes of renewing his courtship?

Chapter Fifteen

'I trust you are not going to be difficult about releasing my sister from your betrothal?'

Gabriel closed his eyes briefly before opening them again, the return to the neat view of the garden outside the study window doing little to soothe the blackness of his mood. How could it, when every time he looked out at this garden he would remember that it was Diana who had instructed the gardeners on how she wanted it to appear? Everything about this house had been lovingly restored to its former glory under her instruction—

'Are you deaf, my lord, or merely choosing to ignore me?'

Just as Caroline would always and for evermore be Diana's champion! That would prove awkward for all of them if—*when* Gabriel's betrothal to Diana came to an end, and Caroline and Dominic were married.

He turned slowly, his expression remaining impas-

The Lady Forfeits

sive as he took in the flushed irritation on Caroline's beautiful face as she glared across the room at him. 'I am neither deaf nor ignoring you, Caroline,' he said silkily.

'Well?'

'Well what?

She stepped into the study before closing the door firmly behind her. 'Is it your intention to release Diana from your betrothal without undo fuss?'

Gabriel's mouth compressed. 'To my knowledge, your sister has made no such request of me.'

Those sea-green eyes widened. 'But surely you must know that she will do so?'

'Must I?' he said evasively.

She scowled at him. 'I do not believe you to be either stupid or insensitive.'

'I am gratified to hear it!'

She gave an impatient snort. 'You are being deliberately obtuse—'

'On the contrary, my dear, Caroline, I am trying—and obviously not succeeding—to understand what business it is of yours how or indeed *if* my betrothal to Diana should come to an end.' He looked witheringly at her.

True to character, Caroline did not back down in the slightest. 'It became my business, my lord, the moment my sister, a woman who never cries, only minutes ago began to sob in my arms as if her heart would break!'

Those words were like a sword wound in Gabriel's own chest. He and Diana had parted just over an hour ago, she to go upstairs with her sister, Gabriel to see to his mother's safe delivery to the comfort of her bedchamber where, to his mother's obvious delight, Alice Britton was waiting to welcome her, which Gabriel had arranged whilst still at the Manor. The joy on his mother's face as the two women were reunited was enough to show him in that, at least, he had acted correctly.

Just as he would have to do by releasing Diana from their betrothal?

Diana had assured him when they'd agreed to marry that there was not even the possibility of her ever reuniting with Castle. But it had been a denial she had made in the abstract, in the confidence that it would never happen; her distressed state at learning Castle wished to see her again was evidence of her true feelings in the matter.

Caroline eyed him warily. 'Does it not bother you in the least to learn that Diana is inconsolable?'

He drew his breath in sharply at the mere thought of her in such an agony of emotions. 'Of course it bothers me!' A nerve pulsed in his tightly clenched jaw. 'I am insulted that you might think it would not. I assure you I have no wish to ever cause Diana the slightest discomfort.'

Those sea-green eyes widened in shock. 'I believe you really mean that,' she said wonderingly.

Gabriel scowled. 'I find the disbelief in your tone positively insulting.'

Her expression became quizzical. 'You seem changed since last we spoke, Gabriel.'

His expression became guarded. 'Changed how?'

'Less forceful. Less unyielding. Certainly less arrogant,' she added with a teasing smile.

'Really?' Gabriel rallied drily. 'I am sure your sister will be gratified to hear it!'

'As are we all,' she responded. 'I trust that you *will* speak with her then?'

He nodded. 'You may.'

His expression became grimmer still once she had departed the study, as he contemplated the upcoming—but very necessary—conversation with her elder sister.

'Has that cushion offended you in some way?'

Diana stiffened at the first sound of Gabriel's voice, turning sharply now from where she sat on the *chaise* to see him standing in the open doorway of her bedchamber, dark brows raised over mocking blue eyes.

He had changed from his dusty travelling clothes and now wore a dark-blue superfine, a lighter-blue waistcoat, beige pantaloons and shiny black Hessians, the darkness of his hair still slightly damp from his ablutions.

His very physical presence took her breath away. 'I beg your pardon?'

'You appear to be shredding the tassels on that cushion,' he drawled as he stepped into the room. 'I felt sure it must have offended you in some way.'

Diana looked down at the cushion she cradled on her knees, having had no idea it was even there until he'd brought it to her attention. Or that she had pulled so agitatedly on the silk tassels at its corner that the majority of those silks now lay in a tangle beside her on the blue-velvet *chaise*.

She hurriedly placed the cushion down on top of that tangle before standing up. 'What can I do for you, my lord?'

What, alone together in her bedchamber, could she *not* do for him? He wondered in despair. The ache he felt becoming a physical discomfort as he hardened with the need to take her in his arms and finally make proper love to her.

A totally ridiculous desire when the evidence of her recent tears was there in the heavy darkness of her eyes and the dampness of her creamy cheeks. When her mouth, those full and kissable lips, seemed to tremble slightly before she set them firmly together and raised her chin to present him once more with that familiar air of cool composure.

Gabriel moved to stand before the window that looked out over the square at the front of the house. 'You must be pleased to find yourself back in London?' he commented.

Must she? Why must she? Diana could think of absolutely no reason, other than continuing the search for Elizabeth—a sister who obviously had no wish to be found!

Nor did she appreciate him seeing her in this way, the evidence of her tears no doubt apparent to him. Although she was firm in her resolve that he should never know the reason for them: because she was so certain that, now that they were back in London, he would waste no time in ending their betrothal.

Her back straightened as if her body was in preparation for a blow. 'It is certainly pleasant to be united with at least one of my sisters.'

Gabriel turned to face her. 'I assure you that Vaughn and I will continue our search for Elizabeth, leaving no stone unturned.'

'I implied no criticism of either you or Lord Vaughn, my lord,' she said quickly.

The sunlight shining in the window behind him gave his hair a blue-black sheen, and threw the grimness of his expression into shadow. 'No?' He quirked one dark brow. 'Then perhaps there should have been. Dominic has obviously been unsuccessful this past week, whilst I have been deeply occupied with other matters.'

She gave an acknowledging inclination of her head. 'I perfectly understood that the continuing welfare of your mother was of greater importance to you at that time.'

A frown creased his brow. 'It is a part of the warmth and caring of your nature to always be so concerned with the happiness of others.'

Was it? She was no longer sure. How could she be, when at this moment it was thoughts of her own unhappiness that consumed her? When the certainty of Gabriel having come here to ask her to release him from their betrothal made her feel as if her heart were shattering into so many pieces she might never be able to put it back together again?

She loved him…

Diana could deny it no longer. Could ignore it no longer. She was irrevocably in love with Lord Gabriel Faulkner, the Earl of Westbourne. The knowledge that Malcolm Castle had reappeared in her life had suddenly crystallised her feelings sharply for her. The only man in the world for her was Gabriel and a huge tidal wave of emotions swept over her every time she so much as looked at him. She wanted to reach out and touch him. To be gathered into his arms and kissed by him. To be held by him and know that he would never let her go.

When letting her go was no doubt exactly what he had come here to do…

She could see it in the dark regret in his eyes, in the resignation of his expression, in his restlessness of movement as he began to pace her bedchamber. No doubt seeking, searching, for the appropriate words in which to tell her he no longer wished to marry her.

It was a further indignity Diana found she could not even bear to contemplate. She drew herself up proudly, her face pale. 'I believe it is the correct procedure in situations such as ours for the lady to be seen to end the betrothal?'

Gabriel drew in a sharp breath before once again turning to stare sightlessly out of the window, an icy chill filling his chest at finally hearing her ask to be released from her promise to him. At the thought of having to stand back and watch as she gave all of the warmth and caring of her nature into the keeping of someone else. Of having to witness her marrying another man—even to give her away in church!

Gabriel had entered into their engagement without a care as to which of the Copeland sisters should accept his offer of marriage in the erroneous belief that one young woman would do equally as well as another. He now knew just how totally false that was. There was no other woman like Diana. No other woman with her warmth and tenderness of heart. Her loyalty. Her care for duty. As for her courage—he believed she would challenge the devil himself, if she had need to, and never count the cost to herself.

Because it was what Diana did. What she had done unstintingly for the past ten years, for her family and others, regardless of her own happiness. And it was what she would no doubt continue to do if he did not agree to release her from their betrothal...

He could not ask that of her. Would not ask that of her.

How painfully ironic that he, a man who had lived the last few years of his life with almost complete disregard for the feelings of others, could not bear to be the reason that Diana should suffer even another moment of unhappiness.

He turned to give her a stiff nod of agreement, lids lowered guardedly over any emotion in his eyes. 'I will see to placing the announcement in the newspapers tomorrow, or the day after at the very latest, if that will suit?' No doubt he would have to place another announcement in those newspapers a day or so after that, this time announcing Diana's betrothal to that cur Castle!

Her eyes were a deep and shadowed blue in the pallor of her face. 'I would appreciate that, my lord.'

He nodded tersely. 'Is there anything else you wish to discuss with me?'

What else could there possibly be? she wondered numbly. Gabriel no longer wanted her as his wife or anything else—what else could possibly have any meaning? All the things she had longed to say to him this past five days, the anger and hurt that had been steadily building inside her, had all dissolved into sheer numbness at the occurrence of the very thing she had been dreading.

The end of their engagement. There was nothing else—only an unending agony of emotions that threatened to bring Diana to her knees. She needed him to leave so she could break down and cry without him knowing. 'There is nothing else I wish to say, my lord,' she lied woodenly.

'Very well.' He walked to the door.

Suddenly, confusingly, Diana could not bear to see him leave. 'You—it was very kind of you to arrange for Miss Britton to be here to welcome your mother.'

He came to a halt and turned with a humourless smile. 'You did not believe me capable of kindness?'

She looked appalled. 'I—that's not what I meant! I know that you are.'

His mouth twisted. 'Just not where you are concerned?'

She swore she could hear her heart breaking 'I consider it a great kindness to have released me from our betrothal,' she choked.

'So it is.' His nostrils flared as his mouth thinned, the expression in the dark blue of his eyes now unreadable. 'If you will excuse me, Diana, I really am very busy.' He left the room, closing the door firmly behind him.

As firmly as Diana knew that his heart was, and ever would be, closed to her.

'You are going out?'

Diana came to a halt in the cavernous hallway of Westbourne House the following morning, turning away from where Soames stood ready to open the front door for her own and her maid's departure, to instead face Gabriel as he stood framed in the doorway of his study, knowing that the bonnet and burgundy-coloured pelisse she wore over her cream-and-burgundy-coloured sprigged-muslin gown should have been evidence enough of her going out. 'I intended to go to the shops, my lord,' she nevertheless answered him coolly. 'Your mother is perfectly happy in the company of my aunt and Alice, if that is your concern?'

Gabriel was well aware of his mother's preoccupation, both with the return of her companion, and the reunion with her old friend Dorothea Humphries—a woman he had finally been introduced to yesterday and who seemed to view him more kindly now that he had brought her friend home with him.

Even if he had not been aware of his mother's happiness, his immediate concern was not for his mother, but more for the chasm that had only widened between himself and Diana since they had agreed to end to their betrothal last night.

'Perhaps we might talk in private for a few minutes before you go out?' he asked softly.

That was the very last thing she wished to do, especially as he was looking more devastatingly handsome than usual in a fashionable superfine of chocolate brown, a gold-and-cream waistcoat buttoned over the flatness of his stomach, with cream pantaloons and brown Hessians fitting snugly to the muscled length of his legs.

She swallowed before answering. 'Can it not wait until I have returned, my lord?'

He frowned slightly. 'I would rather it be now.'

'Very well.' She turned to request that her maid wait for her here before she preceded Gabriel into his study. She stood just inside the room as he closed the door behind him and then went to stand behind his mahogany desk. 'I trust it is something important that you feel the need to interrupt a lady who only wishes to shop!' Her attempt at humour sounded flat to her own ears, but she could see by the tightening of his mouth that he did not appreciate even that effort.

And it *was* an effort to try to appear even remotely like her usual composed self after a night of sobbing uncontrollably into her pillow. She had excused herself from having dinner downstairs with the rest of the family on a plea of lingering tiredness from her

journey. She had requested breakfast in her room this
morning for the same reason. Knowing this avoidance
of his company could not continue indefinitely, Diana
had finally decided to take herself out of the house completely for a few hours, but even that had been foiled by
Gabriel.

'You have news of Elizabeth, perhaps?' She looked
hopefully across the imposing desk at him.

'I am afraid not,' Gabriel frowned. 'I had thought, as
you have been so involved in the matter, that you might
be interested to learn what progress has been made in
regard to the Prescotts?'

Her brow cleared. 'You have managed to ascertain
their whereabouts?'

'Not yet.' His jaw tightened. 'But with Vaughn's help
and resources, I have managed to learn more of my
uncle's debts, at least.' He suddenly looked uncomfortable at having revealed that knowledge about Dominic
to her.

Diana gave a rueful smile. 'Do not concern yourself,
my lord; I spoke with Caroline earlier this morning
and I am now fully conversant with Lord Vaughn's
ownership of one of London's better-known gambling
establishments!' Caroline had visited her bedchamber after breakfast and confessed all in regard to the
weeks she had spent alone in London. Despite her sister
having ended up embarking on a brief stint singing in
Lord Vaughn's club, which Diana admitted was far
from ideal, she had nevertheless realised that Caro-

line had been fortunate indeed to land in such a safe pair of hands.

Gabriel quirked a dark brow. 'You are?'

'Yes.' Diana gave a rueful smile at the memory of the shocking tale Caroline had to tell. 'I am very grateful to Lord Vaughn for looking after my sister so well.'

'As am I,' he said grimly.

Diana bristled defensively. 'Caroline is very young.'

'She is not much younger than you are,' he pointed out.

'In years, perhaps,' she conceded. 'I trust that upbraiding me for not maintaining more control over my sister's actions was not one of the reasons you asked to speak with me?'

'God, no!' Gabriel exclaimed. 'I defy anyone to maintain control over that particular young lady.'

'Even Lord Vaughn?' Diana teased.

His expression softened into a genuine smile. 'Vaughn seems to relish the challenge.'

Diana felt her cheeks warm at thoughts of the effective tactics Lord Vaughn might use in order to put an end to Caroline's challenges any time it suited him. 'You were about to tell me something of the Prescotts, I believe?'

He nodded. 'With Vaughn's inside knowledge into the gambling world, I have managed to ascertain the exact extent of my uncle's debts.'

'They are considerable?'

'They are enormous,' he admitted.

Diana shook her head. 'But that does not excuse his or his wife's treatment of your mother.'

'No, it most certainly does not!' Having nothing and no one else to turn his frustrations upon, as Gabriel could not bring himself to feel in the least angry towards Diana for ending their betrothal if it meant she secured her own happiness, he was instead concentrating all of his efforts on finding his uncle and his wife.

'Was that all you wished to tell me, my lord?'

It was all that he *could* tell her! Having spent most of the previous night thinking about her, Gabriel knew he was no nearer to accepting the end of their engagement than he was to bearing the thought of her being in love with another man.

Because he wished to have Diana's love for himself.

Oh, he ached to make love to her again, but that was not all that he wanted from her. He also wanted her gentleness. Her warmth. Her courage and her dignity. Nor did he believe for a moment that Castle was deserving of the unique and beautiful woman that was Diana. Any more than Gabriel believed that he was worthy of those things either.

'Is that not enough?' he rasped.

'Of course,' she accepted coolly, any hopes—futile hopes, admittedly—that he might have reconsidered his decision concerning the ending of their betrothal totally dashed. 'If there is nothing else, I should like to be on my way.'

Gabriel returned her gaze wordlessly for several seconds before turning away. 'No, there is nothing else. Except...'

Diana raised golden brows. 'Yes?'

Gabriel clenched his jaw to stop himself from saying words he should not, words that begged her to change her mind about him. 'What would you like me to say to Castle if he should call again this morning?'

'The truth, of course.'

'Which is?'

'That I am out,' she said before quietly leaving the study.

Once again he could not help but admire her pride and dignity; she had obviously decided she did not intend to make it at all easy for Castle to believe he might recapture her affections.

When, as Gabriel knew perfectly well, her affections for the man had remained constant and unchanging...

Diana had absolutely no idea where she went or what she did for at least the first half an hour after she left Westbourne House, the carriage ride passing as if in a haze. Then, once at the shops, she found it an effort just placing one slippered foot in front of the other. So lost in thought was she, so mired down by the inner misery she suffered at the futility of the love she felt for Gabriel, that it took some seconds to recognise the familiar face she saw pressed against the window of a passing carriage...

Chapter Sixteen

'Beg pardon, my lord, but I have an urgent message to deliver from my mistress.'

In the hour since Diana had left the house Gabriel had not so much as looked at any of the work that had accumulated on his desk after almost a week's absence. Instead he had spent that time composing the announcement of his broken betrothal before throwing it to one side and then sitting behind his desk in brooding contemplation of the shiny toes of his boots as he rested his feet on the desktop in front of him.

He turned now to frown at the young maid who stood so hesitant and uncomfortable in the doorway. 'Yes?'

'Lady Diana said I was to tell you—'

'Lady Diana?' Gabriel echoed sharply, his feet falling heavily to the floor as he sat forwards in the chair. 'You are Lady Diana's maid?' Actually, he recognised her now from that night in his mother's bedchamber at the Manor.

'I am, my lord, yes. And—'

'Did you not leave to go shopping with her just an hour ago?'

'I did, sir, yes—'

'Your mistress has returned from shopping and wishes you to relay a message to me?' Had it come to such a sorry state of affairs between the two of them that Diana did not even feel she could come and speak to him herself?

'No, my lord. Yes, my lord. That is—' the young woman looked slightly discomposed '—Lady Diana does wish me to give you a message, but she has not yet returned from shopping.'

'Then why the devil are you not still with her?' Gabriel demanded as he stood up.

That discomposure turned to a look of panic. 'She sent me back to the house, my lord.'

'And you left her alone in the middle of London, without a chaperon? Unless she was not alone,' he added as the thought of Malcolm Castle suddenly occurred to him. He scowled as he envisaged Diana's quiet dignity as she listened to her erstwhile suitor's pleas for understanding, to his declarations of having loved her all along.

'Oh, she was alone, my lord. But—'

'Come in and shut the door, girl,' Gabriel instructed. 'Now, explain, if you please.'

The maid's hands were tightly gripped together

in front of her as she eyed him nervously. 'It was the woman in the carriage, my lord. Lady Diana saw her and we followed the carriage until it stopped at an inn and the lady got out, then Lady Diana sent me back to tell you that you must come to her there immediately.'

Gabriel would be more than happy to do as Diana asked and go to her. At any time. To any place. 'What woman in the carriage?' Could it be that Diana had spotted Elizabeth? That she had succeeded where he and Dominic had failed so abysmally?

'It was that Mrs Prescott, my lord.' The maid looked primly disapproving. 'Bold as brass she was, riding along in the carriage as if butter wouldn't melt in her mouth. When all the time—'

'Mrs Prescott!' Gabriel thundered. 'And the two of you were daft enough to *follow* her?' When Diana returned he was going to lock her in her bedchamber and throw away the key for behaving so recklessly!

'It wasn't too difficult to do, my lord.' The girl looked pleased with herself. 'There are so many carriages on the streets at this time of the morning, and—'

'So you followed Mrs Prescott to an inn here in town?' Gabriel cut in, having absolutely no time or patience to deal with this young woman's long-winded explanation.

'Yes, my lord.'

'And Lady Diana is there still?'

'Waiting outside, my lord.'

'Take me there now, please.' Gabriel needed to get

to Diana as soon as was possible. He dare not leave her alone anywhere near Jennifer Prescott—that harpy was more dangerous than she looked.

'If you are intending to look inconspicuous in your attempts at window shopping, then you are failing abysmally!'

Diana stiffened at the first sound of that familiar taunting voice, drawing in a slow and calming breath before slowly turning to face Jennifer Prescott, her gaze coolly dismissive as she looked at the older woman. 'I was attempting to decide which hat I might consider purchasing.'

The other woman looked unconvinced. 'As this is one of the more unfashionable parts of town, I seriously hope you decided on none of them.'

The milliner's was, Diana agreed, a particularly unimpressive establishment, but surely preferable to her simply lurking about on the street corner. 'Perhaps you are right.' She gave a falsely bright smile. 'If you will excuse me?' Diana turned with the intention of walking away, her heart thundering in her chest with the knowledge that she should not have allowed Jennifer to realise that she had seen and followed her back to the inn where she and, possibly, her husband were staying.

'I think not.' Surprisingly strong fingers reached out and took a firm grasp of her arm, preventing her from leaving.

Diana raised haughty brows. 'Release my arm imme-diately, madam.'

The other woman took absolutely no account of the request. 'Where is Gabriel?'

'How on earth should I know that?'

Jennifer's mouth twisted derisively. 'Because I have learnt that wherever you are, he is sure never to be far behind.'

If only that were true, Diana yearned inwardly, at the same time as she sincerely hoped that her outward show of bravado was convincing—surely May must have reached Westbourne House by now and relayed her message to Gabriel? 'I believe you will find that you are in error on this occasion.'

The other woman looked completely unperturbed. 'You had a maid with you earlier; no doubt she has gone for Gabriel.' She smiled mockingly as Diana gave a start of surprise. 'Oh, yes, my dear sweet Diana, I was fully aware of your inexpert attempt to follow me. Just as you were intended to do when I deliberately showed my face at the carriage window,' she added with satisfac-tion. 'Charles and I have had someone watching West-bourne House the past few days awaiting your return to town. It was fortuitous indeed that you should ven-ture out alone so soon, thereby making it easy for me to arrange for you to catch sight of me.'

So much for Diana having believed she had followed her stealthily and unobserved!

Jennifer's fingers now dug painfully into her arm and her face twisted into a malicious mask. 'Gabriel?'

Diana knew she could continue to lie, to prevaricate, but what would be the point? Her chin rose challengingly. 'As you say, I have sent my maid back to Westbourne House to inform him of the whereabouts of you and your husband. I have no doubts he will be here directly.'

If she had intended to disconcert the other woman with this announcement then she was disappointed, as Jennifer smiled in satisfaction. 'In that case I must insist that you join myself and my husband at the inn whilst we all await Gabriel's arrival.'

Diana's eyes widened as she realised the implications of this dictate. 'Unfortunately it is an invitation I must decline—'

'Sadly, you will not be allowed to do so,' Jennifer jeered. 'Ah, Charles.' Her gaze shifted behind her quarry. 'Lady Diana has decided to join us at the inn for refreshment whilst we await your nephew's arrival.'

As a ploy to distract Diana's attention it was not very original. If indeed, it was a ploy?

'How pleasant to make your acquaintance, Lady Diana.' The voice that answered Jennifer was lazily charming, and obviously belonged to her husband, Mr Charles Prescott. Obviously not a ploy, then!

Gabriel's frustration and anger, already at a premium after learning of Diana's recklessness in following Jennifer Prescott, only increased when he arrived outside the inaptly named Peacock Inn where Diana's maid had seen her last and failed to find any sign of her.

Where could she have gone? Surely she could not have been idiotic enough to confront the Prescotts on her own?

'Ah, Gabriel, you are come at last…'

He spun round to confront Jennifer, his eyes narrowing as he considered the implications of both the pleasantness of her tone and her complete lack of surprise in seeing him there. 'Where is Diana?' he demanded coldly.

She gave a mocking smile. 'She and Charles are becoming acquainted at the inn. It really is too bad of you, Gabriel, not to have made the introductions yourself, but—'

'Do not play games with me, Jennifer.' The softness of Gabriel's tone was more menacing than any show of anger might have been, even though the thought of Diana alone with his unscrupulous Uncle Charles was enough to turn the blood cold in his veins.

Jennifer's eyes flashed angrily. 'I suppose Felicity has told you all?'

'You suppose correctly,' he said. 'Now take me to Diana before I give in to the pleasure I would find in wringing your neck.'

She looked unimpressed by the threat. 'How anyone could ever have believed I preferred you over Charles eight years ago is beyond my understanding.'

Gabriel's mouth twisted contemptuously as this statement seemed to confirm Diana's suspicion that Charles was the man Jennifer had been involved with all along.

'Most things are beyond your understanding, Jennifer. Now take me to Diana!'

'Gladly.' She eyed him greedily. 'No doubt, with Diana Copeland as our…guest, you will be only too happy to dismiss any charges you may have thought of bringing against us, as well as paying all of Charles's debts!'

Gabriel did not reveal his reaction to this statement by so much of the blink of an eyelid, his long years of forced exile from his family and home having provided him with the ability to hide his inner feelings. It wasn't that he did not have feelings on the subject, only that they were too strong, ran far too deep, to be allowed out of his rigid control. A control that would undoubtedly snap if he were to learn that this vile couple had harmed one golden hair upon Diana's head.

'—and so you see it was easy for Jennifer to claim that she was with child and that Gabriel was the father.'

Diana eyed Charles with distaste as the two of them sat together in a private parlour of the inn. Oh, he was undoubtedly as handsome and charming as everyone had claimed him to be, with his dark good looks so like his nephew's and his own ease of manner. A charming rogue, in fact.

Except Diana found him far from handsome *or* charming. Not only did she despise him utterly for having just confirmed his involvement with the youthful Jennifer eight years ago, so obviously without any thought or concern for the nephew whose reputation he had so casually destroyed, but the pistol he held in his hand, and pointed directly at her, also gave her reason to fear him.

'For her to *claim* she was with child?' Diana repeated mildly.

'Well, yes, of course; she never actually conceived one—Jennifer has never wanted children, and knows exactly how to go about not having them.' Charles smiled lazily. 'We knew, of course, that none of my family would be so indelicate as to demand Jennifer see a physician to confirm the pregnancy. Not the done thing to mistrust a lady's word, don't you know,' he added. 'It also made it so much easier to say she lost the baby only weeks after our wedding.'

In none of Diana's thinking about the past had she ever considered the possibility that Jennifer had never been with child at all! It was unbelievable. Despicable. And so like the Jennifer Prescott she had come to know that she didn't know why she was at all surprised.

Bright blue eyes narrowed on her admiringly. 'I must say, my nephew seems to have done all right for himself now, inheriting the Westbourne earldom and now becoming betrothed to you. So obviously no harm was done to him in the long run—'

'No harm was done!' Diana was so angry she thought she might actually get up and strike the man, despite the pistol he pointed at her so unwaveringly. 'How can you possibly say that when Gabriel was banished in disgrace for something he had not done and apparently never even existed?'

Charles gave a uninterested shrug. 'The existence of a child made the accusation of Gabriel having seduced Jennifer so much more believable. It was Jennifer's idea, of course, and a damned fine one, too, if I do say so myself.' He grinned unabashedly before sobering. 'Now all we have to do is convince my nephew to hand over a sizeable fortune to us, if he wishes to regain possession of his beloved fiancée, and we can all be on our way.'

He talked just as though Diana were indeed that pair of boots she had so recently likened herself to! 'I am afraid in that you will be disappointed, Mr Prescott.' She glared her contempt and dislike of the man.

'How so?' He raised dark brows so like his nephew's.

She gave a smile of pure satisfaction. 'For the simple reason that Gabriel—'

'Will never negotiate with the likes of you,' Gabriel finished firmly.

Diana was both relieved and frightened to turn and see him silhouetted in the doorway. Relieved because he had come to her, but frightened that he might be injured by having done so. She might no longer be betrothed to him, might never know the joy of having won his love, but she would not be able to bear it if anything should happen to him! 'He has a pistol, Gabriel!' she warned sharply.

He looked at her calmly. 'So I see.'

'With every intention of using it on your beautiful bride-to-be if you do not agree to our demands,' Charles informed him.

Gabriel had entered the parlour in time to hear some

of Diana's conversation with his disreputable uncle. 'To that end I intend to remove Diana from your possession.' He crossed the room to take a firm hold of her arm and pull her to her feet beside him. 'Out of respect for my mother's feelings, you both have twenty-four hours in which to remove yourselves from England, never to return.' He looked at each of the Prescotts in turn. 'Failure to do so will lead me to disregard my mother's sensibilities and result in you being arrested and charged with multiples crimes: theft, my mother's enforced incarceration, and now the added charge of kidnapping. All extremely serious allegations.'

'Do something, Charles!' Jennifer prompted her husband fiercely as she moved to his side.

The older man rose slowly to his feet at the same time as he raised the pistol and once again pointed it at Diana. 'You really do not want to do that, old chap.'

'Oh, he really does,' a chilling voice murmured from across the room.

Diana turned to see Lord Dominic Vaughn standing threateningly in the doorway, the pistol in his own hand pointed directly at the waistcoated chest of Charles Prescott.

Diana's knees almost buckled in the relief of knowing Gabriel had not come here alone, that he'd had the forethought to bring his friend with him. As Gabriel had once told her, he had several times trusted Vaughn with his life, and now it seemed he was trusting him with her life too.

'It appears we are at an impasse,' Charles drawled.

'Really?' Dominic said pleasantly, only the icy greyness of his eyes a warning that his mood far from matched that tone. 'I have already shot and killed one villain this past month; I would not hesitate to dispatch another piece of vermin.'

'Do not waste your shot, Dominic.' Gabriel acted so quickly and capably that Diana could barely follow his movements as he used Charles's distraction with Dominic to move forwards and wrest the pistol from his uncle's hand with a mere twist of the wrist.

Charles clutched his arm to his chest, his face turning deathly pale. 'I believe you have broken my wrist, damn you!'

'You cur!' Jennifer turned to glare her dislike of Gabriel even as she tended to her husband.

Gabriel appeared unconcerned as he weighed the weapon he held in his hand before answering. 'No doubt,' he finally said. 'I have no idea what ships are leaving the English docks today and neither do I care, as long as the two of you are on board one of them when it departs.'

Jennifer straightened, her expression one of indignation. 'And how are we to live?'

Hard midnight-blue eyes glittered dangerously. 'Why should I care how, or even where you live, as long as you are both safely out of my sight?'

'News of your own behaviour will cause a scandal—'

'Another one, my dear aunt?' Gabriel eyed her disdainfully. 'I assure you, I am beyond being concerned about any further scandal you might care to create with your lies and deceit.'

'And what of Lady Diana—is she beyond the consequences of a scandal, too?' Jennifer challenged triumphantly.

His jaw tightened. 'She—'

'—will be only too happy to go into a court of law at any time and give evidence against you and your husband for the atrocities you have committed against both Gabriel and his family,' Diana said firmly as she stepped deliberately to Gabriel's side in an unmistakable show of support.

The other woman appeared less confident now as she looked at Gabriel. 'You cannot just dismiss us in this arbitrary way!'

'Oh, I believe you will find that I can and I will,' Gabriel said as he once again took hold of Diana's arm. 'Be on that ship tomorrow or risk finding yourselves arrested and incarcerated on the day following.' The utter coldness of his gaze warned that he meant every word that he said.

Diana gave Dominic a grateful smile as he stepped aside to allow her to leave the oppression of the Prescotts' suite of rooms, keeping his pistol levelled upon the other couple as he and Gabriel then exited the room and shut the door on the indignant faces of the Prescotts.

Diana looked up at Gabriel gratefully. 'I—'

'Don't say another word,' he warned her through

gritted teeth as they began to ascend the stairs of the inn down to the street below.

'But—'

'Best not to speak to him just now, Diana,' her future brother-in-law murmured softly as they stepped out into the sunshine. 'Gabriel is slow to let loose his anger, but when he does it is best to beware.'

Diana looked bewildered. 'But I have done nothing wrong—'

'Nothing wrong?' Gabriel repeated incredulously, his face furious as he turned to hold her up in front of him. 'You followed that woman without thought for your own safety. You allowed yourself to be seen and to be taken to the Prescotts' rooms and held there as their prisoner. Don't you dare interrupt me, Diana!' he said as he gave her a little shake.

'I did attempt to warn you, my dear,' Dominic said sympathetically.

'Stop it, Gabriel!' She pushed against the hardness of his muscled chest—a totally futile gesture as she still suffered the indignity of remaining firmly held in his grasp.

'Perhaps I should take Diana back to Westbourne House, old chap?' Dominic offered pleasantly as two carriages drew up beside them and both grooms jumped down to open the doors. 'It will give you time to walk off some of that temper, perhaps?'

It seemed as if Gabriel had not heard the other man for several long seconds as he continued to glare down at a rather dishevelled Diana for long tense seconds before a sudden stillness came over him. He drew himself up to his full and imposing height and then finally released her. 'That will not be necessary, thank you, Dom.'

Diana turned nervously to Dominic. 'Perhaps it would is best if I go with you, my lord—'

'Dominic will return in his own carriage and you will return to Westbourne House with me.' Gabriel looked down the length of his aristocratic nose at her as he stood waiting for her to step into his carriage. 'And once there you will go immediately to your bed-chamber and remain there until I send for you.'

'I most certainly will *not*!' There were two spots of angry colour in her cheeks as she turned to glare up at him. 'How dare you order me about as if I were no more than—?'

'I gave her every opportunity, did I not, Dominic?' Gabriel turned and spoke conversationally to the other man.

Dominic gave a pained wince at whatever else he heard in Gabriel's tone. 'You did, yes. But she is young—'

'Her youth is no excuse for the danger in which she placed herself and others.' He no longer waited for Diana to step up into the carriage, but instead swung her up into his arms and carried her inside himself, the door immediately closing behind them and leaving them locked in the dark confines of the carriage together.

Chapter Seventeen

Diana immediately began to struggle in Gabriel's arms to be released, a move that proved totally unsuccessful as he sat down on the padded bench seat with her still held firmly in his arms and the carriage began to move forwards.

'You will release me this instant!' she demanded.

'No.'

She stilled. 'No?'

'No.' He did not even glance down at her, knowing that if he did so, he could not be held accountable for what happened next. She had deliberately and wilfully placed herself in danger. Had made herself the victim of any action the Prescotts might have decided to take against her. Damn it, she had calmly sat in a room making conversation with Charles whilst the man pointed a pistol at her!

"Gabriel!" she protested, squirming at the sudden instinctive tightening of his arms.

He released her so suddenly she almost tumbled to the floor, only stopping herself just in time to scramble inelegantly to her knees. And still he did not dare risk looking at her. 'Sit down and do not speak another word until we have arrived back at Westbourne House,' he ordered autocratically.

Diana sat. Not because Gabriel had ordered her to do so, but because a reaction had now begun to set in at the realisation of the danger they had all been in only minutes ago; her legs were now shaking so badly they would no longer support her. The time she had spent with the Prescotts had all seemed so surreal whilst it was happening, but now that she thought back to the unscrupulous Charles Prescott and the way he had so calmly sat and aimed the pistol he held in his hand directly at her...

She clenched her hands tightly together in order to stop Gabriel from seeing their trembling. Although he surely could not have missed the pallor in her cheeks, and the horror in her shadowed blue eyes, if he bothered to look at her. Which he did not. Instead, he sat across from her in complete self-containment as he silently continued to look out of the carriage window at the people milling about on the busy London streets. Almost as if he had forgotten she was even there!

She turned away as her eyes filled with the heat of her tears, blinking rapidly in an effort to stop them from falling down her cheeks. It was humiliating enough that

Gabriel had been put to the trouble of rescuing her from the clutches of the Prescotts; she could not bear for him to see her crying at his haughty dismissal of her.

'Diana—'

'Don't touch me!' She turned, her face flushing with temper as she glared fiercely across at him as he sat forwards on his seat with the obvious intention of doing just that; her humiliation really would be complete if she now broke down in tears at the slightest hint of softening towards her in his manner.

Gabriel drew in a sharp breath before sitting back against the plush upholstery to resume his previous silence, his eyes narrowing briefly on Diana's flushed face before he turned away; she could not have demonstrated any more clearly how abhorrent she now found the prospect of his touch.

Diana was vastly relieved when the carriage came to a halt outside Westbourne House, the groom having barely succeeded in folding down the steps before she moved down them to hurry into the house. Only to come to an abrupt halt in the hallway as Caroline emerged from the drawing room with Malcolm Castle at her side!

'Malcolm insisted on waiting once he knew that you had returned to town yesterday,' Caroline informed her happily.

'Indeed.' Diana turned a frosty gaze on that young man. 'To what do I owe this pleasure?'

'I will tell you everything once we are alone.' Malcolm's face was alight with his own pleasure in seeing her again. He was a little under six feet in height, with fashionably styled golden hair and a handsome evenness of features, his brown eyes first widening and then narrowing on the man who had just stepped into the hallway beside Diana. 'Lord Gabriel Faulkner, I presume.' He bowed formally.

'You presume correctly.' Gabriel's tone was even as he inclined his head. 'If you wish to talk privately with Mr Castle, Diana, then you may use my study—'

'But I do *not* wish to talk with Mr Castle, privately or otherwise.' She did not even glance at Gabriel as she instead gave Malcolm a sweepingly disdainful glance, at the same time wondering how she could ever have believed she found his insipid good looks in the least attractive! 'Indeed, I have no idea what he is even doing here.'

'Diana!' her sister gasped.

'I believe Malcolm is perfectly capable of speaking for himself, Caroline.' She gave her sister a quelling glance. 'Well?' She eyed the man coldly.

Malcolm flushed uncomfortably. 'I have come to beg your forgiveness, Diana, and to ask you to marry me. I made a mistake when I ended our friendship and have told Vera so,' he continued in a rush as her expression remained distant.

'Then I suggest you return to Hampshire post-haste and beg Miss Douglas's forgiveness instead of mine,' she said in a bored voice, 'for I will not have you.'

His eyes widened. 'But—but—'

'But we are no longer betrothed, Diana,' Gabriel murmured as he stood at her side.

She turned those frosty blue eyes on him. 'And?'

'And so you are now free to marry where you also love,' he explained, scowling at the very thought of her marrying this indecisive young man. Neither was he enjoying being a witness to this conversation in the slightest. Oh, he acknowledged that Diana was perfectly within her rights to want to punish Castle for having ended his friendship with her in favour of a woman with a fortune. But the man had admitted his mistake and was here now pleading for her forgiveness.

Diana gave a humourless smile. 'In saying that, are you presuming I am in love with Mr Castle?'

Gabriel looked surprised. 'Of course.'

'Of course you love me, Diana.' Malcolm crossed the hallway to take both her hands in his. 'You have always loved me—'

'Your conceit really is beyond belief!' Diana said exasperatedly as she extricated her hands from his clinging grasp. 'I am going to say this only once, Malcolm, and so I suggest that you listen carefully. I may have believed I loved you once, but I know now that I did not. I have never loved you. I *will* never love you.'

'But—'

'You don't love him?' Gabriel repeated slowly.

'I have just said that I do not,' she confirmed irritably.

'But you broke off our betrothal because he'd come back to you!' he exclaimed.

She snorted. 'I did not break off our betrothal at all, my lord—you did! It was very clear you no longer wished to be engaged to me.'

'Diana!' Malcolm protested.

'Diana?' Gabriel murmured softly.

'Yes, that is correct, I am Diana!' She crossed the hallway with a flounce of her skirts, her face flushed, eyes glittering. 'A warm, flesh-and-blood woman who is tired of being passed between you two gentlemen as if I have no will or emotions of my own!' She glared from Malcolm to Gabriel.

Gabriel could only gaze back at her with complete admiration, even though he was still totally bemused by this whole conversation; damn it, he would not have let Diana go at all if he had not thought her to be in love with Castle, would have fought with every measure at his disposal to prove to her he was worthy of her himself.

She turned as she reached the bottom of the staircase. 'You, sir, are conceited and lily-livered!' she told a stunned Malcolm Castle. 'And you—' she turned that blazing glare upon Gabriel '—are so embittered by the past that you cannot see the worth of marrying a woman who loves you when she is standing right beneath your arrogant nose! Now, if you will excuse me, gentlemen. Caroline…' she nodded briefly to her incredulous sister '…I wish to go up to my bedchamber now. And I hope not to be disturbed by any one of you!' She ran swiftly up the staircase.

'Gabriel?'

He dragged his gaze away from Diana as she disappeared round the corner to turn and look enquiringly at the thoroughly dazed Caroline.

'What just happened?' she asked.

Gabriel grinned at her. 'I believe your sister has at last rebelled against subjugating her own needs and desires in order to please everyone else and has decided to please only herself,' he said.

'And she was quite magnificent about it.' Caroline came out of her daze to turn and look pityingly at Malcolm Castle. 'It would seem that you are not the man my sister loves, after all.' She began to smile, that smile turning to a chuckle, then to outright laughter. 'I must say, Gabriel, I much appreciated her comment about your arrogant nose,' she teased.

Gabriel was still trying to decide if that remark had really meant what he hoped it had, or if it were merely wishful thinking on his part. Could Diana, after calling him embittered and arrogant, really have also implied that she was in love with him?

'Is that the same innocent cushion as yesterday that you are destroying, or perhaps another one?'

She should have known that Gabriel would choose not to listen to her wish for privacy—he had never heeded her wishes before, so why should he begin to do so now? She placed the cushion down on the *chaise* and stood up, her profile turned determinedly away from him. 'Has Malcom gone?'

'I am sure he cannot have gone far away if you have

changed your mind about marrying him,' he said, testing the water.

'I have not changed my mind in the slightest!' Her eyes sparked furiously as she finally turned to him. 'How he had the audacity to come here at all is beyond me.' She frowned. 'What do you want now, Gabriel? To reprimand me once again for what happened earlier this morning? Or perhaps you wish to upbraid me for refusing what is, after all, an advantageous offer of marriage for someone as without funds as I?'

Gabriel's admiration for her intensified; Caroline had been in the right of it earlier—Diana in this mood was truly magnificent! Her eyes shone as bright as the sapphires they resembled, her creamy cheeks were flushed, her lips red and inviting, and the gentle swell of her breasts was made all the more eye-catching by quickly rising and falling with her agitated breathing. Truly, wondrously magnificent!

'If that is the reason you are here, my lord, then I believe I should tell you now that I do not care!' she carried on before he had the chance to reply. 'Either about the Prescotts or Malcolm Castle.' She began to pace the bedchamber. 'The Prescotts are both too despicable and too beneath contempt to waste my time discussing them any further, and Malcolm can just go to the devil!'

Gabriel was fascinated…no, totally mesmerised by Diana in her present mood of rebellion. 'I totally agree.'

She gave him a startled glance. 'You do?'

'Oh, yes,' he murmured softly. 'Diana, why did you ask to be released from our betrothal?'

Her cheeks flushed. 'I told you, I did not—'

'*Why*, Diana?'

'Because *you* wished to be free of it!'

'I made no such statement—'

'There was no need for you to do so when your every word and action since your mother's return to health has shown that you no longer have need of or require a wife.'

'And *that* was the reason you brought an end to our betrothal?' Gabriel stared at her in disbelief.

She raised her proud little chin. 'You have made it more than obvious recently that you have no further need of my company, let alone wish to take me as your wife.'

'An earl is always in need of a wife, Diana.'

She gave dismissive movement of her shoulders. 'Then no doubt once you are established back amongst the *ton* you will eventually settle for some suitable and accommodating young woman.'

'Suitable and accommodating…' Gabriel murmured consideringly. 'And what if I would prefer that my wife be strong-willed and courageous rather than suitable and accommodating?'

'Then no doubt you will find a woman with those qualities amongst the ton, too.'

'And if I have already found her?' he wanted to know.

She swallowed hard. 'Then I would say that you have acted even more quickly in finding my replacement than I had anticipated.'

'And if *you* are the woman to whom I refer?'

Diana looked at him wordlessly for several long seconds before her back stiffened and her chin once again jutted proudly. 'I do not appreciate your toying with me in this way, my lord.'

'But you will agree with me that you *are* strong-willed and courageous?' he teased.

'You gave me every indication earlier that you considered me reckless and headstrong!' she protested indignantly.

'It takes a certain courage and will to be both of those things, too,' he acknowledged ruefully.

Diana huffed. 'You are talking nonsense, my lord.'

'I am indeed,' he conceded. 'I am discovering love does that to a man.'

She gave a snort. 'Appreciative as I am of Lord Vaughn's assistance earlier, I have no wish to discuss him now, either!'

'Lord Vaughn?' Gabriel repeated in utter confusion. 'But—'

'My lord, I have decided that if I cannot have what I wish in my marriage, then I will not marry at all.' She could see herself years from now, the elderly and spinster aunt to her sisters' children—

'And what is it that you want from marriage, Diana?' Gabriel prompted huskily.

She gave a sad smile. 'Something that is completely beyond your comprehension.' Yes, as time passed she would become an aunt to her many nieces and nephews, and no doubt be considered as slightly eccentric by the rest of her family, and as the long and lonely years passed her by—

'Diana, if I were to get down upon one knee and beg you to marry me, would you at least consider it?' Gabriel suited his actions to his words as he knelt before her and took her hands in his. 'I have been a fool,' he continued urgently. 'A blind, insensitive fool! But I am a blind and insensitive fool who is also deeply, irrevocably in love with the woman who happens to be right beneath my arrogant nose.'

Diana stared down at him as if he had completely lost his senses. 'Get up, do, Gabriel.' She attempted to pull him to his feet and failed miserably as he refused to be moved.

'Marry me, Diana!' he urged passionately. 'Marry me and allow me to love you until the day I die and beyond. Say yes, my darling, and I promise I will worship at your beautiful feet for the rest of my life.'

Perhaps it was she who had lost her senses? Gabriel could not really be kneeling in front of her saying these wonderful things to her! He could not! Could he?

He gave a choked laugh as he obviously saw the bewilderment in her expression. 'Dominic warned me of how it would be if I ever fell in love; to my shame, I chose to dismiss his warning.' He drew his breath in sharply. 'I do love you, Diana; I realised some days ago just how much. So much, my darling, that my very happiness depends upon your every word and smile. These past days of even thinking of living without you, of some day watching you marrying another man, has been an agony I wish never to be repeated.'

'But you became so cold and distant whilst we were at Faulkner Manor and after we got back,' she said.

He sighed. 'I believed you must think less of me because of my blindness to both the events in the past and my neglect of my mother.'

'I could never think less of you because of those things, Gabriel,' she insisted. 'You and your family were lied to and deceived by your uncle and aunt, and you could have had no idea of their treatment of your mother. Once you did learn of it, you put the matter right immediately. No, Gabriel, I could never think less of you because of those things,' she repeated firmly.

His hands tightened about hers. 'Then will you not consider marrying me? Will you not put me out of this agony of uncertainty and instead make me the happiest man alive?'

Diana could see by the lines of strain that had appeared beside his eyes and mouth that he spoke only the truth. The complete, unvarnished truth. Gabriel loved her! Really loved her. He could no more bear the thought of living without her than she could bear the thought of being parted from him!

She drew in a shaky breath. 'I do not need to consider marrying you, Gabriel—because I could marry no one else. I love you so very much, my dear darling love!' She placed her hands on either side of his face as he got slowly to his feet and looked up at him with that love shining brightly in her eyes. 'Whatever I once thought I felt for Malcolm is nothing in comparison to what I feel for you. What I know I will *always* feel for you. I love you so very, very much, my darling Gabriel.'

He could barely breathe as he slowly lowered his head and his lips claimed hers in a kiss that showed her just how deep and overwhelming his love for her was—and she returned it whole-heartedly.

'Everyone will be wondering why we did not appear for either luncheon or dinner,' Diana said, scandalised.

'The fact that no one has come in search of us shows that Caroline did not leave them wondering for long!' Gabriel lay back upon the pillows of Diana's bed, his arms about her and her head resting upon his shoulder as she snuggled into his side, the long length of her golden-red curls a warm caress against the bareness of his chest.

The hours since they had confessed their love for one other had been ones of pure bliss for both of them, as they made long and delicious love together, and then talked softly of the misunderstandings of the past few days, before making love again. 'As soon as we have the strength to leave this bed I intend taking you to the best jewellers in town and buying you the biggest sapphire ring we can find,' he announced with satisfaction.

Diana glanced up at him. 'I do not need fine jewels to know that you love me.'

His arms tightened about her. 'Maybe not, my love, but I need to place my ring upon your finger as a warning to other men that you belong to me.'

She laughed softly. 'Can there be any doubts as to that?'

'Hopefully not,' he muttered.

'Definitely not!' she protested.

Gabriel sobered. 'I do think that perhaps we should not delay the wedding for more than a few days or so.' He smiled to himself, knowing that despite his previous intentions, he had been so enthralled by the beauty and pleasure of their lovemaking that he had lost all control and consummated their marriage ahead of the actual ceremony. 'Perhaps a double wedding with your sister Caroline and Dominic?' he suggested.

'Perhaps,' she said quietly.

'Only perhaps?' Gabriel turned to look down into Diana's slightly pensive expression. 'You are not having second thoughts? Now that we have made love, have you decided that—'

'Hush.' Diana placed slender fingers against his beautifully sculptured lips. Lips that had kissed and explored parts of her body that still made her blush to think of. 'I have told you that I love you, Gabriel, and I do.' She gazed deeply into his eyes. 'I love you. All of you. Now and for ever.'

Gabriel's arms tightened about her, only slightly reassured. 'But you will only "perhaps" marry me?'

A slight frown creased her brow. 'I do not believe that either Caroline or I wish to be married without Elizabeth present.'

'Of course.' He finally relaxed, relieved by the obvious explanation. 'Then Vaughn and I must find her as quickly as is possible.'

'I am afraid you must, yes,' she agreed.

'Never be afraid to ask anything of me, Diana.' His eyes glowed lovingly down at her. 'Whatever I have, whatever I am, it all yours, and always will be.'

No woman could possibly ask for more than that from the man that she loved and who loved her in return.

* * * * *

A sneaky peek at next month...

HISTORICAL

IGNITE YOUR IMAGINATION, STEP INTO THE PAST...

My wish list for next month's titles...

In stores from 6th January 2012:

❑ The Lady Confesses – Carole Mortimer

❑ The Dangerous Lord Darrington – Sarah Mallory

❑ Marrying the Captain – Carla Kelly

❑ The Unconventional Maiden – June Francis

❑ Her Battle-Scarred Knight – Meriel Fuller

❑ Alaskan Renegade – Kate Bridges

Available at WHSmith, Tesco, Asda, Eason, Amazon and Apple

Just can't wait?

1211/04

Mills & Boon® Online

Discover more romance at
www.millsandboon.co.uk

 FREE online reads

Books up to one
month before shops

Browse our books
before you buy

...and much more!

For exclusive competitions and instant updates:

Like us on **facebook.com/romancehq**

Follow us on **twitter.com/millsandboonuk**

Join us on **community.millsandboon.co.uk**

Visit us Online

Sign up for our FREE eNewsletter at
www.millsandboon.co.uk